DEATH
IN THE
CARDS

*Also by Sharon Short
in Large Print:*

Death by Deep Dish Pie
Death of a Domestic Diva

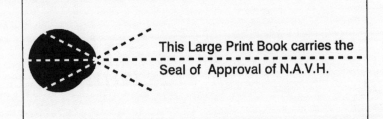

DEATH
IN THE
CARDS

A Stain-Busting Mystery

Sharon Short

WHEELER
PUBLISHING

Published in 2005 by arrangement with Avon Books, an imprint of HarperCollins Publishers, Inc.

Wheeler Large Print Cozy Mystery.

The text of this Large Print edition is unabridged. Other aspects of the book may vary from the original edition.

Set in 16 pt. Plantin.

Printed in the United States on permanent paper.

Library of Congress Cataloging-in-Publication Data

Short, Sharon Gwyn.
    Death in the cards : a stain-busting mystery / by Sharon Short.
       p. cm. — (Wheeler Publishing large print cozy mystery)
    ISBN 1-59722-002-7 (lg. print : sc : alk. paper)
    1. Toadfern, Josie (Fictitious character) — Fiction.
2. Women detectives — Ohio — Fiction.   3. Self-service laundries — Fiction.   4. Ohio — Fiction.   5. Large type books. I. Title. II. Wheeler large print cozy mystery.
PS3569.H594D427 2005
  813′.54—dc22   2005006826

To David,

with whom life is a far
greater joy than I could
ever have predicted

As the Founder/CEO of NAVH, the only national health agency solely devoted to those who, although not totally blind, have an eye disease which could lead to serious visual impairment, I am pleased to recognize Thorndike Press★ as one of the leading publishers in the large print field.

Founded in 1954 in San Francisco to prepare large print textbooks for partially seeing children, NAVH became the pioneer and standard setting agency in the preparation of large type.

Today, those publishers who meet our standards carry the prestigious "Seal of Approval" indicating high quality large print. We are delighted that Thorndike Press is one of the publishers whose titles meet these standards. We are also pleased to recognize the significant contribution Thorndike Press is making in this important and growing field.

Lorraine H. Marchi, L.H.D.
Founder/CEO
NAVH

★ Thorndike Press encompasses the following imprints: Thorndike, Wheeler, Walker and Large Print Press.

Acknowledgments

In the course of writing this novel, I was reminded by events in my personal life of the importance of a team. And so, I must thank a delightful team who helped make this book happen.

Thanks to Ellen Geiger, agent, and Sarah Durand, editor, for wisely reminding me to "keep the whimsy!" And thanks to my family team: David (who has infinite patience), Katherine (who helps keep me organized), and Gwendolyn (who really does make the best grilled cheese sandwich ever).

About the stain removal techniques in this book: I've tested each one but please know that what works on one type of fabric might not work on another. If you want to try them . . . Josie says, please test first in an inconspicuous area of the item you're cleaning! That said, congratulations to the winners of Josie's second "Stain Busters" Contest:

- Louis Mackey, for fluffing rugs with salt in the wash tip

- Barbara Heckart, Pat Smith, and Katherine Shephard for the rust stains removal tip

- Karen Poe, Deb Hollister, and Linda Summers Posey for the blood removal tip

1

*That there is a devil, there is no doubt. But is he
trying to get in . . . or trying to get out?*

This was the only commentary my Aunt
Clara Foersthoefel — may she rest in
peace — ever made about religion, and she
made it often until the Sunday she quit
church.

At least, she quit attending the Paradise
Church of Almighty Revelations, a fundamentalist, nondenominational congregation
that still meets in a log building on the
outskirts of Paradise, Ohio, just down the
road a piece from the Happy Trails Motor
Home Court.

Uncle Horace and I fancied sleeping in
on Sundays, the only day our family-owned
laundromat closed. But on that Sunday
some fourteen years ago, when I was about
fifteen, our slumber was shattered when
Aunt Clara came slamming in the back

door, proclaiming she'd quit her once-beloved church, and giving as her answer to our question of why: "that there is a devil, there is no doubt. But is he trying to get in . . . or trying to get out?"

It was the last time she ever uttered that saying.

Then Aunt Clara herself slept in for two Sundays in a row. The Sunday after that, she roused Uncle Horace and me from slumber, made us put on churchgoing clothes, and turned us all into demure Methodists, which I have been ever since.

I never knew just where Aunt Clara's devil saying came from. Was this Aunt Clara's personal theory? Or a doctrine she'd heard the Almighty Revelations pastor, Dru Purcell, preach on some fine Sunday morning? Truth be told, I never quite understood it, either. All I know for certain is that it still gives me the willies.

A few years after Aunt Clara uttered her saying one last time, Uncle Horace died. Aunt Clara passed on two years after that, and I inherited the laundromat. In the years since then, Aunt Clara's devil saying slipped from my thoughts entirely.

Until the morning a few weeks ago, back in late October, when I met Ginny Proffitt, and suddenly Aunt Clara's adage seemed like more than just a scary old saying.

It seemed like prophecy.

I'm Josie Toadfern, owner of Toadfern's Laundromat, and a stain expert. Self-taught and proud of it. Best stain expert in Paradise, Ohio. Or in Mason County. Or in Ohio. Maybe even in all of the United States.

After my aunt died, I took over the laundromat that had been my uncle's (my aunt helped with the laundromat but worked full-time at a local pie company) and eventually renamed it Toadfern's. I also took over the guardianship of my aunt and uncle's only son, Guy Foersthoefel, an adult with autism who lives at Stillwater Farms, a residential home fifteen miles north of Paradise. My life has been plenty busy in the nine years since I took over the laundromat (I'm twenty-nine now). I didn't have much time to dwell on the past or contemplate the distant future — my thoughts and actions were firmly embedded in the present and near future, and I liked it that way.

At least, that's how I felt just a few weeks ago on a Friday morning in late October. I was happily anticipating the weekend. That evening, I was going on a date with my boyfriend, Owen Collins, to a local "haunted" corn maze, and I planned to relax with him Saturday evening after working in my laundromat all day. Sunday, after church, I'd tutor my literacy student, Hugh Crowley, and after that, I'd visit my cousin Guy at Stillwater Farms. For Sunday night, I envisioned more snuggling with Owen. This pleasant rhythm would be accented with chats with my best friends — Winnie, Cherry, and Sally — or by reading a good book.

As I contemplated my upcoming calm weekend, I staggered across the parking lot of the Rhinegolds' Red Horse Motel, my gait awkward because I embraced a large laundry bag overstuffed with fluffy ecru towels and washcloths.

But my load didn't stop me from letting my thoughts drift from the pleasures in my immediate future to the perfection of the autumn morning. The pleasantly crisp air. The cloudless sky blue with a hue that can only come in autumn, as if it's taken the heat of an entire summer to burnish the sky into deep cobalt. The huge oak tree that grew right out of the asphalt by the motel's entrance, my ultimate destination.

I love that tree and the fact that the Rhinegolds paved around it back when it was a sapling and have never cut it down. The tree was a brilliant orange red, the perfect counterpoint to the vibrancy of the sky.

The autumn colors were, ironically, made more vibrant by the fact that we'd suffered a long spell of drought from late summer into autumn.

Across from the Red Horse was Beeker's Orchard, acres of apple trees laden with Jonathans and Red Delicious and Winesaps. Just a glimpse of the orchard made my mouth water from the taste-memory of hand-pressed cider and home-made applesauce.

With all that sensory input, who could blame me for gazing around, taking it in — and not seeing the woman crossing the parking lot?

The woman herself, it turned out.

We ran smack into each other. She bounced off the front of my laundry bag with a loud "oof!" I dropped the bag and staggered around, stunned from the surprise impact.

I regained my balance and took a good look at the woman, sprawled on the asphalt, knocked out cold right by the sign pro-claiming, RED HORSE MOTEL, VACANCY, COLOR TV, POOL, AIR CONDITIONING, an ultramodern amenity when the sign was put up in the 1950s.

I ran over to the woman and knelt beside her. She wasn't breathing and her eyes were closed. I held my hand over her face and didn't feel any breath. My heart started racing, my throat tightening. Oh Lord, I thought. I've killed her!

I told myself to stay calm, to remember the steps for CPR I'd learned in a Red Cross training class. I'd checked her breathing; now I needed to check for a pulse. I started to move the sapphire-studded gold watch on her wrist.

But my fingers had barely brushed the watch when the woman jerked back to life, sitting up so suddenly she nearly butted heads with me, grabbing my wrist before I could say a word. Then she twisted my arm back, pinning me, right side down, to the asphalt lot. She knelt down, put her face by mine. I looked at her with just my left eye, the right one being squished closed. All I could manage in protest was a gargley-sounding "Hey!"

"You think you can rob me here in broad daylight?" the woman demanded. Her eyes were a pale gray. It's hard to imagine eyes that color blazing, but they did. Her reaction to our situation was so over the top that normally I'd find it funny. Me, trying to rob someone? I don't look like I could pull off a heist at a church rummage sale even with the pastor's blessing.

But there was something about those pale gray eyes burning with a cold fury — and about my twisted arm starting to throb in her viselike grip — that made this a definitely not-funny situation.

Then, suddenly, the woman's eyes softened into a normal gaze and she released my arm. I rolled to my back, sat up, and started butt-scooting away. "What was that all about? I wasn't trying to rob you —"

"Aw, sorry about that," the woman said gruffly. She jumped up nimbly and brushed herself off. I stopped scooting. "Got mugged twice in the same month in L.A. Twitchy about that kind of thing ever since. Kinda like a post-traumatic disorder but just for muggings."

I smiled a little at the woman's attempt at humor as she reached a hand down to help me up. I studied the hand she offered instead of taking it right away — after all, she'd just twisted my arm with it. Her hand was broad and manly, despite the carefully polished hot-pink nails and the sparkly rings adorning every finger. No wonder she'd been mugged, if she went around like that in big cities.

I wasn't sure I wanted to take this woman's hand — my arm was still hurting where she'd twisted it. Then again, I was a little unsteady and there was something very insistent about that hand, so I took it. The woman gave a strong, easy yank, and I came back up on my feet lightly.

I studied the woman. She was about my height — just shy of five feet three — but, unlike me, athletic-looking even though she was wearing a warm-up suit. Usually people who wear those haven't warmed up for years to do anything more strenuous than a channel-surfing marathon, but this woman's arms were folded tight across a flat abdomen. Even her jawline looked toned, a pretty good clue that the rest of her was in shape.

Her athletic aura was at odds, though, with the rest of her appearance: artfully applied makeup, gold jewelry, tanning salon tan, and a perfect brunette bob. She was so coiffed, she looked allergic to sweat.

And that warm-up suit. Both pants and jacket were a patchwork of turquoise and hot pink, each triangle distinguished from the other by gold brocade. And she wore matching hot-pink, high-top sneakers.

I swayed a little.

16

"You okay?" the woman asked.

"Sure, fine," I said. I wasn't about to tell her that the contrast of her outfit with the autumn colors around us was making me nauseated. "But on the pavement . . . you weren't breathing. . . ."

"Self-induced deep meditation. My breathing is extremely shallow in that state. It's my automatic response to trauma. And a self-healing technique. I became an expert in it in the 1960s — when that kind of thing was more popular and I was in my open-minded twenties."

I was surprised — the woman didn't look a day past 50. I made a note to myself to look into meditation.

"So, tell me why you ran into me," the woman added.

"What? We ran into each other! I admit, I was distracted by the beauty of the day, but you must not have been paying attention to where you were going, either. I mean, with my big laundry bag, I should have been pretty noticeable. What was distracting *you?*"

I eyed the laundry bag, a bulky lump to our left on the Rhinegolds' motel parking lot. Thank the good Lord the contents hadn't spilled to the pavement.

When I looked back at the woman, her

eyes were hard and narrow, and for a moment that chilly, creepy feeling I'd had before edged toward me. But suddenly the woman laughed, a great hearty laugh.

"You're kinda feisty. I like that," the woman said, giving me an appraising look. "Wouldn't have expected it, though."

Gee, thanks, I thought, starting toward my laundry bag.

"I was on my way to a meeting."

I looked at her. "What?"

"You asked what was distracting me. I have a meeting I'm going to —"

"Me, too," I said. After dropping off the laundry with the Rhinegolds, I planned to meet my friends Cherry Feinster and Sally Toadfern (who's also my cousin) for coffee and gossip before a rare Friday morning outing. "I'm running late."

Her eyebrows went up. "Really," she said. I gulped, feeling unaccountably guilty at my white lie. I wasn't running late; as usual, I was running a bit early, but I wanted to get away from this woman.

"It's time we met properly," the woman said. "My name's Ginny Proffitt. I'm here for the psychic fair. As one of the psychics."

I gulped again. Great, I thought. With my luck, she was probably the only one who really could read minds.

18

I knew about the psychic fair, of course. For one thing, Paradise has a population of just fewer than three thousand, and not much happens without everyone knowing. For another, a few months ago I'd rented the spare apartment on the second story over my laundromat — I live in the other apartment — to Damon and Sienna LeFever. They were a twenty-something couple from Paradise who moved out to California for a few years, then returned a few months ago to open their new business: Rising Star Bookshop and Psychic Readings, just down the street from my laundromat. They sold New Age books and did tarot card readings and they were hosting a psychic fair at Paradise's only motel, the Red Horse.

In the *Columbus Dispatch*, I'd seen ads for Columbus-area psychic fairs, gatherings of psychics who do readings and balance chakras (I wasn't quite sure what that meant) and sell crystals. But this would be Paradise's first.

And Ginny Proffitt was the first psychic I'd ever met, with the exception of Great-Aunt Noreen Toadfern, who was said to be gifted with dreams that foretold calamitous events. Great-Aunt Noreen had looked like a loon. Ginny looked well tended. Neither one looked like my idea of a psychic.

Ginny smiled at me. "Don't worry," she said. "Most people are surprised when they find out I'm a psychic. I guess they expect gypsy skirts and loopy earrings."

I forced myself not to gasp. She'd just described my expectation. "I'm Josie Toadfern."

"The laundromat owner," she said.

I glanced at my laundry bag on the pavement. It definitely didn't take a psychic to figure that out. "I was just dropping off the Rhinegolds' weekly linens."

"They told me about you when I asked about laundry facilities," she said. "I just got here a few hours ago, but I'm sorry to say I didn't have time to do my laundry before I came. So I packed a suitcase of dirty clothes, thinking I could do my laundry once I got here."

I kept my face still while thinking *ew*. I didn't want to be interested in this woman or her story. But my natural curiosity took over. (My school-years nickname was Nosey Josie, but I prefer to think of myself as inquisitively gifted.) Who packs dirty clothes on purpose? Who is so busy they can't even wash a few clothes before traveling?

Ginny Proffitt smiled and answered the question I hadn't asked out loud. "I'm in the process of closing down my business and selling it off. Had some last-minute details to take care of and couldn't get to the laundromat." She plucked at the arm of her warm-up suit. "This is clean, though." She held out her hand. "Nice to meet you, Josie."

I took her hand. "And you." We exchanged a firm handshake, and I started to pull away, but Ginny held on to my hand.

"The least I can do after all this is give you a complimentary palm reading," she said.

I resisted an eye roll, remembering Great-Aunt Noreen holding forth at the Toadfern family reunion every year, telling the kids about how she'd dreamt only the night before of someone drowning. Our reunions were held at the man-made Licking Creek Lake State Park, shelter B, by the shore.

"I really am in a hurry —" I started.

"Nonsense," said Ginny, firmly turning my hand in hers, so that my palm faced up. She stared into it. "I know the LeFevers did the best they could recruiting people, and of course everyone's always drawn to the tarot readers because of the colorful cards, but between you and me, I'm the only real psychic here. Oh, the others get

21

occasional vibrations, I'm sure, but for a real reading, I'm the one to see. I do palm and crystal orb readings, plus dream interpretation. This reading will be quick since we're both in a hurry —" with that she glanced up with a knowing smirk, and I flushed — "but come by later for an in-depth consultation."

I tugged my hand, but she held on firmly. "You know, I appreciate your offer, really, but —"

Ginny stroked the center of my palm with her forefinger. "Ah. Long lifeline. That's nice."

I gave in to my earlier impulse and eye-rolled, since Ginny was staring at my palm. What else would psychics say? Hey, kid, you're gonna die soon? They wouldn't get too many repeat customers that way.

"Hmm. But I see some problems in the near future. You're going to be worried about someone very dear to you . . ."

Who doesn't worry about their loved ones?

"Health may be an issue soon for someone you care about . . ."

Flu season's just around the corner, I thought.

"A time of turmoil and turbulence is coming . . ."

Bet she says that to everyone a month

before Thanksgiving. Family get-togethers have that effect on a lot of people.

"But you'll find the strength to work through it."

Pumpkin pie leftovers can do that.

"An issue that's been bothering you will become more important to you . . ."

Gee, could we get any more vague?

"Do you have a boyfriend who's hidden important facts about his life from you in the past?"

What? I rolled my eyes to a standstill and stared at Ginny.

Ginny looked up at me. "Hmm. Stay open-minded but protect yourself, dear."

I relaxed. I bet she said that to all the single women, and she could guess my single status from my lack of wedding band.

"That's about all I see . . ."

Thank the good Lord!

"Except . . ."

Ginny's grasp tightened. "Oh my! You have a spirit guide!"

Time to start eye rolling again. Let me guess, for only $29.95 I could come to her booth later and find out how to harness the energy . . .

"A teacher . . . not just now, but a teacher from your past. You dream of her.

A Mrs. Aaa . . . No! A Mrs. O, something. Mrs. Ogdon, Ogmore . . . I can't quite get the name. Doesn't matter," Ginny said. Her eyes were distant, as if drawn to something only she could see, her voice awed, but not, I thought, with what she was saying, more as if she never stopped being surprised by her own ability to probe a stranger's psyche. My psyche.

"When she comes to you in dreams, you want to dismiss her as just a figment of your imagination. But Mrs. O was important to you in ways you didn't realize when she was living, and she's more important to you than you want to realize now, and . . ."

Ginny's mouth kept moving, but suddenly I couldn't hear any of her words. I could only stare into her cool gray eyes.

And I could only hear Aunt Clara, as if she stood behind me, muttering . . .

"That there is a devil there is no doubt . . . but is he trying to get in or trying to get out?"

2

"Girlfriend, you look like you've seen a ghost," said Sally Toadfern, one of my twenty-seven first cousins on my daddy's side, and the only one I count as a close friend. She took another long drink from her coffee cup and eyed me thoughtfully.

"Maybe she's reacting to something she ate," Cherry said. "Or smelled. Once in Junior High Home Ec class, when Mrs. Oglevee was showing us how to steam broccoli, Josie went pale like that right before she threw up —"

I blanched at the mention of Mrs. Oglevee. Cherry and Sally swayed away from me. I was sitting between them at the bar at the back of the Red Horse Motel's restaurant.

"Did you have to mention that?" I asked Cherry.

Cherry runs Cherry's Chat N Curl,

located right next to my laundromat, and she has a memory for details — which customer prefers the green apple-scented shampoo, which one needs a wee more ash blond in her tint to keep from going bluish. And Cherry has a way of putting her gift for recollection to use by recalling my most embarrassing memories better than I do, and sharing them with everyone in vivid detail.

"Josie hasn't liked steamed broccoli since," Cherry went on. "Come to think of it, neither have I."

"She's never been much on ghosts — or ghost stories," Sally said.

"Which is why you told them to me every chance you got," I snapped at Sally.

Though we were only sipping innocent cups of coffee, we were seated at the bar because the dining room behind us was being rearranged for the psychic fair.

Sally was chuckling. "Yeah, I did, didn't I? But my stories never seemed to bother you as much as when Great-Aunt Noreen would tell us her freaky dreams about us all drowning at the family reunions . . ."

"Quit it, both of you! I'm fine."

Sally stopped chuckling and cracked her knuckles. Cherry puffed her glossy red lips up into a precious pout. Both of them gave

26

me hurt little glances.

I was lying about being fine, and they knew it. If I told them that Ginny Proffitt had seriously spooked me, they'd probably tease me. Not that I'd blame them. It was the kind of thing that invited teasing. But I wasn't in the mood for it.

You see, most of Ginny's "reading" of my palm had been generic fluff, but somehow she'd tapped into a truth I hadn't ever told these two, or my friend Winnie, or my boyfriend Owen: I do, in fact, have dreams in which I am visited by Mrs. Oglevee, my Junior High history and home-ec teacher. Mrs. Oglevee died four years after retiring and one week before she was supposed to go on a luxury Riviera cruise, for which she'd saved from her meager teacher's pay and by substitute teaching after retirement. As you might imagine, Mrs. Oglevee is not in a good mood in my dreams. But she does love to give me much unwanted advice and criticism. Just as she did in real life.

I've always chalked up these dreams to simple explanations, like enjoying a fried garlic-bologna sandwich too close to bedtime. But how could I explain away a total stranger like Ginny Proffitt knowing about my dreams, when I'd never mentioned them to anyone? I pushed the question to the back of my mind while pushing a smile to my face.

"So, tell me what's new with the two of you," I said brightly.

"The triple-threats have stopped eating everyone's glue, but rumor has it their teacher is still considering a career switch to sales," Sally said, referring to her sons' — Harry, Barry, and Larry — kindergarten experience so far. She shrugged and added flatly, "I have a kitchen cabinet install this weekend." Sally owned the Bar-None bar on the edge of town — having just bought it from her ex-mother-in-law — but she also did odd carpentry jobs when she could. She struggled, but got by as a single mom. (Her ex-husband Waylon Hinckie, a.k.a. the Rat, had taken off with a honey on a Harley when potty training the triplets got to be too much for him.)

"No date for me tonight," Cherry said, sighing. Sally and I cut each other a look. We thought it was just as well Cherry had broken up with DeWayne Forrester, her most recent beau. His idea of a romantic date was going to the Burrito Barn for the double-wide burrito special. Plus he'd been two-timing her with Robin Seales. But Cherry hates to be without a fella.

"I guess I'll go over to her place for line dancing," Cherry added, jerking a thumb at Sally.

Then Cherry and Sally went silent and glared at me. I knew what this was — emotional blackmail — and I wanted to throttle them for it. Both of them would normally be talking over the top of each other with a lot more info than that.

They thought I couldn't bear their stony silence.

And they were right. I broke down right away.

"All right," I said, "I'll tell you what's bothering me. I was more or less mugged, right out in the parking lot."

"What? Mugged? Oh my God, we need to call the police!" Cherry dug into her big purse, which was silk-screened with a black-and-white photo of Marilyn Monroe, Cherry's hero, never mind that Marilyn died a decade and a half before Cherry was born. Sally and I had gone in on the bag for Cherry's thirtieth birthday party, held after hours at the Bar-None. That — and a lot of bourbon — had helped make up for the fact that we'd teased her unmercifully about turning thirty a year before us.

"Damn it, where's my cell?" Cherry cried. Mascara, lipsticks, tissues, Tootsie

Rolls, and other assorted goodies all plopped out onto the bar.

Sally was on her feet, hands on her hips. "What'd the guy look like? I'll take care of him." She cracked her knuckles again.

You've gotta love friends like this. Or else you'd kill 'em.

I put a hand on Sally's shoulder, tried to press her back down to the barstool. "It wasn't like that. I said I was *more or less* mugged. I'm fine. For pity's sake, here's your phone, Cherry, but don't dial 911." I plucked her cell phone out from under a pile of tissues and York Peppermint Patties.

I myself had just gotten a cell phone a month before, after Guy had fainted at Stillwater. The incident had scared me because Guy's health has always been excellent. After that, I got the cell because I wanted the Stillwater staff to be able to reach me anytime, anywhere.

Sally picked up a patty, unwrapped it, plopped it in her mouth, and said around it, "I thought you were on another diet, Cherry?"

Cherry gave her a look. "Those are just for breath freshening," she said, with a defensive sniff. I considered pointing out the lower fat grams of Tic-Tacs, then thought better of it. "And you gave us a scare, Josie Toadfern. Explain yourself."

I helped Cherry sweep everything back into her purse. Sally plucked up another Peppermint Patty before Cherry could swat her hand. Sally does not diet. She has a firmly toned hourglass figure, even after birthing triplets, damn her. Cherry and I are, well, pleasantly plump.

"The psychic fair is going on this weekend —"

"We know," said Cherry.

"— and I was delivering the Rhinegolds' laundry order when I met one of the psychics. A woman named Ginny Proffitt. And she, well, she forced a psychic reading on me!"

Sally and Cherry stared at me.

Sally crumpled up her York Peppermint Patty wrappers. I swallowed. Only Sally could make squashing two one-square-inch pieces of aluminum foil look intimidating. Well, maybe Ginny Proffitt could, too.

"That's it?" asked Sally. "Some little old lady in a gypsy skirt wants to tell you 'love is around the corner and don't forget to buy a lottery ticket' and you can't say 'no, thanks'?"

"She wasn't little. Or old. Or much of a

lady, for that matter. She was pushy and her prediction was much more spooky than that."

Cherry clutched my arm, looking suddenly alarmed. "She didn't say you were going to be in a wreck, did she? 'Cause once at the county fair me and Marcia Jean went to see the gypsy lady —"

"I said she wasn't like a gypsy lady —"

"And when Marcia Jean wouldn't tip the gypsy lady, she hollered that Marcia would be in a wreck, and sure enough, she was. Fractured her fibia in both legs!"

"You mean tibia —" I started.

"How long was the wreck after the prediction?" Sally asked skeptically.

"Twelve years. But still —"

"I'm sorry I brought it up," I moaned.

"C'mon, Josie, tell us what she said," Cherry pleaded.

I paused. I couldn't tell them about my dreams about Mrs. Oglevee. Sally would never let me hear the end of it. And Cherry would give me a list of questions for Mrs. Oglevee, no doubt about her future love life and whether or not she should add a new line of styling gel to her salon.

But I had to tell them something. "I have this same dream over and over," I said. "It's — it's about drowning in the lake.

32

Like Great-Aunt Noreen always said we would do. And it's got all of these specific details, like the color of the swimsuit I'm wearing —"

"Bright orange bikini?" Cherry asked.

I frowned at her. "Navy one-piece."

Cherry frowned back. "Hmmm. That doesn't sound so bad. I mean, if this is a nightmare, bright orange bikini would be more fitting —"

"For pity's sake, it's my nightmare!" Okay, it was my imaginary, white-lie nightmare. But still. "Anyway, the point is, there's no way this woman could know the details of my dream, but she looked at my palm, and the next thing I know, she's telling me all about it. Don't you think that's creepy?"

"Don't the psychic fair organizers rent the apartment next to yours?" Sally said.

"Yeah. Damon and Sienna LeFever. So what?"

"Well, so what if you hollered out some details about your dream in your sleep without knowing it and they heard it and mentioned it to this Ginny?"

I felt a surge of hope, and then frowned again. "I don't holler out in my dreams."

"You sure about that? Lots of people do and don't realize it."

Cherry gave me a sly look. "Yeah, Sally's right. You should check with Owen."

I didn't say anything. She and Sally'd been trying for weeks to get me to say if Owen and I sometimes spent the night together. I figured it was none of their business.

Sally chuckled, and put down two dollars to cover her coffee and a tip. She stood up. "C'mon, let's go see what we can learn about this Ginny Proffitt."

"What? No — we'll be late for the tour!"

The LeFevers had organized a tour for the fair's psychics to Serpent Mound, the largest serpent effigy in the United States, created by the Fort Ancient Indian culture sometime between A.D. 1000 and 1500. The mound — which is about three feet high and coils for about 1,300 feet atop a plateau overlooking the valleys around it — has been a Ohio Historical Society park for about a century and is a National Historic Landmark. Which means lots of nearby school groups visit it.

But because it is believed to have been created for religious or spiritual purposes, it's also long been a draw for followers of New Age beliefs, which included many (although not all) of the psychics coming to the psychic fair.

I'd been invited along on the LeFevers'

34

tour of the Serpent Mound because I'd staunchly defended the LeFevers against the ranting rage of Pastor Dru Purcell, leader of the Paradise Church of Almighty Revelations that my Aunt Clara had attended long ago, then abruptly quit. Dru had crashed several Chamber of Commerce meetings demanding we rise up against the force of the devil, as he called it, moving into our town in the form of the LeFevers and their new business, Rising Star Bookshop and Psychic Readings. I'd spoken up for freedom of religion, business, and expression — all of which are intertwined — and said we should welcome and support the LeFevers.

I made the same statements at a city council meeting at which Pastor Purcell had called the LeFevers "dangerous weirdos" and demanded Paradise be rezoned free of businesses "based on or catering to psychic phenomena, Wicca, or other alternate New Age beliefs." Several chamber members wavered toward Pastor Purcell's point of view, until I pointed out that we in Paradise benefitted from visitors to Serpent Mound, which besides being a historical monument was a draw for many New Age visitors because of the mound's spiritual nature. So, in effect, our entire town's economy catered to what Pastor Purcell decried as spiritually dangerous. Why, I'd said, besides selling gas to Serpent Mound visitors who passed through town, Elroy's Gas Station and Body Shop even offered a fine selection of Serpent Mound postcards and souvenirs. (At that, Elroy went a little pale and looked nervous.)

In the end, my argument prevailed and the LeFevers opened Rising Star and happily planned for what they hoped would be the first of many psychic fairs in Paradise. And as a thank-you, the LeFevers invited me to join their tour of Serpent Mound and to bring some friends. Winnie Porter was working the bookmobile and my boyfriend Owen Collins was teaching at the Masonville Community College, so I'd asked Cherry and Sally, who'd happily agreed, thinking a tour of Serpent Mound with a bunch of psychics (instead of teachers and fellow students) would be a "hoot."

"The tour doesn't start for another half hour," Cherry was saying, drawing me back to the present conversation. She clutched her short skirt's hem so she could slide off her stool with some modesty. She pulled two dollars from her Marilyn Monroe bag and put them on the bar.

"Look, I overreacted, let's just let it go —"
I said, but my friends had already headed
away from the bar into the dining room. I
looked at the bar. My cup of coffee was
still half full.

But I tossed down two bucks, too, and
went after Sally and Cherry, hoping to
catch up before they could offend Paradise's
guests — the visiting psychics — by calling
them gypsy women. That would most
definitely not be a "hoot."

3

The dining room had been rearranged for the psychic fair. The square tables were lined up in rows and cleared of their usual trappings — sweetener packets, paper napkin dispensers, salt and pepper shakers labeled *S* and *P.* The tables were covered with white, spotless tablecloths, which gave me a wee swelling of pride.

The cloths had come out of the Rhinegolds' storage room, after having been entombed there for nearly a decade, and I'd been hired the previous week to wash and de-stain them just for this event. Rust spots from our town's water had emerged on the tablecloths, not an uncommon problem with old linens. But lemon juice and sunlight had taken care of the rust spots, and a careful washing on the delicate cycle had made the cloths almost as good as new.

The chairs were placed on either side of the rows, I reckoned for psychics on one side and . . . well, what would you call people getting their futures read? Psych-ees? . . . on the other. The room was mostly empty, except for two women unpacking boxes behind one of the tables, and Damon LeFever, huddled over in one of the booths.

These booths, plus a few tables, had been left available for diners. Usually, the Red Horse just serves drinks and snacks in its combined bar and dining room. Luke and Greta Rhinegold, the Red Horse owners, were in their seventies and Greta had given up cooking full menus about five years before, due to her arthritis. But for this event, the Red Horse would offer hot dogs, hamburgers, and chips.

A corner of the dining room was blocked off with movable panels to create a private area, whether for the psychics or some other purpose, I wasn't quite sure.

The only other people in the dining room were two women who looked like a mother and daughter. They were arguing in low voices, but we could hear them because the room was nearly empty.

"Geez, ma, how many times do I have to tell you? All those brochures would have made the table too crowded," the younger woman was saying. The strength of her voice was a surprise, coming from behind a sheath of long blond hair that hung down her back and in her face. She was very thin and dressed in jeans and a pale blue T-shirt that didn't quite meet her jeans' waistband. She wore thick-soled shoes with chunky high heels.

"But, Skylar, what if we run out like we did last time? I just don't think fifty flyers is enough." The older woman was a little heavier, a little shorter, and had short, cropped blond hair. But she, too, wore jeans and a blue T-shirt and high-heeled chunky shoes. I shuddered at that. I've always thought that dressing alike on purpose was a little creepy. I wondered whose choice it was and guessed the mom's.

Sally frowned at me. "Shouldn't they know exactly how many brochures they'll need, I mean, if they're psychic and all?"

"Lord, what I could do with that child's hair with braids, if I just had a chance," Cherry moaned, wiggling her fingers.

"Hush, you two," I said in a harsh whisper. "Why don't we just let this whole thing drop, okay? We don't want to be late for the tour. C'mon, it's a gorgeous day, we'll wait outside . . ."

"For pity's sake, Josie, we have a whole half hour before the tour leaves," said Cherry. She started toward the two women who were still arguing over whether they had enough brochures. "Yoo hoo! Oh, psychic ladies!"

I moaned.

The women stopped talking, and stared at the three of us. At least, the older woman did. The younger woman's features were still hidden behind her hair, so it was hard to tell.

"We're hoping to find a woman named Ginny Proffitt. Do you know where she is?"

They kept staring.

"Maybe they prefer you communicate with them mentally. You know, think what you want to say to them, and they'll pick it up on their brain waves," Sally said.

"Good idea," Cherry said. She closed her eyes, scrunched up her face in such intense concentration that I knew she was going to have mascara smudges from her upper lashes below her eyes. Then she started moaning, in a long, flat "O-o-o-om."

Now the two women were really studying us. The younger one had even tucked her hair behind her ears, so her eyes were clear to stare at us. She had a sweet, innocent face.

I'd had enough. I walked over to the women. "Hi. I'm Josie Toadfern. Sorry about my friends. I reckon they've never met psychics before." I paused. The women's expression hadn't changed, except now their staring was focused on me. And I couldn't tell what they were thinking. The irony of the fact that I wished I had the power to know wasn't lost on me, and it made me smile, and relax a little. "I reckon I haven't, either."

The younger woman sighed. "That's okay. We get jokes all the time about our calling." Hmmm. I'd never thought of being a psychic as a calling. More like something that would be thrust on you, whether you wanted it or not. Kind of like flat feet.

"People think psychics automatically just know things — like what people are thinking, or precise details about the future —" she glanced over my shoulder at Sally and Cherry. I'd heard them shuffling toward us, but the shuffling stopped with the woman's glance — "as if we can just look such things up, as if being a psychic means having access to some otherworldly encyclopedia. It's more like the ability to get an impression, through intuition, like . . ."

I must have looked confused — which I

was — because the young woman trailed off. Then she smiled, as if something bemused her, a private joke. "I'm Skylar Temple. Well, really, Skylar Smith. But for business, I took a pseudonym."

She thrust out her hand. Her shake was surprisingly flimsy. "This is my mom, Karen Smith."

I turned to the older woman, but she wasn't paying any attention to me. She was looking worriedly at her daughter. "Skylar, really, why do you tell people that about your last name? It ruins the whole effect."

Skylar rolled her eyes. "My mother, my manager."

I pushed back a laugh. Skylar would fit right in with Cherry and Sally and me, although I guessed Skylar to be in her early twenties. Cherry and Sally had finally shuffled up beside us.

"You know, you have the most beautiful hair." Cherry's fingers waved near Skylar's hair. "It would be perfect in braids."

Skylar lifted her eyebrows. "You're good with braids?"

I said, "She owns Paradise's only beauty salon. Braiding's her specialty — although she also does buns and blue heads."

We all laughed, except Karen, who kept a fretting look on her face. "I am her manager. But she never pays any attention to me, even though I'm the one who discovered her talent, which she inherited from my mother, God rest her soul."

"You're not a psychic?" I asked, surprised.

Karen gave a twittering laugh. "Oh no, not at all. But Skylar — well — Skylar has a gift with dream interpretation. She also does Tarot reading —"

"Ooh, Josie, here, got mugged with a palm reading and a dream interpretation, on her way in! From a Ginny Proffitt," Cherry chimed in. "You all know her? We're hoping to find her. Or find out more about her."

The Smiths went stonily silent again. Uh oh.

Then Karen turned to her daughter, "See? I told you. You should have protested your table assignment! But do you ever listen to me? Not about the brochures, not about that awful Ginny Proffitt! I hate that woman! I'm not psychic, but even I know this is going to be a disaster!"

With that, Karen stomped off toward the curtained area. She thrust aside the curtain so hard the whole structure wobbled. She was surprisingly strong for such a petite woman. Skylar stared after her mom, looking at once embarrassed and worried.

"What's behind the curtain?" Sally asked, breaking the uncomfortable silence. "The Wizard of Oz?"

Skylar looked back at us, regaining at least the appearance of composure with a quick laugh. "Right now, a bunch of boxes — participants' brochures, a few items for sale at the tables. By tomorrow afternoon, when the psychic fair opens, it'll be an area for specialty seminars. How to balance your chakras, things like that."

Sally grunted. "I don't even know how to balance my checkbook."

"Well, don't ask me about that — or about chakras. I know a little, but it's not my specialty."

"Psychics have specialties?" said Cherry.

"Sure," Skylar said, "like in most any profession. I mean, you do hair, but your real passion is braiding. My gift is in dream interpretation and Tarot reading, just like mom said. Ginny Proffitt focuses on palm and orb reading —"

"Orb?" Cherry said.

Skylar smiled. "What most people think of as a crystal ball. But Ginny also does dream-interpretation."

"I take it you two are competitors in the dream interpretation department?" Sally asked.

Skylar's smile faded. "My mom and Ginny are competitors — ever since a psychic fair last spring in Illinois. Ginny's table was beside mine then, too, and she grabbed all the attention. I still did just fine — and I prefer a much more relaxed approach — but Ginny's a real self-promoter."

She turned, pointing to the table that was next to hers. She and her mother had been blocking it from our view, and we'd been so focused on her mother's stomping off that we hadn't noticed the red tablecloth on the table next to Skylar's.

Now that Skylar had moved, we could also see the large clear crystal ball, on an ornate gold stand, with four dragons holding up the ball, displayed on a red tablecloth embroidered with gold stars, and the professionally printed display poster that read, GINNY PROFFITT, SEER AND PROPHETESS. PALM AND ORB READINGS . . . DREAM INTERPRETATION . . . YOUR FUTURE REVEALED! She also had a huge stack of full-color, promotional brochures.

I looked at the black-and-white, printed-at-the-local-copy-shop flyers on Skylar's plain, white tableclothed table. I could see why Karen felt intimidated by Ginny, on her daughter's behalf.

"Wow," said Cherry. "Think I could get her to redesign the front window to my hair salon?" I resisted an eye roll. I swear, sometimes I think Cherry wouldn't know tacky if it jumped up in all its big-haired glory and bit her on her pierced (with just the tiniest of diamonds, I admit) nose.

"Does she come out wearing a turban?" Sally asked.

Skylar laughed again. "No. But she wears a specially made gold lamé robe. And she wanted a dry-ice machine. Fortunately, for this fair at least, Damon and Sienna nixed that idea. Rumor has it Ginny was furious."

"But she seemed pretty down to earth when I met her," I said. "Overly aggressive maybe, but not the gold-lamé-robe-type." Although the warm-up suit had been pretty flashy, kind of like Dolly-Parton-does-step-aerobics.

"Yeah, but she forced a palm reading on you. And told you all about this dream you have repeatedly, about drowning in an orange bikini . . ." Sally said. I could tell she was still angry at Ginny on my behalf.

"Drowning can represent feeling overwhelmed," Skylar interjected wisely. "Now the orange bikini — hmm. That's one I'll have to think about . . ."

"The orange bikini was my idea of what to wear in a drowning dream," Cherry said. "Josie was wearing a navy one piece when she drowned in her dream."

"Oh, well, that just represents being overly responsible," said Skylar with a dismissive wave of her hand. "You know, the kind of person who's always looking out for other people, doesn't cut loose much . . ."

Well, thank you very much, I thought. And just what does it mean that I dream of my dead Junior High teacher giving me unwanted advice?

But out loud, I said, "Don't Ginny's tactics put off her customers, though? And wasn't everyone supposed to have white tablecloths?" I knew this because of my role in laundering the cloths.

Skylar smiled knowingly. "Ginny Proffitt is very popular. She has groupies, a discussion group on her Web site, and a self-published book of her philosophies that will sell hundreds of copies this weekend. She's the draw for this fair, and everyone knows it. That's why if she wants a red tablecloth, she gets it."

"But no dry-ice machine," I said. My gaze strayed back to the crystal ball. There was something very appealing about its perfect orb shape. Soothing. But all I saw through it was a distorted view of the brochures on the other side, kind of like looking through a warped magnifying glass. I wondered what someone like Ginny saw when she looked through it.

Skylar shrugged, fingering the Celtic cross she wore around her neck. "Damon and Sierra are brave souls. Like the rest of us, Ginny's self-promotion tactics make them nervous. She plays to all the stereotypes the rest of us are trying to overcome and she gives her clients specific predictions."

"Isn't that what psychics are supposed to do?" Sally said.

"We see it more as giving impressions of possible challenges a client might face. And Jesse and Sienna have asked Ginny to keep her predictions to that level — not 'your husband will die in a week,' but just saying if she senses ill health for a loved one. Damon even warned her that she'll be asked to leave if she gets too specific. At the Illinois fair, Ginny predicted just that — the husband dying — to a client, and the poor woman collapsed in hysteria. Of course, Damon's warning has angered Ginny, who is already spreading gossip on the psychic Internet list servs that Damon and Sienna don't really know what they're doing, this being their first fair."

Cherry went behind the table and pointed at the crystal ball. "So she uses this crystal ball to see the future, huh, like that poor woman's hubby dying?" I shook my head. Cherry heard what she wanted to hear — and like a lot of people, what she wanted to hear was that there is some specific way to know the specific future. She tapped the ball with her long red fingernails. "Wake up, wake up! Am I gonna get back with DeWayne, or are we through for good?"

I gasped. Sally rolled her eyes. Skylar frowned and waved her hand over the top of the ball. "Don't do that, okay?"

Cherry jumped back, suddenly looking nervous. "What, is it bad luck or something? You know, I did feel a little zap when I touched it . . ."

"That was static electricity," I said.

Skylar took us all in with a single glance — and I could read just what she was thinking. That the three of us were nuts. Great. Three native Paradisites had just managed to out-weirdo the so-called weirdos in less than ten minutes.

"It's just disrespectful," Skylar said. "Even if I don't much like Ginny, either, I have to speak up for her personal effects.

That's her orb for gazing, and it's tuned now to her own energy. Sort of like my Tarot cards are tuned to me."

Cherry withdrew her hand. "Sorry," she squeaked meekly, now staring at the ball as if it might take on a life of its own and attack her somehow.

"Josie! Josie, I need your help!" That was Damon, hollering as he bolted over to us from his booth. "There's no way that Sienna and I can lead today's tour!"

"Is she feeling poorly this morning?" I asked hopefully — which made Skylar give me a funny look — but I knew that Sienna and Damon were trying to have a child and not having any luck. The previous month she'd felt queasy two mornings in a row and was all excited that she was experiencing morning sickness. It turned out she had the flu.

Damon shook his head. "Nothing like that. It's our store! Someone must have broken in last night — the place has been trashed! Crystals, incense, amulets, books everywhere." Tears welled in his eyes. "I don't understand. I'm sure we locked up and set the alarm like we always do. We wouldn't have known about it until Monday —" The Rising Star was closed for Friday and the weekend because of the psychic fair, where all of Damon's and Sienna's customers would be anyway. "— but she'd left her tour notes in the back office and went in to get them just a half hour ago . . ." Damon's voice trailed off shakily.

I patted his arm, Cherry swooped in for a bear hug that made Damon gasp, and Sally swatted her fist into her palm, muttering about what she'd do if she caught the jerks who'd messed with her friends.

"Is Sienna okay?" I asked.

"She's shaken up, but fine," said Damon, pulling out of Cherry's hug. "But she's filing a police report with Chief Worthy, who isn't being all that helpful."

That didn't surprise me. I'd overheard John Worthy at Sandy's Restaurant — a popular local diner across the street from my laundromat — complain that he feared the LeFevers' business would attract all kinds of weirdos who would do who knew what kind of vandalism. I'm not sure exactly how an interest in tarot cards or supernatural books makes someone a vandal. The only crime I'd known to happen because of their business up until now was that the first (and only) time I went in, my sense of smell was assaulted by the overwhelming fragrance of patchouli incense.

But now someone had vandalized their

business. The poor LeFevers. I knew they'd put everything into their business, and had taken out pretty large loans, too.

". . . and of course Chief Worthy wants Sienna to give an accounting of what may have been stolen, but she says the place is such a mess that it's going to take hours for her to straighten out the inventory to figure out what's missing." Damon put his hands to his head and moaned. "We'll have to cancel the tour and I just don't know how we can focus on making this fair a success with this . . ."

"Damon, you're not really going to cancel the tour, are you? I was really looking forward to it," Skylar said. "Everyone was . . ." She trailed off as we all looked at her. "I'm sorry. I know how that sounds." She looked at Damon. "I'm really sorry that happened to your business. But to miss Serpent Mound . . ." Skylar shook her head sadly.

"Serpent Mound is an important spiritual site. Visiting it was part of the draw for coming here for several of the psychics, especially Ginny Proffitt," Damon explained to us. "We were all looking forward to attuning ourselves to the wise spirituality of the ancient ones who created it."

Cherry started to giggle, but I elbowed

her before Damon noticed.

"Everyone's going to be so disappointed," Damon concluded, looking sad, in a little-boy-who-lost-his-puppy sort of way. It made me feel sorry for him, even though I wasn't quite sure what to make of his "attuning" and "ancient ones" talk.

Apparently, his sad face got to Sally, too, because she said, "Aw, hell, Damon, why don't you have Josie here lead the tour. She knows all about Serpent Mound."

"What? What are you talking about?" I cried. "I don't know more than anyone else who's from around here."

"Don't you recollect the project you did on Serpent Mound for eighth grade local history class?" Sally turned to Damon. "She even did a to-scale clay model."

"Hey — I think I remember that," said Cherry. "It was really cute. With little flags and all, identifying the important parts . . . like, you know. The head. The tail. The middle."

I flinched. How had Cherry managed to pass anything other than beauty-school braiding?

"Yeah," Sally said. "It even impressed old Mrs. Oglevee. And Josie never impressed her."

I flinched again — this time at the mention

of Mrs. Oglevee. "Well, I was always fascinated by Serpent Mound . . ."

"And still are," Cherry said. "We were on the bookmobile last week at the same time and I was getting the latest issue of *Elle*, and Josie had all these books about Serpent Mound, which Winnie had gotten especially for her from some other library."

Winnie Porter is our bookmobile librarian and a good friend. She'd wanted to come on this tour, but had been called into a special meeting at the main Masonville library branch.

"Well, now," I said, "I do have an interest, but my knowledge is pretty general. I'm sure Skylar and everyone else would want to know pretty specific things," I said.

Skylar sighed. "Oh, yes. I've always heard that part of Serpent Mound's power comes from the unusual shape of the land it's built on, but I don't know much more than that."

"Well, the rocks underlying most of Ohio are flat, but a five-mile diameter of land on which the Fort Ancient people built Serpent Mound has an unusual underlying topography of folded-up bedrock. Usually that's caused by volcanic activity or a meteor strike, but that's not at all the case at Serpent Mound. It was caused by a cryptoexplosion, which means an explosion of gas from within the earth," I said. "The gases built up and finally exploded, forming underlying layers that make up some gentle contours, and some sharp rises in the land. It doesn't look all that different from the rest of the rolling hills of southern Ohio, until you climb up the observation tower, and then . . ." I trailed off, realizing everyone was staring at me in amazement. Too late, I clapped my hand over my mouth.

"Josie, you really could fill in for Sienna, especially if we get her notes," Damon started, then looked crestfallen again. "I rented a van for this excursion. I was going to drive —"

"Aw, hell, Damon, I can drive," said Sally. "I can drive anything."

"And I can point out the sights on the way there, while Josie looks over Sienna's notes," Cherry said.

"You know, this could work!" Damon sounded happier again. "What do you say, Josie?"

What could I say? They were all four of them looking eagerly at me. And — as I'd explain over and over again later on to anyone who'd listen — I just wanted to help.

So of course, I said yes.

4

"And to our left, we have a cornfield!"

Cherry, who was in the front passenger seat of the full-size van, swiveled around to face the rest of us. I was in the seat behind her, which meant I was facing her, but she ignored me, gazing over the top of my head at the passengers behind me. When I nervously glanced over my shoulder, I noted that all eight — Skylar, her mom Karen, and six other psychics — were craning to look out the windows on the left.

No Ginny Proffitt, though. We had waited for her as long as we could, but finally decided that the meeting she had mentioned to me must have gone on longer than planned. Several people were worried that Ginny would be angry about us leaving without her, but everyone needed to get back in time to set up for that night, so Damon reassured everyone that he'd be sure to bring Ginny on a private tour of Serpent Mound after the psychic fair ended. Everyone seemed relieved by that solution, and I wondered how many people had been on the receiving end of Ginny's wrath, which I'd experienced in the Red Horse parking lot.

"The cornfield belongs to the Crowleys," Cherry went on. "who have lived in the Paradise area for four generations . . ."

I turned back around in my seat and stared out the window on my right at another cornfield, which looked just like the one on the left, although the Fowler family owned it.

"If you get a break tonight from the psychic fair, you might want to visit the Crowleys' gently haunted corn maze. The maze, cut out of an acre of corn, will have young ghosts, goblins, and witches —" Cherry giggled, apparently confusing psychics with witches, "— and other Halloween characters from the United Methodist Church of Paradise's Youth Group. The maze is a fundraiser for the Crowleys to offset some medical bills of a family member — a ten-year-old-boy — who has cancer."

A murmur of sympathy arose behind me, and I felt a wave of sympathy, too, which never lessened even though I'd heard the story many times. I attended church with the Crowleys and knew that young Ricky Crowley-Ypsilanti had childhood Hodgkin's disease, a form of lymphoma. Ricky was lucky in that his disease was in stage I, meaning found in only one lymph node area, and so far he had responded well to chemotherapy.

But the emotional and financial burden was tough on his family. His mama, Maureen Crowley, was divorced, had just lost her job as a secretary in Cincinnati, and didn't have any health insurance. Ricky's grandpa, Ed Crowley, had passed away from a heart attack the previous August. Maureen and Ricky had moved back to the Crowley farm, with Maureen's mama, Rebecca, who still grieved for her husband, and with her Uncle Hugh, Ed's brother. Just a week before the psychic fair, Ricky had taken a bad turn and was in Children's Hospital in Cincinnati.

Most everyone in Paradise offered comforting words and prayers to ease the Crowleys' emotional hardship, and we'd held several fundraisers to help with the financial difficulties, too. Cherry had donation cans at each station in her hair salon, and Sally had organized a line-dancing marathon at the

Bar-None, and I'd coordinated a chili-spaghetti dinner at church.

(Chili-spaghetti is Cincinnati-style chili — more of a sauce, seasoned with chili powder, nutmeg, and even a bit of chocolate — served on spaghetti and topped with mounds of grated cheddar cheese for a "3-way." Onions or beans makes it a "4-way," both makes it a "5-way." I prefer my chili-spaghetti "4-way," with onions.)

The "haunted corn maze" had been Ed Crowley's idea, but after Ed died, the Crowleys lost heart in it, until Pastor Lamb, at the Methodist Church, turned the idea over to the youth group, which had worked with Hugh Crowley to make it happen.

"Now, the haunted corn maze opens tonight," Cherry was saying, "and it will be open Saturday night, too, and the next two weekends as well, through Halloween."

I was looking forward, myself, to going on a date to the corn maze that evening with Owen. Maybe afterward we could stop by the Bar-None, and then . . .

The Ford swerved, jolting me out of my daydream.

" 'Possum!" Sally called out. "Sorry 'bout that." Sally was driving the van, a Ford 350 SuperDuty valued at about

$40,000, Damon had said nervously when he handed the keys over to her. Sally had assured him she'd once chauffeured a rock band.

(Damon looked so worried about Sienna and his business and the upcoming weekend that I didn't have the heart to tell him that Sally'd been paid in six-packs and cigarettes, the band was a rockabilly gig thrown together by Sally's brother Garret for a weekend contest, and the "coach" was a 1965 VW microbus that they'd had to abandon in favor of a Greyhound when Sally stripped its gears beyond redemption.)

I glanced down at Sienna's notes. Sienna's cramped handwriting was hard to decipher. Poor Sienna and Damon. We'd stopped by the Rising Star on our way out of town to drop off Damon and pick up the notes. I'd only glimpsed the damage through the store's front pane window, but it looked even worse than what Damon had described.

Who would have done such a thing? My first thought — which I hated — was that it was Pastor Dru Purcell and his followers, wanting to mess up the weekend for them. But would even Dru stoop that low?

"After you've set up your crystal balls and things, come on out to the Crowleys this evening to visit their corn maze,"

Cherry was saying. "Your goal is to find a map piece in each section of the maze, until you have a complete map."

"That sounds truly a-maz-ing!" said Samantha Mulligan, a pet psychic who sat behind me.

I groaned.

"I'd love to go!" hollered Max Whitstone, a large, muscular man wearing a Stetson and, despite the chill of October, a T-shirt that showed off dragon tattoos on his biceps. Perhaps predictably, Max and Cherry had already hit it off, although if Max couldn't foresee that a love connection with Cherry would probably be a bad idea, I didn't have much faith in his palm-reading prowess.

The van suddenly jerked again. "Sorry!" Sally called out cheerily. "Didn't see that curve coming."

"Damon promised a smooth ride," whined Maggie Langguth from the back of the van. Balancing chakras was her specialty. "This is disturbing my inner equilibrium!"

I turned around in my seat, pulled up on my knees, and faced all eight psychics. I ignored Cherry's poke in my back, swallowed hard, smiled and said, "Well, we sure do appreciate Cherry's comments about, um, rural lifestyles around Paradise. Now, we'll be at the entrance of Serpent Mound soon. The mound was originally attributed to the Adena culture, circa 800 B.C. to A.D. 100, who created two burial mounds also at the site — as well as other burial mounds found in southern Ohio. But a third burial mound, near the serpent's tail, was known to have been created by the Fort Ancient culture, which existed much later, from about A.D. 1000 to 1500. The most recent excavations uncovered wood charcoal, which was carbon dated to the time of the Fort Ancient culture, so the belief now is that these people were the actual creators of Serpent Mound . . ."

I told myself, Josie, everything's going to be just fine . . . you'll get through this tour, then never have to see any of these people again.

Too bad I didn't have my own crystal ball, one that would really work. I'd have jumped right out of that van and into the nearest cornfield.

From the top of the observation tower, we could see everyone else — except Cherry and Max — seated cross-legged in a circle near the head of the Serpent Mound. Maggie was leading some kind of meditative ceremony to, as she put it, "tap into the universal power of the ancient earth mother."

I took that to be some kind of prayer.

Sally, Cherry, and I had been invited to join in — which I thought was mighty generous of the group — but we declined, Sally and I because we just needed a break, and Cherry because she was eager to go off "exploring" (mmm hmmm) with Max.

During our self-guided tour and lunch — poor Sienna had prepared a cooler full of sandwiches, cookies, and sodas — we'd come to know most of the psychics better. They were enraptured by the mystery and spirituality of Serpent Mound. The psychics were a mixture of beliefs — mostly Christian, Wiccan, and one self-professed "seeking" (which I think pretty much describes everybody) — but unified in their fascination with the Mound.

I felt peaceful, standing up in the observation tower, overlooking the earthen works and the meditative ceremony. Did this place inspire a sense of peacefulness because I knew the Fort Ancient people had created for themselves a spiritual, mystical place, or was the place peaceful in and of itself, and that's why the ancient ones had chosen it?

"You reckon this place has spooks?"

Sally broke into my musing. She never was one for contemplation.

I shrugged. "I don't think so. I think the psychics are just trying to get in touch with the spiritual nature of this place by getting in touch with their own inner natures."

Sally shook her head. "Too complicated. Me, I just would like a night to go two-steppin' and beer drinking."

Sally had little time for just fun, with her three sons, and no daddy around to help, although she'd commented often about how she was better off without Waylon Hinckie, the Rat.

"But you know, as flaky as their beliefs seem to be, they do kinda grow on you," Sally said, looking fondly down on the circle of psychics, as if they were a litter of puppies instead of just people with beliefs different from what Sally and I had been raised to accept. "And you did a nice job on the tour."

I was surprised at Sally's compliment. "Thanks," I said. "But I'm glad it's over. Nothing can go wrong from here, right?" All I had to do was keep my fingers crossed that Sally'd get us all back to the Red Horse in one piece. Then I'd go home, freshen up, and go out on my corn-maze date with Owen. I was looking forward to that, and the quiet normalcy of the coming weekend.

"Nah, nothin' can go wrong," Sally was saying, "except by the end of this weekend, he's gonna break her heart."

Sally pointed to the path below, where Cherry and Max walked arm in arm, Cherry regarding Max with giggly adoration.

"Poor Cherry," I said. "You'd think she'd learn to recognize man trouble, even when it comes nicely packaged with Stetsons and tattoos."

"Yep," said Sally. "I surely hate to see my girlfriends get their hearts broken."

I looked away from the path to Sally. "My heart is gonna be fine," I said.

"You sure about that?" Sally asked.

I held her gaze as long as I could, then finally broke away to look again at the earthworks. It wasn't that her gaze was too hard to hold. I'd won my share of staredowns with Sally. It was just that I wasn't sure how to answer her question.

I knew Sally didn't like my boyfriend, Owen Collins, because she sensed that he'd hurt me. And he had, although I hadn't told her the details — that for the first nine months we dated, he'd withheld the truth of his past, that he'd once been married, had a twelve-year-old son, and had, in a fight he hadn't started, accidentally killed another man, and so had spent time in prison for manslaughter. It wasn't my place to share Owen's story with Sally, not yet, but because she sensed he'd hurt me, she was wary of him, and said we came from different worlds. She said sooner or later he was bound to get tired of Paradise and move on to better places, and she knew I never would because of my cousin Guy.

"Besides," I said, "I've had my heart broken before. I can deal with it." Cherry and Max disappeared behind a tree.

Sally gave a short laugh. "Breakin' up with John Worthy back in high school doesn't count, sister." She calls me that when she's annoyed with me, even though we're cousins. Maybe it has something to do with the fact that she has six brothers and no sisters.

"Does, too," I said, elbowing her. "The bum left me high and dry for junior prom."

"I offered to set you up with Bo!" Bo was a biker buddy of her ex-husband — and both men were fifteen years older than us.

"Oh, that'd have saved my heart from pain." We laughed.

The silence between us became comfortable again.

Then Sally said, "You know, them people down there, maybe they're onto something. Great-Aunt Noreen might have scared us near to peein' our pants with her talk of dreams about us drowning over at the lake, but Mamaw still says the gift of sight runs deep back into our family. I've always thought it was hogwash, but Mamaw's right about a lot of things."

"I wouldn't know," I said. Mamaw Toadfern had stopped talking to my mama when Mamaw's son, my daddy, ran off when I was a baby and never got back in touch with anyone ever again. When my mama ran off, too, a few years later, Mamaw turned the silent treatment on me — never mind that I was seven. Many members of the Toadfern clan, who didn't want to make Mamaw mad, didn't talk to me, either, unless they had to come into my laundromat when their washers broke or the water tables ran low on their farms after a drought. A notable exception was Sally and a few other cousins, who'd already ticked off Mamaw about all kinds of things. In Sally's case, that was marrying a wild biker and then buying a bar to run. (Mamaw was a strict Pentecostal.)

"Well, true," Sally said, "but the point is, maybe there's something to at least a few folks having a gift of prophecy. And I can tell, Josie, that that Ginny Proffitt woman spooked you with whatever she said she saw in your palm. And I don't think it was really about navy blue swimsuits, either."

I stared down at the earthworks. Here it was, my chance to tell someone about my recurring dream of Mrs. Oglevee. I'd never considered sharing it before.

Max and Cherry fell over from behind the tree — literally — with Max right on top of Cherry. Even from our distance, we could hear Cherry's "oof." But that didn't stop Max from kissing her or Cherry from responding.

Sally sighed. "Might as well buy the bourbon and chocolate for next week now. He's gonna bust her heart wide open."

"Yes, he will. He's known for that kind of thing."

Sally and I both jumped and turned. Karen was right behind us. She was breathing quite evenly, given that she'd just climbed dozens of steps. "I saw them going at it as I came up the path. It's just desecration, pure and simple."

I glanced back at where the psychic group (minus Max) had gathered. They had finished their ceremony and most were milling about now along the Serpent Mound path.

Sally waggled her eyebrows at Karen. "You think the Fort Ancient people never got it on? Maybe their spirits appreciate Max and Cherry's homage to the life force."

Karen snorted — primly, somehow — at that. "Max would pay homage to the life force with anything in a skirt that's not dead. He's even flirted with my Skylar, although he's old enough to be her father —"

"— and I'm old enough to take care of myself," said Skylar, who came up the steps to the lookout sounding weary, though not from her trek. "Really, Mom, leave poor Max alone."

"He's just lucky Ginny's not here. She'd tell him off for desecrating a spiritual hot spot," Karen said, a little sulkily.

"But not Cherry? She has some choice, after all, in whether or not to play tonsil hockey with Max," Sally said. Two more people came up — Maggie, the chakra balancer, and Samantha, the pet psychic.

Skylar laughed. "Ginny'd just warn Cherry to beware of Max — that he's incredibly charming, but grows weary of his companions quickly. And she should know."

"But they were together for three years, weren't they?" Samantha said, huffing every few words. I liked her for that. Karen, Skylar, and Maggie's ability to bounce up all those steps without getting out of breath was a wee bit annoying.

"Max and Ginny were dating?" I asked.

"Living together," said Karen. "Unwed." She put a whole lot of negative judgment into that one word. I was surprised to realize she was a conservative psychic follower — not a likely type, I'd have thought, but I guess it really does take all kinds.

"Until Ginny dumped Max. But not because of his flirtatious nature. Just because she tired of him," said Maggie. "At least, that's the talk, and it doesn't surprise me. Ginny uses people for her own purposes, then dumps them." I looked at little, plump, soft-spoken Maggie. She sounded so bitter.

"Is that why Ginny didn't come on the tour — because of Max?" Sally asked.

"I don't believe so," said Samantha. "Ginny is quite capable of ignoring Max, although Max really hates her for dumping him. Male ego and all that."

"I'm amazed Ginny would miss this. Isn't she from here?" Maggie said.

Sally and I looked at each other, startled.

71

We knew most everyone from around this area, but neither of us had heard of Ginny Proffitt before today.

"From the Columbus area," Karen said. "She told me about Serpent Mound, how much she loved coming here as a kid. This was at the Chicago psychic fair, before the fair started and she took so many of Skylar's potential clients away. If I'd known she was going to do that, I'd never have talked to her. I've really got to talk to Damon and Sienna about moving Skylar."

"Mo-o-om," Skylar started.

"Now, sweetie, your mom is just trying to watch out for you," Samantha said kindly. "Unfortunately, that is Ginny's way. She always wants all the attention, all the focus on her, and —" Suddenly Samantha stopped, her soft round face going rigid, as she stared into the trees.

"Are you okay?" I asked anxiously.

Maggie swatted me on the arm. "Hush!" she hissed. "She's tuning in."

Sally looked around nervously. "What? What? Don't tell me there are Fort Ancient spirits you all can see."

Maggie pointed at the tree below us. I stared at the tree. Sally stared at the tree. And all we saw was a tree. Even Max and Cherry had moved on from behind it.

Then, finally, I saw what had snagged Samantha's attention — a gray squirrel, up on a top branch, sitting up on its hind legs, its front paws dangling. Samantha was perfectly still as she stared at the squirrel. The squirrel was perfectly still as it stared back at her.

Then, suddenly, Samantha threw her arms up in the air and let out a wail that sounded like "whee-w-w-whree-eee!!"

The squirrel shot up into the tree as if it had been launched from a cannon, disappearing from our sight.

Samantha — quivering and shaking — wiped sudden tears from her eyes. Sally, I noted, was quivering, too, and wiping at her own eyes, but I had a feeling it was from a very different emotion than what had motivated Samantha, who was now hollering, "Oh, thank you, dear Xavier!"

I looked around. "Xavier?" Had I forgotten a psychic?

Maggie swatted my arm again. "The squirrel. She's thanking him for the message."

I was confused. "Message? I didn't hear anything."

Samantha gave me a look, again surprisingly hard for such a little, soft woman. "He told me," she said with great dignity, "that all will be avenged for me this weekend."

"That was mighty nice of him," Sally said, barely holding back her laughter. "You leave him any messages?"

Samantha gave her a look of such seriousness that even Sally quickly sobered. "Xavier had forgotten where he'd left a stash of acorns. I reminded him."

With that, she turned and started back down the steps. Karen watched after her, clearly awestruck. She sighed. "I do so admire psychics' talents." She patted Skylar's arm. "Yours are the best, of course, sweetie."

"Thanks, Mom," Skylar said, through gritted teeth. They started down the steps, too.

"Most everyone's headed back to the van. We need to get back to the motel to finish setting up. You did a great job leading the tour," Maggie said, turning toward the steps.

"Wait — what do . . ." I paused, wanting to keep the incredulity out of my voice as I spoke the next words. "What do you know about Samantha's message from the squirrel — that she'll be avenged this weekend?"

Maggie turned back around. "My guess is that Samantha interpreted whatever the squirrel channeled to her" — Maggie said this with complete seriousness — "to mean

74

that Ginny will in some way be humiliated this weekend. Samantha and Ginny were business partners once, and, so I hear, it didn't end well. Somehow, Ginny ended up with most of the assets, and Samantha basically had to start over."

Maggie shook her head. "Poor Samantha. The stress almost destroyed her abilities, but fortunately she met a duck at the park near her house, and after several conversations with him, Samantha was back on track. She moved to Milwaukee and rebuilt her business. She's probably better off without Ginny, but I don't think she's ever quite gotten over it."

Sally contained herself until Maggie had gone down the steps, then erupted with laughter.

"Keep it together," I snapped, grumpy because I knew I'd also been tempted to laugh. "I need you to help me get everyone back on the van so we can head back to Paradise."

"Aww, Josie, can't Xavier come too?" Sally called after me, as I started down the steps.

I didn't let her see it — but her comment made me smile.

"Thank you for touring with us! On our

way back to Paradise, I'll point out some of the sites we missed on our way over here," Cherry was saying, fifteen minutes later, as Sally pulled the van out of its parking spot.

We were all present and accounted for on the van, and, I thought with relief, my duties were over.

"As we exit, you'll see on your left a large soybean field where a local man sighted a landing of an alien spaceship."

The group behind me gasped. I wasn't sure if this was in awe at this report, in annoyance that perhaps Cherry was making fun of everyone (which I didn't think to be the case . . . I thought she was just enjoying being Ms. Tour Guide), or if it was because as she flipped her hair behind her right shoulder and turned to look to the left herself, a largish red mottled hickey was revealed on her neck.

"Of course, when the man reported it to the local authorities, they pooh-poohed his claims, despite the fact that burn marks in a circular pattern were found in the field that could never be explained . . ."

As Sally went on, and everyone else craned to look at her hickey, I stared out my window to the right. Tonight, I told myself, I would have a fine, relaxing time with Owen . . .

Then I saw them. Ginny Proffitt and Dru Purcell. Standing in the parking lot, facing each other. Talking — but, I could tell even behind the window that made their conversation mute to me — in a quiet way. Not the screaming I'd have expected from Dru.

What was Ginny doing here? Had she finished up her mysterious meeting and come to meet us for the end of the tour?

That seemed believable . . . but what was Dru doing here? This wasn't exactly his kind of place. One of his Sunday School teachers at the Paradise Church of Almighty Revelation, so I'd heard, had been so severely reprimanded for suggesting a youth group field trip out here, that she'd become a Lutheran.

Then, I saw him lift his glasses, wipe his eyes and pull Ginny to him in a tender, gentle embrace.

The meeting Ginny had rushed to, I knew with startling clarity, had been this — to meet Reverend Dru Purcell at Serpent Mound. As Dru hugged her, Ginny looked over the top of his arm . . . at me. At the bus. And she grinned. And pushed him away enough to give me a wave.

Then Dru pulled away from her and looked over at our van, at me staring out at them through the window, and a look of fear — then anger — came over his face.

And Aunt Clara's saying came drifting through my mind again . . .

5

"That there is a devil, there is no doubt. But is he trying to get in, or trying to get out?"

I clearly recall the first time I heard Aunt Clara's saying. It was a few months after she and Uncle Horace took me in from the local orphanage, after my mama ran off.

I was seven, eating my after-school snack of molasses cookies and milk in the kitchen, and trying not to squirm in the hot tweed dress Aunt Clara had sewn for me on her old treadle Singer. It was Indian-summer hot, but to Aunt Clara, October in southern Ohio meant crisp candy-apple weather, and that was that.

Aunt Clara stared out through the kitchen window at Buster Toadfern — a distant cousin of mine on my daddy's side (Aunt Clara and Uncle Horace being on my mama's side). She kept washing her Ball canning jars while muttering and staring and shaking her head.

Aunt Clara had hired Buster to clear out the tomato vines from the large vegetable garden that filled half of the backyard of our house on Plum Street. She'd already put up sixty quarts of juicy red tomatoes, but I'd heard her tell Buster that morning to be sure to save all the green tomatoes.

Some she'd fry in corn meal batter, the rest she'd can as relish. Aunt Clara's grand plan was to be so frugal that there'd always be money to take care of Guy. To Aunt Clara, green tomatoes were an important part of that plan.

"What's a matter, Aunt Clara," I asked. "Did Cousin Buster throw out the green 'maters?"

At my question, Aunt Clara went quiet, so fast and hard that her bun quivered in the wake of her sudden stillness.

Then, keeping her gaze on Buster, she said: "That there is a devil, there is no doubt. But is he trying to get in, or trying to get out?"

The answer made no sense to me, but even with all my tweed, it sent a shiver creeping over my skin, as if something had crept up behind me and breathed down my neck. Still, I pressed on.

I wouldn't get my nickname — Nosey

Josie — for another nine years. And what some people call nosey, I call curious. I like to think of my natural curiosity as a gift that I was born with, a gift that lay dormant in me just waiting for the right moment to spring forth. And somehow, when I heard my aunt's devil saying the first time, it sprang.

"What's that mean, Aunt Clara? How can you tell if he's in or out? The devil, that is? And how can you have no doubts about such a thing? And —"

Aunt Clara gave me a hard look over her shoulder, her bun still aquiver. "Never you mind, Josie Toadfern. Just never you mind. Finish up and get to your homework . . ."

I told Owen about this memory that night, after the Serpent Mound trip, on our corn maze date. When I finished my story, Owen repeated the devil saying thoughtfully, mulling it over.

Somehow, now that he was musing on Aunt Clara's old adage, I felt better, safer, more relaxed. So relaxed, that I sighed contentedly as I leaned into Owen's shoulder. I was warm, because of my heavy coat and hat, because of the toasty fire flickering before us, because (best of all) of Owen's presence. I was sated — we'd dined on roasted weenies, at one of the fire rings in the field by the Crowleys' corn maze, and from a thermos sipped cups of spiced cider I'd prepared. And now I was also relieved, having told Owen about Aunt Clara's statement, my first memory of it and how it came back to me when I met Ginny Proffitt, and about having to lead the tour at Serpent Mound, and about seeing Ginny and Dru there, together, embracing.

What more could a girl want?

Another s'more, I decided.

I leaned away from Owen just long enough to pick up the confection, roasted marshmallow and chocolate square sandwiched between graham crackers. Then, I leaned back into him and bit into the s'more. Mmmm. Yummy, gooey, crunchy chocolaty bliss.

Owen Collins is not only adorably cute — long, blond ponytail, blue eyes, lanky build — he is also extremely bright. And even though he has three PhDs — in religion, philosophy, and psychology — his smarts don't just come from book learning. (Not that I don't appreciate his love of books. I love books too. In fact, our shared book mania was part of what drew us to each other.) He has deep-down, peer-into-your-soul, stay-up-late-and-ask-lots-of-what-if-questions smarts.

So I knew if there was sense to be made out of my day — and my weird reaction to Ginny — Owen would tap into it.

"On the one hand," Owen was saying, "your aunt's quote is a classical conundrum. Do our downfalls come from our inner demons — metaphorically speaking, of course — or from outer demons, such as temptations?"

I swallowed and was tempted to take another bite of the s'more without commenting, but overcame my temptation and said, "I'm not sure my aunt was speaking metaphorically. Before becoming a Methodist, she was a member of the nondenominational Paradise Church of Almighty Revelations, a very fundamentalist group." Then I took another yummy bite of s'more. Some temptations are not meant to be resisted for too long.

"And what bugs me about that is that Dru Purcell still pastors that church, as he did when Aunt Clara attended," I went on. "And for the first time in years I remembered my aunt's saying when I met Ginny Proffitt. And it turns out Ginny Proffitt has some connection to Dru Purcell even though Dru claims to hate Ginny and all the psychics. But before he saw our bus, he was hugging her most tenderly. Then he looked so horrified when he saw us, and she looked so pleased. I think she set him up to be seen with her, that she wanted us to see them together."

Owen sighed. "All right. Let's back up a minute. Do you agree that your aunt's saying is best interpreted figuratively?"

I gazed at the lazy tongues of fire lapping up into the night, then into the darkness beyond the fire circle. My gaze swiftly returned to the fire. I snuggled closer to Owen. "That surely is my preference," I said. I ate the final bite of my s'more and longed for another, but I'd eaten the last one. We were down to just graham crackers. Those, I thought, would make a good snack later with peanut butter.

"Good," Owen said. "Some psychologists interpret so-called psychic phenomena as a highly tuned subconscious ability to notice and interpret subtle clues in a person's mannerisms, tone of voice, and so on. Maybe you just subconsciously picked up on clues that indicate Ginny's struggling with an inner, or outer, figurative demon, and that's what brought the saying to your mind."

I pulled away and stared at Owen. "Are you sayin' I'm psychic?"

A playful grin teased up the corners of his mouth, eroding his studious and serious expression. "Never! Just highly intuitive. And sensitive." He trailed his fingertips over my brow. "Mmmm, yes, very sensitive, I'd say . . ." Yum. I liked this. S'more, s'more, I thought.

His grin widened. "Plus . . . you're nosey."

I groaned and gave him a playful punch on the arm, and he laughed. He knows how much I hate my old high school nickname — Nosey Josie. Even when it fits. Which in this case, it surely did. Just what was the connection between Ginny and Dru?

Suddenly, Owen looked serious again. "But I think there's something else about Ginny that bothered you. You said she somehow knew about a particular dream you've been having. I'm here to listen if you'd like to talk about it, Josie, if that would help."

I looked away. Sally had asked me earlier what my dream really was about. I'd been saved from answering by Karen coming up the steps to the observation tower. Now, there was no one nearby. We had this particular fire ring to ourselves. A group of Ranger Girls was at the nearest ring, but they weren't likely to come over to interrupt us. Ranger Girl–cookie-selling season wasn't until next spring, after all.

Here was my chance. I could open up to Owen about something that was, on the one hand, so silly, and yet, on the other, was so disturbing to me, much more than recalling my aunt's saying upon meeting Ginny. How did she know about my dreams about Mrs. Oglevee? And why did I have those dreams, anyway? I'd sloughed them off as just a bizarre glitch in my subconscious, but now, the fact of them bothered me.

And I'd been hurt that Owen had held back the truth about his past for so long, even wondering if he'd ever have told me if he hadn't essentially been forced to by his own slip of the tongue, when he'd told a mutual acquaintance a tale about his past that didn't fit with the past he'd told me. So, if I expected openness and honesty from him, shouldn't I give him the same?

Of course.

So I opened my mouth to speak. And here's what came out: "It's just this silly dream I have about wearing an orange bikini in public."

I pressed my eyes shut. Oh crap. That was Cherry's spin on my previous lie about the dream. I'd said navy one-piece. She'd said orange bikini. And in any case, apparently I couldn't bring myself to open up to Owen.

He was silent for a long moment. "I think you'd look great in an orange bikini, Josie," he said softly.

It was a compliment, and yet there was something sad in his voice — as if he knew, somehow — thanks to his own highly tuned subconscious ability to notice and interpret subtle clues in my mannerisms and tone of voice — that I wasn't telling the truth.

Our mood, thankfully, lightened once we were inside the corn maze.

The maze was cut out of an acre of corn, then divided into nine sections, each section marked by plastic ribbon of a different color or design (hot pink, white with blue polka dots, bright green, and so on). At the start of the maze, you got a piece of paper, with a key at the bottom (for example, hot pink equals section one) and a large three-by-three grid, which would form the base of the maze map. In each section was a mailbox, which contained that section's "map" and rolls of tape. The idea was to tape that section's map onto the correct spot of the grid. Eventually, you'd have an entire map of the corn maze — the "reward" for the challenge.

One of the tricks to navigating a corn maze — or, I reckon, any maze, although I've never been in a non-corn maze — is to stick to only left-hand or right-hand turns. We'd right-hand-turned our way past a witch, a goblin, a princess, a ghost, and a Dracula, who was really Lenny Longman. He was one of the stars of the East Mason County High School basketball team and the dreamboat of the Paradise Methodist Church youth group.

Lenny had on an old basketball jersey that had been muddied and cut with slits, rubber bloody fangs, streaks of dirt on his face, and twigs and leaves sticking out of his hair, to signify his rising from his burial site. He was also wearing a huge grin, mostly because several members of the basketball cheerleading squad kept getting "lost" over and over in his section. It didn't seem to frustrate them, though. They giggled every time they walked past Lenny, who made a big show of lunging at them.

We'd just gotten our second-to-last map piece from Lenny and were in the next section. For the moment, we had this corner of the maze to ourselves.

Owen widened his eyes and wiggled his fingers at me. "I vant to suck your blood," he said in a bad Dracula imitation, "so you can be my cheerleader forever!"

I giggled, and pounded at him as he pulled me to him and then started to dip me. "You know I never made the squad!"

"But you have such delightful pom-poms, my darling . . ."

My next wave of giggles was thwarted by his kiss. Not bloodsucking, thankfully, but definitely blood-heating . . . until we heard the proverbial bloodcurdling shriek.

But it wasn't playful, or coming from Lenny's quadrant. It was coming from outside the maze. And was followed by the words, "Get off of our property! Or we're callin' the police!"

Owen and I stood up quickly. I shone my flashlight on the map. "We're here," I said, pointing to the northwest corner of the maze on the map, "and the hollering's coming from right about here — which is right by the road." I grabbed Owen's arm. "Come on. Let's see what's going on."

"We don't know our way out of the maze yet," Owen said. "Whatever's going on will be over by the time we get there."

"Short cut," I said, folding up the maze map and stuffing it into my purse. Then I turned my flashlight to a break in the back wall of corn. It was bad corn-maze etiquette, but someone had obviously gotten tired of trying to figure out the maze, and had crashed on through. Several stalks of corn were bent backward, leaving a gap just wide enough for a person to edge through sideways.

I went on through and trotted a few steps before stopping to look around and gain my bearings. We were right by the road, near the entrance to the Crowleys' corn maze.

And then I saw what all the hollering was about. "Oh, for pity's sake, would you look at this, Owen?"

Dru Purcell and a dozen or so others had gathered at the entrance with signs. The entrance was well lit, so I could make out the wording — HALLOWEEN IS EVIL! BE A-MAZED BY GOD, NOT CORN-MAZED BY THE DEVIL! JUST SAY NO TO PAGAN HOLIDAYS!

I gasped.

"This is private property," Hugh Crowley was hollering at Dru. "You have no right to be here, messing with our fundraiser and scaring our customers! What do you have against our corn maze, anyway?"

"If it were simply a corn maze, that would be fine," Dru shouted back. "Or if it were populated by people dressed as Bible characters, say."

"Jesus and Moses in a corn maze?" Hugh sounded incredulous.

But Dru took his comment seriously. "Yes, my brother, yes, Amen! Young people dressed as Jesus and Moses, passing out Bible scriptures . . . what a testament of faith that would be . . ." His voice started to tremble with the wonder of a biblically populated corn maze until his wife, Missy, poked him.

"But instead, you have young people dressed up in costumes of the devil!" Dru shouted.

"Now, look, Pastor, let's go talk quietly as two men of God." I recognized the voice of my own pastor, Micah Lamb, although I couldn't see him. I had to smile. Pastor Micah had a gift for finding common ground among people. "We don't want to disturb this fundraiser for these good people . . ."

"I don't recollect any of the volunteers dressing up as a devil." That was Rebecca Crowley. I couldn't quite see her, either. Her voice was trembling. "Just some ghouls and princesses and witches . . ."

"It's the holiday of the devil," Dru said, his voice stretching with infinite patience. Poor lost soul, his tone proclaimed. His followers shouted "Amen," and Dru was off, sermonizing, shouting "tonight we protest this evil corn maze, tomorrow night the evil psychic fair!" His voice drowned out Hugh and Rebecca, and even Micah.

"This is ridiculous," I said. "Owen, let's go see if we can help Pastor Micah to get Pastor Dru and his cronies to leave the poor Crowleys alone."

Owen didn't say anything. I turned back to look at him.

And gasped again — but this time, not in consternation. In surprise.

I'd hurried out through the split in the corn, my gaze focused straight ahead. Owen had sidled out more slowly and had seen what I had missed in my hurry: two feet, sticking out of the corn in the corner of the maze. Owen was shining his flashlight on the feet wearing hot-pink high-top tennis shoes.

Where had I seen shoes like those before? And then I remembered. On Ginny Proffitt's feet. Just that morning.

I ran over to Owen's side, stared into the corner of the corn maze, all sound — the ruckus just down the road, the night bugs' chattering, the corn shocks' dry papery rustling in the wind — giving way to a high buzzing in my head.

I forced myself to breathe slowly, to focus on the body in the corn stalks, lit by our high-powered flashlights.

"It can't be," I muttered. "She's —" my voice trailed off and I finished the thought silently: supposed to be at the psychic fair.

But there was no mistaking that the body was Ginny Proffitt's, swathed in her gold lamé robe, wearing her high-top hot-pink sneakers. Her crystal ball and its holder were by her head, turned so that we could see only the left side and the ghastly hole from a bullet. God only knew what the right side of her head, pressed against the ground, looked like, where the bullet had exited.

My stomach roiled at the thought, and then I started shaking. "Owen?" His name came out in a thin mewl. But it was enough to draw him to me, and, although shaking himself, he hugged me to him, and I turned my face to his shoulder, away from the sight of poor dead Ginny Proffitt.

6

After we found Ginny's body, I immediately called 911 on my cell phone. Owen stayed by her body while I got Rebecca away from the ruckus at the front of the property. I left Hugh and Pastor Micah still arguing with Dru and his followers.

At first, Rebecca thought I was trying to tell her I'd called the police because of the ruckus. She'd started shaking, tears streaming down her face as she said, "Josie, I wish you hadn't called the police. We don't need any more trouble from Dru Purcell. We can handle it."

Her comment struck me as odd. She made it sound as if Dru had given her family trouble before that night. I hadn't heard talk of any trouble between the Crowleys and Dru. Now, I knew the Crowleys, like me, went to the Methodist church, avoiding Dru's hard-line yet growing following, but as far as I knew they'd been friends with the Purcells a long time. Dru and Ed, in fact, had been star quarterback and running back, respectively, on the East Mason County High School football team, taking the school all the way to the state finals, where we lost against West Mason County High School. That was back in the early 1970s — a few years before I was born — but still, I knew about it because everyone still talked about it, the biggest football victory East High had ever experienced. That kind of thing becomes town lore.

So I was curious what Rebecca meant by her comment implying they'd had trouble with Dru in the past, but I didn't get a chance to ask. I heard Owen saying, "Get back in the maze!"

I grabbed Rebecca's arm and pulled her after me. We got to the outside corner of the maze in time to hear a group of cheerleaders giggling as they walked on the other side of the corn stalks, and one saying, "I wonder what all the hollering is about out there?" and another giggling, "Who cares! Let's go back to see Lenny!"

I turned to tell Rebecca gently that she might not want to go forward and see what Owen had been keeping the kids from —

but when I looked at her, I realized she had already trotted over to Owen, huffing with the effort. Rebecca's fifty-plus and a bit on the heavy side. Her body went rigid as she stared down at Ginny. She turned and walked a few steps away, then crumpled to her knees and put her hands to her face and began sobbing.

I went over to Rebecca, knelt down beside her, and put my arms around her. She remained stiff, at first, and then leaned back into me, letting me hold her as she kept crying. I reckoned that this was too much for her, what with having lost her husband Ed just two months before, and now worrying about Maureen and Ricky.

Her family and the Methodist youth group had only wanted to raise money to help Maureen and Ricky, but it surely hadn't gone well — the protest by Dru and his followers was bad enough, but finding one of the psychics dead at the maze . . . this was just too horrible for Rebecca.

In the meantime, Dru and Hugh kept shouting at each other, while Pastor Micah tried to calm them down, with Dru's followers every now and then shouting a hearty "Amen!" in response to Dru's rhetoric, unaware that a most unholy scene was just yards away.

But when the first police car arrived, most of Dru's followers silently wandered off. Dru, Micah, and Hugh stopped shouting as Chief John Worthy got out of his police car and started toward them. Then all three men began talking at the same time to Worthy, but no longer shouting, so I couldn't hear what they were saying.

"I'm taking Rebecca over to Chief Worthy," I called to Owen.

"I'll keep watch here," Owen said grimly.

"Come on, Rebecca," I said. "We have to go talk to the police."

I thought I'd have to help her up, but suddenly she stood up, shaking me from her so hard that I went from kneeling to landing on the ground with a hard thump. She wavered for a moment, as if she were light-headed, and then squared her shoulders and marched over to the men.

It took her a second to get their attention. She turned and pointed past me to where Owen stood by Ginny's body. Then Rebecca slumped into Hugh, who put his arms around her. They stayed in a tight embrace, swaying together under the light, as if stuck in a sad little dance.

Chief Worthy said something into his hand radio, then unclipped a flashlight from his belt, turned on the light, and trotted up the gently sloped field toward me. Dru followed him. I frowned at that. Shouldn't Dru stay back, with the Crowleys?

Worthy stopped when he got to me. He wasn't even huffing a little. He's always been in fantastic shape. So annoying. He turned the flashlight on my face. His stamina isn't the only annoying thing about him.

I squinted. "Could you get that out of my eyes?"

He lowered it a little. "Mrs. Crowley said the body is over here, but she wasn't sure who it was."

"Ginny Proffitt. One of the psychics from the psychic fair over at the Red Horse Motel this weekend," I said, then gave a brief explanation of how Owen and I had come out of the maze through a break in the cornstalks to see what all the shouting was about, and then found Ginny's body.

"Who did you say you found?" Dru Purcell had finally caught up with Worthy and huffed out his question between gasping breaths. He was not in shape like Chief John Worthy. But he was still annoying.

Worthy frowned at him. "This is a crime scene, Pastor Purcell. I want you back over by the light with the Crowleys."

I ignored Dru. "Do you want me to wait over there, too? I can direct the other officers over here —"

"I was patrolling in the area and that's why I got here first," Worthy said, cutting me off. He was directing his comments solely to Dru. "When the other officers and the emergency crew get here, direct them over this way. And wait by the light pole. I'll have questions for both you and —" he finally cut me a glance "— Ms. Toadfern." He looked back at Dru. "Make sure she doesn't stick her nose in where it shouldn't be."

I turned and started walking quickly back down the slope to the light pole, Deputy Dru huffing along right behind me. God only knew what he'd do if I kept right on walking past the light pole and to my car to wait for Owen — which I was tempted to do. Probably grab me and shout, "Citizen's arrest! Praise the Lord!!"

Not a pleasant thought. So, I did as Chief Worthy had asked and stopped by the light pole. I leaned against the pole, stared at the few buggy critters flying around in the light. At least it wasn't spring, when the bugs would have been swarming.

"Josie?"

I glared at Deputy Dru.

He drew in a long, shuddery breath, his potbelly jiggling behind his suit jacket, which strained at the button. "Now I know, Josie, we've had our differences in the past —"

I rolled my eyes. Having "differences" would mean, say, one person liking pork rinds and the other wanting tater tots. Our differences were more like, well, barbeque-flavored pork rinds versus salad with non-fat dressing. Or like heaven and hell. (And my own theology is that heaven will have pork rinds with all the flavor and none of the fat.)

"— but won't you join me in a word of prayer for the fallen soul —" he waved a hand "— over yonder?" He held out his hands, expecting me to take them. Sweat glistened on his palms and brow. If he took off his jacket, I just knew I'd see sweat stains on his underarms.

"Don't you want to know who we're praying for?"

"Rebecca said it was one of them psychics," Dru Purcell said. "So I'm sure their soul is lost. But despite my moral obligation to fight their Satanic influence, it's also my moral obligation to pray for their soul even as it wends its way to the fiery depths of hell . . ."

He broke that last word into two syllables, as if hiccupping in the middle of it, lifting his hands to the heavens, or at least to the sparse autumnal bug population in the light.

"The dead person is Ginny Proffitt," I interrupted harshly. "She appears to have been murdered."

For a moment, Dru went as solid as if he'd glanced Gomorrah over his shoulder. His hands dropped to his side. I thought he was going to fall straight over. Then he drew a handkerchief from his pocket, and put a trembling hand to his brow, wiping away the sudden beading of sweat.

In that moment, he stopped being a caricature of himself, of the identity of righteous, knows-it-all preacher he'd created for himself. He looked lost. Scared. Confused. He looked simply . . . human. I felt a surge of pity for him.

"You knew her, didn't you? I mean, personally," I said softly.

He put the handkerchief away and stared at me as if trying to figure out who I was. Then he looked around as if trying to figure out where he was and how he'd gotten there. For a moment, I thought maybe he'd snapped. Could a person get amnesia all of a sudden, just forget who he was because of something terrible he'd heard? Did Ginny mean that much to him?

"Pastor Purcell? You knew Ginny Proffitt?" I asked again.

Suddenly he looked at me, his dark eyes intense. "Yes, young lady, I knew her. I knew her to be a force of evil come to our town. A practitioner of the dark arts. A follower of —"

"No, I mean you knew her personally. I saw you with her at Serpent Mound. You were embracing, as if you were old friends," I said. Or lovers. But I didn't have the guts to say that.

Dru gave me a long look. Finally, he said, "No. I do not know Ginny Proffitt personally."

"I saw you with her at Serpent Mound."

He shook his head. "I was not there with her. I was not there at all. The place should be razed, in my opinion. You know I've spoken out on that many times." Oh yes, I knew. Dru's absolute certainty in his self-made brand of Christianity really did extend to wanting to see thousands-years-old remnants of an ancient civilization destroyed. "You must be mistaking me for someone else."

"You're pretty unmistakable," I snapped.

Dru glared at me. "I was not at Serpent

Mound with Ginny Proffitt."

"You're counting on me being the only one who saw you, just because mine was the only face you saw looking outside the bus? But you can't be sure I'm the only one who saw you," I said. "And it's a small town. Word will get around."

He gave a short laugh. "It hasn't yet. And what are people more likely to believe — my word, or yours and a van full of psychics no one wanted here in the first place?"

"Most people in Paradise were fine with the psychic fair," I said. "The only opponents were you and your followers. And I've never really understood why. What are you so afraid of?"

He started to speak, but I held up my hand and went on. "No, I don't want the same old answer about the dark arts. I want to know why you personally are so afraid of these people. And of Ginny Proffitt in particular."

A brief shadow of sadness passed over his face. Then the know-it-all mask he usually wore returned. "I got the names of the psychics from the fair brochure and researched them on the Internet. They all have Web sites advertising their dark arts," he said with disgust. "The other psychics are misguided, of course. Some even proclaim to be Christian as they practice their black arts. But like the LeFevers, Ginny Proffitt is a self-avowed Wiccan. A follower of Satan."

"Being Wiccan isn't the same as following Satan," I said. "In fact, Wiccan is just the opposite — a very peaceful, loving belief system. At least get your facts right. Besides, did you know that Wicca, although still small, percentage-wise, is the fastest-growing religion in this country, according to some surveys?"

"All the more reason to stamp it out quickly," Dru said.

I sighed. There would be no convincing this man to be more open-minded . . . or to admit he'd been with Ginny at Serpent Mound. I stared back up at the light. I was through trying to talk to him.

John Worthy, followed by Officer Corey Spalding and Owen, came down the rise to us.

"I'm going to have to ask each of you some questions. Shouldn't take long," he said.

I jerked a thumb at Dru. "Ask him about how he met Ginny Proffitt at Serpent Mound today."

"I have no idea what she's talking about, Chief," Dru said.

I glared at him. "Sure you do. And you know I know."

After that, Owen and I answered Officer Spalding's questions. He didn't have many. Owen and I told him all we knew, which wasn't much.

As we walked quietly back to the grassy parking area, we saw the ambulance, carrying Ginny's body, pull out silently onto Mud Lick Road.

We remained quiet until we got to Owen's old BMW.

"I don't much feel like being alone tonight," I said.

"Neither do I," Owen said, giving me a gentle smile.

7

There's something about the scent and the quietness of my laundromat when I first enter it — before customers come, before the washers and dryers are humming and thrumming — that's always comforting.

Most mornings, I notice it, that moment of "ahhh" when I first come in through the back door to my storage room/office, but I also take it for granted.

Not so, the morning after Owen and I discovered Ginny Proffitt's body in the back corner of the corn maze. I turned the key to my laundromat's back entrance, stepped in, shut the door behind me, then leaned against it and closed my eyes. I didn't even bother to snap on the light just yet. I breathed in slowly. Ahhh.

The smell of clean, fresh laundry. The soapy smell of the small boxes of laundry detergent I keep on hand to sell to customers (at only a small markup) mingling with the scent of fabric softener sheets.

You know, smell is the most underrated of all the senses. But it's a very personal thing, even though it's hard to describe. How do you describe the smell of green tomato relish as it's being cooked and canned? I'm not sure. But just the phrase "green tomato relish" brings back the memory of Aunt Clara and her determination to make sure Guy would always be provided for.

How do you describe the smell of fabric softener sheets? Even the marketing writers aren't sure. They just put "clean laundry fresh" on the box. But still, the scent means a lot of things to me: comfort. Purity. All's in order and right with the world.

Some people have that reaction to chocolate chip cookies or fresh bread — some homey memory of coming home from a bad day at school to the comfort of that scent. Me, I remember many a day of trudging home from school, feeling down after John Worthy — now the chief of police — and his pals teased me for being Nosey Josie. I'd stop by the laundromat on the way home, to help Uncle Horace. And I'd step in and smell that clean, soapy, laundry scent, and somehow, I'd know that things would be okay.

And that's how it felt as I slowly breathed in the air of my laundromat the morning after the discovery of poor Ginny Proffitt's murdered body.

After a few minutes, I opened my eyes and snapped on the light. I shrugged off my jacket and hooked it on the coatrack that had always been back there. For a moment, I felt a pang, wishing I could see my aunt and uncle's coats — both tweed, threadbare, the only coats I remember them having — hanging side by side on that rack.

I shook my head to clear it. I'd taken the day off the previous day, I reminded myself, and no doubt I had orders to catch up on. Plus the day would be busy. Not only was it Saturday, but we'd suffered a long dry spell, a drought, really. That — and a sudden unseasonable cold spell with temperatures earlier in the week plunging below freezing — had made for more vibrant autumn colors, but it had also meant that the water tables were low. We were fine in Paradise proper, but the folks who relied on well water out on farms would be coming in to town to do their laundry, as they'd want to preserve their water for cooking, livestock, and bathing.

I sat down at my desk to sift through the previous day's mail, but my mind immediately started drifting back to the night before, replaying images.

The most pleasant ones were from spending the night with Owen. We went by my apartment, above the laundromat, and I picked up a change of clothes. I knocked on the door of the LeFevers to tell them the news about Ginny Proffitt, but they weren't home, which didn't surprise me. The psychic fair that night was running until 10:00 p.m. and it was about 10:45 p.m., but I reckoned they were still at the Red Horse, attending to details for the next day of the fair.

I wondered again what had drawn Ginny away from the fair, and how the LeFevers had reacted when they realized their star psychic wasn't there . . . or had Ginny been there part of the evening, then slipped out?

I drove my car over to Owen's, following him, since I knew I'd want to be back at the laundromat early, well before he'd want to be up and about.

We showered together after we got to Owen's place, both feeling the need for cleaning after what we'd witnessed at the corn maze. After that, still damp, we snuggled in his bed . . . and kissed . . . and then some . . . and after *that,* he dozed off.

For a long while, I just snuggled awake against Owen's chest, finding comfort in the slow, even rhythm of his breathing, in the clean scent of the Zest soap we'd used on each other. Finally, I fell into a long sleep that was restless but that at least wasn't interrupted by any visits from Mrs. Oglevee.

In the morning, I woke up early — around 5:30 a.m. — and dressed quietly. I drove into town and went to Sandy's Restaurant for biscuits and sausage gravy with a side of sausage and hash browns and coffee — lots of coffee. I hoped the caffeine would help me shake off my tiredness.

I ate by myself at my usual spot — third stool from the right at the counter — and took in the talk buzzing in the booths behind me. There weren't too many people at Sandy's at that hour — two guards on their way to work at the state penitentiary over by Masonville, an elderly couple, the Greatharte sisters — but they were all talking about Ginny Proffitt's murder. The Greatharte sisters were saying how they were going to the psychic fair that day and Joe (one of the guards) was admonishing them that his pastor, Dru Purcell, had preached against all such foretelling the previous Sunday.

Henry, the other guard, allowed as how his mama had practiced Bible-cracking, which is closing your eyes to ask a question of God, then letting the Bible fall open where it may, then poking your finger onto a page, and taking whichever verse your finger lands on as God's answer. He didn't see all that much difference between Bible-cracking and, say, going to a crystal ball gazer, and if it was good enough for his mama, it was good enough for him, a sentiment that seemed to comfort Heffie and Bessie Greatharte.

Bless you, Henry, I thought, as he and Joe left, debating the Godliness of Bible-cracking versus other means of intercessory communication with the good Lord.

When Sandy came over to hot up my coffee, I put down an extra-large tip of three bucks and said to her, "I was at the Serpent Mound yesterday."

"Uh huh," she said, in her voice made baritone by years of smoking. Today she was wearing her favorite T-shirt, a black one with the words, WHO ASKED YOU? in bright yellow.

Sandy's customers come for the good home cooking.

Well, she hadn't asked me, but I told her anyhow. "Saw Ginny Proffitt there. With Dru Purcell. Hugging."

Sandy lifted her eyebrows and overflowed my cup. I grinned at her. She hurried away, not bothering to clean up the spill, scratching her teased-up hairdo with the eraser end of the pencil she usually keeps tucked behind her ear.

I pulled a wad of paper napkins from the dispenser, sopped up the spill, and felt a little song spring forth in my heart as I sipped my coffee and watched Sandy talking animatedly with Bea, the morning cook.

They turned and stared at me. I nodded, gave a little finger wave, thought "what the hell," and left another buck on the counter.

Then I went to my laundromat, where I took in the comforting scent and sat at my desk and stared at my mail without really seeing it. I told myself I really ought to check the bin, tucked in a corner behind the front counter, for any orders that might have been dropped off the previous day.

But I was distracted from that task by a knock on my back door. I got up, went to the door, opened it, and was surprised to see Hugh Crowley standing there.

He looked weary, the heavy lines in his

face more deeply grooved than ever.

Rebecca and Maureen and Ricky Crowley's problems were getting all the attention now, but the truth was that Hugh's life hadn't been any easier. Hard work and a hard life had etched his face, with lines and a settled look of resignation and soft sadness in his eyes.

Hugh had dropped out of school forty years before, when he was just thirteen, to help his father run the farm. He'd never done well in school, and saw himself as the "dumb" one compared to his little brother Ed, three years younger than him. When Mrs. Crowley took ill, Hugh stayed home to help with the farm and to be sure his little brother could stay in school, although Ed had his share of chores on the farm.

It hadn't been easy for Ed, either, I reckoned. He'd had school, football, and farm duties to juggle, and no doubt a ration of guilt over big brother Hugh dropping out to make sure Ed could pursue his dreams.

Then as soon as Ed graduated from high school in the early 1970s, he joined the military, swearing he wanted nothing to do with the farm ever again. By then, Hugh had married and had one son. Hugh and his wife, Lily, and Hugh Sr. managed the farm just fine for quite a few years. Hugh's son Sam and his bride Jenny moved in with Hugh and Lily. Sam and Jenny loved the farm life, and each other, and their son, Matt.

But driving home from Gatlinburg, Tennessee, where they had celebrated their tenth wedding anniversary, Sam and Jenny were in a car wreck that took their lives. Hugh raised Matt as best he could, while tending to Lily, who had breast cancer. Lily died six months after the wreck. Hugh's father, who by then was in his nineties, died a few months after that.

After that, Ed didn't re-up for the military. He changed his mind about the farm, and came home with Rebecca and their only child, Maureen. Hugh focused on Matt and when Matt graduated from high school and wanted to go away to Ohio State University to study agricultural science, the whole family was proud.

When Matt called home to say he'd switched his major to fine arts and wanted to be a photographer, Ed was furious, but Hugh gave him his blessing.

Last year, Matt moved to Seattle.

A lot of this — the tragedy of the wreck, Lily's breast cancer — I knew about because everyone in town knew.

And most people in town knew about

Matt moving to Seattle to pursue his dream of being a photographer, although they mostly shook their head and clicked their tongues over the impracticality of such a goal, and in such a far-off place, too.

I knew about the discord Matt's decision had caused because Hugh had told me.

And I knew something else that no one outside of Hugh's family knew.

Hugh was illiterate.

He'd struggled with reading all through school. Ed had helped his big brother as much as he could, but after Hugh dropped out, he lost much of what he'd learned. Then Lily had covered for her husband. After she passed on, and Ed and Rebecca returned, Ed again helped Hugh.

But after Matt left, Ed was so furious at him for abandoning his family, as he saw it . . . even though Matt had made the same choice that Ed had made years ago . . . Ed refused to read any of the letters that Matt sent home to Hugh.

About six months ago, Hugh had a confidential talk with my good friend Winnie Porter, who is the Mason County Library bookmobile librarian and a volunteer tutor and coordinator for the county's literacy tutoring program. I'd just completed my tutor training and so Winnie had assigned me as Hugh's tutor. And Hugh had been a diligent student, even after Ed died from a heart attack two months before and the burden of the farm fell, again, to Hugh.

Normally, we met at my laundromat, in my combo storage room/office, on Sunday afternoons when my laundromat's closed. Our tutoring was scheduled for after church but before I went for my weekly visit to see Guy. I'd given Hugh a key to my office so he could let himself in if I was running late.

So I was surprised to see Hugh at the back door of my laundromat on a Saturday morning, especially after all that'd happened out at the corn maze the previous night.

"Mornin', Josie," Hugh said. He sounded tired already. "I just came by to give you this." He held his hand out to me. In his palm was my spare back door key.

I didn't take the key. "Hugh, why? You want to meet somewhere else?"

Hugh shook his head. "No, Josie. I can't meet any more at all. Rebecca needs me. All her time's tied up with Maureen and Ricky, and after what happened last night, she can barely think. I've got to focus on keeping the farm going. No time for book learning." He smiled thinly. "Never would've thought way back when I was in school I'd be sad to say that."

He pushed his hand toward me, urging me with the gesture to take the key. But I wasn't about to let Hugh give up on himself quite that easily. I stuffed my hands in my jeans pockets.

"Now, Mr. Crowley, let's talk about this."

I stepped back. Hugh didn't move.

"I'll make a fresh pot of coffee. Have to get it ready for the customers, anyway." I always have a fresh pot of coffee on a little table at the front of my laundromat.

Hugh glared at me.

I lifted my eyebrows.

He sighed, put the key back in his pocket, stepped in, muttering, "Women. Ornerier than mules."

I turned my face to hide my smile, then went and made the coffee.

A little bit later, we sipped coffee from styrofoam cups, both of us sitting behind my desk, just like we do during tutoring. I gave him the desk chair — it's sturdier and easier on his back, which I know gives him trouble every now and again — while I sat in a plastic chair from my laundromat. It'd taken me a month to convince him to let me do him this favor. I'd finally won out by standing through an entire lesson. He'd called me ornery then, too, but he's taken the wooden chair without comment ever since.

"I don't like talking outside the family, but truth is Rebecca's fit to be tied about what happened to that poor psychic woman last night. Says no one will come to the corn maze now and we won't be able to raise money for Ricky's care," Hugh said.

I didn't think that was the case. In fact, I thought, more people might give in to the gruesome side of their human nature and go on out to the Crowley corn maze just to gawk. But Hugh was usually a man of few words, carefully chosen, so I thought it best not to interrupt him on the rare occasion that he felt like talking.

"Rebecca says we ought to shut the whole corn maze down, even though Chief Worthy said we could still let people in, except the section the police have taped off. I designed the maze in nine equal sections, so I can reroute around the closed section." Hugh took a sip of coffee. The cup trembled in his hand. "With her worrying over Maureen and Ricky or driving down to the hospital in Cincinnati, I can see the farm's going to need all the attention I can give it.

Besides redoing the corn maze, I need to work on the books and plan for next spring. Lots of repairs needed on the barn and tractors. Now's the time to do it with harvest over, before the cold really sets in.

"But I can't neglect any of that for my studying for our sessions." Hugh took another sip of coffee, looked at me. He was old enough to be my daddy, but there was something about his sad eyes that rendered his deeply lined face boylike, and made me want to hug him. Such a thing would have scared him, though, so I stayed put. "I don't want to let you down, Josie."

"Mr. Crowley, you don't need to worry about letting me down. You've given your whole life to other people and to your family's farm. Maybe you oughta think about not letting yourself down."

Hugh shook his head slowly. He put his cup on my desk, reached in his pocket and pulled out the key again, holding it out to me. "That's not my way," he said.

I put my own cup down and crossed my arms. "Fine. Don't come here anymore then." Hugh looked a little surprised, and even a little hurt. The tutoring meant more to him than he would admit. "I'll come out to your place Sunday afternoon. That way you'll be available to your family in case there's an emergency."

He shook his head. "It's not just the meeting times, Josie, it's studying in between —"

"And we'll just meet every other week," I broke in. Aunt Clara and Uncle Horace had taught me better than to interrupt or sass my elders. But they'd also taught me never to give up on a person. "That way you can take a little longer to get each lesson down. Of course, you can call me any time you need help or have a question."

"But —"

I held up a hand. "This way, we won't lose what you've achieved, but you won't feel under so much pressure and you can still be there for your family."

Hugh stared at me for a long moment, and I held his gaze, stubbornly keeping my arms crossed. No way was I taking back that key.

At last he sighed, and shook his head again. "Ornery woman," he muttered.

I smiled and finally uncrossed my arms. I took his rough, calloused, thick hand in mine and closed his hand over the key. "Keep it," I said, "for when you're ready to go back to once a week tutoring."

Hugh stood up, put the key back in his pocket. "Now about tomorrow. Maybe week after next would be better —"

"I'll be there at 2:00 p.m.," I said.

"But —"

I stood up. "You missed last Sunday 'cause of finishing up the corn maze. Tomorrow. 2:00 p.m."

Hugh went out the back door muttering "ornery" under his breath.

I grinned to myself and went out into the laundromat and opened up the front doors.

8

Just as I'd predicted — from common sense, no crystal ball or tarot cards needed — my laundromat was even busier than usual for a Saturday morning, what with the water tables low outside of town.

Again, I meant to check the bin in the corner behind the front counter for orders from the previous day, but I got too busy, too fast.

I showed Gurdy McGuire my trick for making throw rugs look like new — adding a half-cup or so of table salt to the wash water.

And I showed Matt Peterman how to get the Silly Putty out of his daughter's frilly go-to-church dress — pouring rubbing alcohol over the putty, rubbing, and repeating until the Silly Putty disintegrates or can be pulled right off.

Of course, just as Sandy's Restaurant

had been buzzing with talk of Ginny Proffitt's death, my laundromat was, too. Most of it was the same, contemplation about which of the other psychics had killed Ginny.

In between helping my customers and catching up on the mail and bills in my back storeroom, I considered the psychics who'd known Ginny. Many of them had had motives, I realized, thinking back on the previous afternoon's trip to Serpent Mound. There was Karen Smith, who wanted Ginny to stop stealing "child prodigy" Skylar's limelight. Max Whitstone, Ginny's ex-boyfriend. Could he be jealous? Even dear old Samantha Mulligan, the pet psychic, who'd lost money on a business deal and who'd gotten a message of vengeance from Xavier the squirrel.

And I couldn't discount Damon and Sienna LeFever. Ginny had given them such a hard time, spreading rumors about their supposed incompetence. I shivered at the thought of the LeFevers, my neighbors and tenants, as killers.

But all the psychics had been busy at the fair the previous night, I thought, as I went over to the ironing board behind my front counter to start on an order of shirts, fresh from the dryer, for Harvey Grieshop, who runs the Paradise branch of the Farmers and Merchants Bank. Ada Grieshop had brought them in that morning. The shirts reminded me I really ought to check under the counter for any orders from the previous day, but again I put it off. Ada had asked for a rush order on Harvey's shirts.

I started ironing the sleeve of a blue oxford. When would any of the psychics have had time to kill Ginny? Unless, of course, one of them left the fair, maybe to have a secret meeting with her, which could have gone badly . . .

And speaking of secret meetings, I thought, what about Ginny's meeting with Dru Purcell? I knew I'd seen them together, no matter what he said.

People were talking about that, too. I'd stirred up some juicy gossip by dropping the news at Sandy's that morning. Maybe, I thought, it'd force Dru to tell Chief Worthy about the meeting, and that would help Worthy figure out who killed Ginny . . .

Or maybe my gossipmongering would just make me the next victim, I thought, as Missy Purcell stormed in the front door of my laundromat.

Believe me, she wasn't coming in with a laundry basket. Missy lives in town, where the water pressure's fine, and has her own washer and dryer. And from the fury in her eyes, she wasn't coming in to ask if she could leave off religious save-your-soul-from-hell tracts, as she did from time to time. (My countertop's always too crowded for those. Although there's plenty of room for the Ranger Girls'–cookie-sale flyers.)

She stopped in front of my counter, her strawberry-blond topknot quivering in the aftermath of her sudden stop right beside me. The smell of her hairspray was overpowering. I coughed. The sound seemed too loud in my laundromat, which had gotten suddenly quiet when Missy entered. Suddenly, no talking — just the hum of the washers and dryers, the low buzz of the TV at the front of the laundromat, by the kiddy picnic table, and the vending machines, the sound of my cough, and Missy's hard breathing.

I went back to ironing another of Harvey's shirts — this one white with gray pinstripes. "Countertop's still too crowded, Missy," I said.

"I know what you've done," Missy said. She was speaking low, but I knew everyone in my laundromat could hear her. "Chief Worthy came out to question my husband about him meeting with that evil Ginny Proffitt woman."

I pressed my lips together to hold back a smile, then spritzed starch on the shirt collar. Missy coughed this time. Hmmm. Maybe the collar could use a bit more starch. Spritz, spritz.

"Dru didn't ever meet with that woman," Missy said, after she finished a fit of coughing. "And he told Chief Worthy so."

I slammed the iron down, looked up at Missy. "You know, it might help Chief Worthy figure out who killed Ginny Proffitt if Pastor Purcell would be honest about meeting with her. She might have said something to him that would be an important clue. He might think it's nothing, but something she said might fit with something the chief learned at the crime scene —"

"You think you're so smart, don't you, Josie Toadfern?" Missy interrupted with a smirk. "Like I told Chief Worthy — and he believed me because of course I always tell the truth — Dru was home with me all morning!" With that, Missy turned for the door.

"Oh, Missy, could you pass on something to Pastor Purcell for me?" I called sweetly.

She looked back at me.

"Tell him there's one other besides me who saw him meet with Ginny Proffitt."

A look of fear flashed in her eyes, and I knew she knew Dru had met with Ginny. They could discount just one eyewitness, especially since everyone knew that Dru and I had come to harsh words in the last Chamber of Commerce meeting. Now, most folks wouldn't think I was a liar, but they might be convinced I was clinging to my mistaken beliefs out of my dislike for Dru. But she and Dru couldn't discount another witness.

Hmmm. So there was something there between Dru and Ginny — something Dru and Missy wanted to keep hidden. Even to the point of lying to Chief Worthy.

Unfortunately for me, the other eyewitness wasn't likely to come forth to testify, at least not on the streets of Paradise.

Still, it gave me an amount of satisfaction to look right in Missy's watery blue eyes and say, "The other witness was . . . God."

Missy snorted at that, whirled around, and practically knocked over Winnie Porter, who was coming in the front door of my laundromat as Missy was going out.

But Winnie was too distraught to even react to Missy knocking into her, then continuing out the door without so much as a "sorry."

"Winnie, what's the matter?" I asked, while hanging the gray pinstripe on the clothes rack on wheels behind me. I had three more of Harvey's shirts to go, but they could wait for a good friend like Winnie.

Winnie almost never gets distraught. She's a fifty-something librarian who dresses like the 1960s hippie she wishes she'd been but never was, living up in Masonville as she has all of her life. South central Ohio was never exactly part of the flower-powered peace, love, 'n' rock 'n' roll culture. Still, Winnie favors Birkenstock sandals (with socks, in October), and long, swirly peasant skirts and peasant blouses. She now wears her gray hair in a short-cropped do, the better to show off her dangly earrings and wide, engaging smile, always at its brightest when she's recommending the just-right book to a bookmobile patron, or reading to a child.

But today, her face was crumpled up in misery.

Winnie leaned her forearms on the counter. She was shaking. "Oh, Josie," she moaned.

"Winnie — what's the matter? Is it

Martin?" When I'd seen Winnie on the bookmobile the previous Wednesday, she'd told me that her husband, Martin, had been having shortness of breath that worried her.

"No, Martin is fine. The doctor says he just needs to work out. He's up at the Big Sam's in Masonville checking out treadmill prices today," Winnie said. "I came by to tell you what happened at the library meeting yesterday afternoon."

The meeting, I recalled, that Winnie'd been attending while I was on the psychic tour to Serpent Mound. "Wasn't it just a regular monthly staff meeting?" Winnie doesn't like the monthly meetings of the library branch and department heads — she'd much rather be out on her beloved bookmobile — but as head of outreach services, she's obliged to go. This, though, was beyond her usual complaining.

"Oh, Josie, the director announced yesterday that we're going to have to cut back services because of how much money we've lost in the state funding cuts," Winnie said. "Fewer hours. Part-time staff cut back." Winnie's chin trembled. "And no more bookmobile."

I stared at her in disbelief. "No bookmobile?" Paradise relied on Winnie's twice-weekly visits for books. Teachers at Paradise Local Elementary relied on Winnie's visits, too, to supplement the offerings of the school library. My heart fell.

"I suggested we cut back on something else temporarily — maybe periodicals and video purchases, or a few hours at the main library, but the director said that since most of the tax base for the library is up in Masonville, the bookmobile would have to go."

A solitary tear coursed down Winnie's cheek. She sniffled, wiped it away.

The bookmobile was Winnie's life . . . and a lifeline to Paradise and many other small communities that dotted the outskirts of Masonville.

I glanced at Harvey's shirts. They'd just have to be late.

"Winnie, we're doing something about this."

She shook her head. "I already talked to the director. I don't think anything can be done about the bookmobile unless we have a levy that passes next spring to get back some of the funding the state's cut."

A whole winter without books coming to Paradise? I thought of Mrs. Beavy, who doesn't drive and would have a hard time getting up to Masonville. A whole winter for her without her beloved romance and mystery novels? I thought about Hugh Crowley and how he was just learning to read and how he was looking forward to checking out a few books from the bookmobile's children's section to read to his grandnephew Ricky. I thought about my own need to read.

I grabbed Winnie by the shoulders. "Winnie, Paradise isn't taking this without a fight. We'll petition to get the bookmobile back, and then we'll petition to get a levy on the ballot next spring that everyone will vote for so none of the programs or hours have to be permanently cut!"

And that's how, again, I put off checking for orders from the previous day. Winnie and I spent the next hour getting everyone we could — and most people were very supportive — to sign our handwritten petition to get back the bookmobile.

And truth be told, I might not have thought to check at all if Chip Beavy hadn't come in that morning.

And Chip wouldn't have come in if his grandmother hadn't sent him in on account of the bookmobile petition, word of which had already spread through most of Paradise.

Funny how things work like that, isn't it?

One thing leads to another until pretty soon a whole mess of things end up connecting in ways you'd never predict.

Anyway, Chip did come in. "Josie, Mamaw sent me on over here. She wants me to sign that petition and to know if I can write her name in for her, too."

"Is she doing okay?" The Widow Beavy was a favorite customer of mine, but I didn't see her quite as often now that she had her own washer and dryer, a good thing, since she's eighty-something and doesn't get around quite like she used to. She only lives a street over, on Plum Street, but it's still too hard for her to tote over her clothes. I do her rugs and comforters for her at the laundromat, though, as her washer and dryer are too tiny to handle such things.

"She's fine — well, her hips bother her every now and again — but she's just busy, what with sorting things out for the historical society." The Paradise Historical Society had recently inherited a 1930s' era estate house that was once in the Breitenstrater family, of Breitenstrater Pie Company fame, one of Paradise's major employers. The house would be home to the historical society and its holdings. Mrs. Beavy was in charge of overseeing the new displays of items for the museum, which was supposed to have its grand opening at Christmas.

I grinned, knowing Mrs. Beavy was joyous in her busy-ness.

"Mrs. Rowentree came by the Breitenstrater house" — in the way of a small town, the building would be called that for decades, never mind that it was now owned by the Paradise Historical Society — "and told Mamaw all about the petition. She called me and told me to get in here and sign it for both of us. And to tell you she's not so busy that she doesn't still want you to drop by next Thursday afternoon for a visit."

Since Mrs. Beavy had started doing most of her laundry at home, I'd started dropping by for a cup of coffee and a slice of her famous secret-recipe buttermilk pie every other Thursday evening, after closing up the laundromat.

I handed Chip the petition. "Tell her I'll be there."

"Will do," Chip said, signing his name carefully, then adding his grandmother's name on the next line.

Chip handed me back the petition and started for the door, then stopped. "Oh, Josie, I hope it's okay I put the suitcase right behind the order bin. It wouldn't fit."

I frowned, confused. "Suitcase?"

"You didn't see it yet? A customer — I think she was one of the psychics — left it off yesterday. Didn't want to leave her name or any directions about what she wanted done. I'm assuming it's filled with dirty laundry. She said you'd know who it was from and what to do."

My heart plunged. I swallowed hard. "Was she wearing a brightly colored warm-up suit?"

Chip nodded. "And hot-pink high-top sneakers."

The suitcase — Ginny Proffitt's, I knew, even though Chip hadn't directly said that and the suitcase bore no name tag — was a lot like one my Aunt Clara had once had. Hard-sided, made of shiny rigid plastic in a tan tortoise-shell swirl. Metal latches. Empty, it weighed far more than the average person could easily carry. Last made long before the wheeled, soft-sided, pullout-handle variety, maybe back in the 1950s. On eBay, this would be a collectible.

I studied the suitcase back in my office/storeroom, somehow feeling the need for a little bit of privacy.

I remembered my Aunt Clara's from the

one and only trip she took — to Florida, for her sister's funeral. She sat in the kitchen, crying at the table, while the cab — which Uncle Horace had hired to come all the way down to Paradise from Masonville, to take Aunt Clara to the airport over in Cincinnati — waited in front of our house on Maple Street. The neighbors watched from their front porches. A cab was an unusual sight in Paradise.

Aunt Clara cried because she didn't want to leave Guy, even knowing he was safe at Stillwater, for the four days the trip would take. While Uncle Horace told her it would be okay, he told me to carry her suitcase down to the cab. I was fourteen, but that suitcase was as heavy as if it were filled with the flat fossil-ridden stones from the bottom of Licking Creek. I tried to hoist it down the steps. The cabbie stomped out his cigarette right there in Aunt Clara's bed of mums and came and got the suitcase for me.

While the cabby's back was turned — even he grunted, loading the suitcase in the trunk — I fished the cigarette butt out of the bed and put it in my pocket, knowing Aunt Clara would really pitch a fit if she saw a cigarette among her mums. We'd probably never have gotten her off to her Florida sister's funeral. Then I ran back in and fetched the little square makeup case that matched the suitcase. The makeup case was much lighter, holding as it did only Aunt Clara's comb and bobby pins, for securing her long braid up in a knot, and her Pond's Cold Cream — her only concession to vanity.

That night, I went out in the backyard and tore off the filter and tried to smoke the cigarette, but it set me to coughing so hard, Uncle Horace heard me and came out and found me. He asked me if I'd gotten the cigarette from my no-good cousin Sally Toadfern, who even then smoked unfiltered cigarettes, and I told him no. I've always been grateful that he believed me, just sent me off to bed early with no questions, and never mentioned it to Aunt Clara.

Aunt Clara's suitcase was smooth and unmarred. The only time I saw her use it was on that trip to Florida. But Ginny's version was beaten and dented and scratched from years of hard use. Aunt Clara'd had no chances for travel, as Ginny seemed to have. I smoothed my hand over the suitcase's surface. I thought it said something about Ginny that she carried such an old, out-of-style suitcase — but what? That she was cheap?

Or had the suitcase belonged to Ginny's mother or some other relative, so that Ginny'd kept the suitcase all these years out of sentimentality? She hadn't seemed at all the sentimental type. But then, I'd only met her in the parking lot, when she'd foisted that reading on me, and then seen her once with Dru, at Serpent Mound.

I was spending all this time thinking about the outside of the suitcase, I knew, because I was fearful of opening it and seeing what was inside.

I shook my head to clear it. In the parking lot, Ginny had said she hadn't had time to launder her clothes before coming out here and she'd bring them by the laundromat. That's all the suitcase would contain, I told myself.

I started to open the metal latches on the top of the suitcase, then stopped. The suitcase might just contain dirty laundry, but it was the dirty laundry of a woman Owen and I had found dead. It was possible that something could be in there that would shed some light on her death or prove that it wasn't suicide, as Chief Worthy apparently believed. I should turn it over to him.

But it couldn't hurt to take a look first, I

reasoned. Then I'd turn it over to the police.

I unlatched the luggage and opened it up. For a second, I closed my eyes, wincing at the sickening smell that immediately filled my storeroom: mustiness. Filth. Body odor.

I opened my eyes and looked in the suitcase, which held only one item of clothing: extra-large bibbed overalls that had once been white, but were streaked with many different colors of paint and dirt. On top of the bibbed overalls was a plain white handkerchief that was also paint- and dirt-splattered.

Ginny had written on the handkerchief with a black felt-tip pen:

Josie —
In case anything happens to me, know this:
That there is a devil, there is no doubt.
But is he trying to get in . . . or trying to get out?
Mrs. O will help if you start from the end
And go to the beginning to find out.

Peace,
Ginny.

For a long moment, all around me seemed to fall away and I knew only the nasty smell of the dirt-ridden overalls and the words of Ginny's note, ringing in my head.

Then, as if from a great distance, I heard the ringing of something else . . . a telephone . . . but I seemed to be in a trance, unable to react to it.

How did Ginny Proffitt know my aunt's old saying? It wasn't a common saying. And yet, she'd known it . . . just as she'd known about my dreams of Mrs. Oglevee. And she had used this saying in a message that, judging from the phrasing she used, she'd written right before her death . . . *in case anything happens to me.*

I grabbed up the handkerchief. It seemed an odd thing to go with the overalls. The handkerchief was an ordinary men's handkerchief, plain other than the white-on-white striped border, no monogrammed initials or other detailing. But it seemed an oddly delicate, almost feminine, companion to the old painter's overalls, which were men's size.

The telephone ringing stopped. My initial reaction of freezing creepiness melted away and frustration took its place, like an itchy rash. Why had this woman turned to me for help? And how had she gotten into my head, knowing about my aunt's saying and my occasional dream visits with Mrs. Oglevee? Why couldn't she have just left me a normal message, say, a recording on my voice mail. Something like "Hey, Josie, it's Ginny Proffitt and I think so-and-so is going to kill me at the maze tonight?" Better yet, why couldn't she have just bypassed me completely and gone to the police with that concern?

Maybe she had, I thought. Maybe she'd felt unsatisfied with Chief Worthy's reaction to her fears, found him too dismissive.

The door from my laundromat swung open. Quickly, I stuffed the handkerchief in my pocket and slammed the suitcase shut. Both movements were instinctive reactions. Something told me that I didn't want just anyone knowing about Ginny Proffitt's luggage and its contents.

I hefted the suitcase off of the top of my desk and quickly stashed it under the desk as Chip Beavy walked in. Of course, my effort to hide the bag wasn't necessary where Chip was concerned. After all, he'd taken it from Ginny to begin with. But I hadn't known who was coming into my office.

I wanted to ask him more about what Ginny said when she dropped off the suitcase, but something about Chip's expression stopped me. He looked worried.

"I answered the phone for you out front." He nodded at the phone on my desk. "You'd better pick up. It's Don Richmond."

I inhaled sharply. Don was Stillwater's director. I visit Guy every Sunday at Stillwater, and if something was going on that couldn't wait just a day, then it couldn't be good news.

My heart clenched. Oh Lord. Guy was in good health, although I worried about the fainting spell he'd had, but there could have been an accident . . .

The old handkerchief with Ginny's recent cryptic note in my pocket and the strange old suitcase with its stranger-still contents stashed under my desk slipped completely from my mind, as if I'd never seen, smelled, or touched either one. I reached for the phone on my desk.

9

The week Aunt Clara had to go to Florida for her sister Jeanne's funeral, a killing frost came early to Paradise. Uncle Horace and I felt it coming in the cold snap in the air, sitting on the front porch of our little house on Maple Street. We were sitting on the porch swing, having glasses of iced tea I'd made.

Uncle Horace was dozing and I was thinking about how someday maybe I'd get away from Paradise. Does anyone at age fourteen want to live forever in the town they grew up in?

My mind was wandering with visions of me traveling to some of the places I'd read about in books Winnie — even then, I called her Winnie — had given me on the bookmobile. Far away exotic places. Like Greece. Or Nepal. Arizona, even.

And I knew I'd go to these places someday because a fortune-teller had told me so at the Mason County Fair. The woman, looking uncomfortable in her too-hot gypsy garb — I reckon she knew it was an expected cliché — had also told me that on my travels I'd meet someone handsome and smart and funny, who'd appreciate my finer qualities. My insatiable curiosity, for example. My love of good books.

But a chill wind swept over the front porch, nudging the porch swing so that Uncle Horace jolted awake, and I was whisked away from my Greece-Nepal-Arizona-cute-boy dreams back to our porch, back to the sound of the last of the summer bugs every now and again giving a lonesome chirp, the fall silence between their chirps drawn out as if the cold had stolen their breath. Suddenly, the iced tea glass was too chilly in my palm.

"Heard on the radio today there's a chance of the first killing frost come early tonight," Uncle Horace said. He kept a radio going in the laundromat for his customers. Years later, the TV at the front of the laundromat would be my innovation.

"Yeah," I said. "Want me to make us coffee instead? Maybe slice us some more apple pie?"

Uncle Horace yawned. "No. I'm still full from that delicious dinner, Josie." I'd made tuna casserole, and put extra crumbled potato chips on top, since Aunt Clara wasn't there and couldn't harp on me for being wasteful. "But I'm also worrying about your Aunt Clara's tomatoes."

We swung back and forth in the chill wind, thinking about her tomatoes out back of the house, a dozen bushes laden with still-green tomatoes.

On the one hand, Aunt Clara wouldn't want anyone else to do the canning. I helped, of course, but she never let me do any of it on my own, because she was afraid I wouldn't do it just right and the jars wouldn't seal or the jellies wouldn't gel and we'd have a basement full of poisonous green beans and green tomato relish and runny jelly. But truth be told, I'd helped with every step of the canning for several years now, and knew I could do it myself.

I also knew Aunt Clara would be heartbroken if she came back from her sister's funeral and found we'd let a killing frost take the green tomatoes. To her, it would be a failure in frugality that might mean Guy wouldn't get the care he needed at some point in the future. No green tomato relish today could spell financial disaster in the future.

But Uncle Horace wasn't going to give me direction about what to do. He ate green tomato relish without complaint, but such matters were not in his department. I could just let the tomatoes go, and no one would criticize me.

And so I found myself sitting in the front porch swing, somehow faced with a decision that, at fourteen, I could only sense was much greater in its import than whether or not the green tomatoes out back were saved from a killing frost, only to be minced into relish. The burden of the tomatoes' fate weighed heavily on me.

Finally, I said, "Guess I'd better go pick the tomatoes. I'll fix and can the relish tomorrow after school."

Uncle Horace hopped up quickly, and I realized he was relieved at my decision. "I'll help you pick them," he said. "That's all I can do," he added, his voice a little sorrowful.

Truth be told, he made fried bologna sandwiches for us the next few suppers, so I wouldn't have to cook dinner as well as work with the tomatoes. Aunt Clara had to stay an extra two days in Florida because her other sister, Doreen, had a fainting spell at their sister Jeanne's funeral and everyone was afraid maybe it was a heart problem for her, too (although it just turned out to be that she'd passed out from skipping breakfast, even though she was diabetic). I made us fried green tomatoes to go with the bologna sandwiches the rest of the week, until Aunt Clara came home. And I canned twenty-four pints of green tomato relish.

When Aunt Clara, who I later heard didn't let anyone see her cry at her sister's funeral, saw the twenty-four pints lined up on the counter, gleaming like a crop of liquid emeralds, she burst out crying and hugged me without saying a word.

Was my memory of the green tomatoes I first canned on my own an odd thing for my mind to drift to while I sat out in the hard plastic, butt-numbing chairs in a waiting area at Mason County General Hospital? Maybe.

But while waiting for Guy's tests to be completed, I'd already gone through five issues of magazines such as *Good Housekeeping* and *Home Town Cooking*, and jotted down on the back of a bank deposit slip, fished from the bottom of my purse, two recipes: one for Light and Creamy Pumpkin Pie (a simple recipe that would be good for some future church carry-in) and another for healthy Applesauce-Bran

Muffins (a nod to my never-ending battle to lose fifteen pounds). Deep down, I knew I'd make only the pumpkin pie.

Then I'd grown weary of scanning recipes and housekeeping tips and can-this-relationship-be-saved? advice, and let my thoughts wander. Maybe it was the cooking theme that brought to mind the first batch of green tomato relish I'd ever canned by myself. In any case, my thoughts drifted to that week when Aunt Clara had been gone to her sister's funeral, and I'd rescued the green tomatoes instead of letting the frost get them.

I'd wondered then why Aunt Clara had cried over those green tomatoes I'd saved, but now, sitting in the hospital, I understood what Aunt Clara had immediately known when she saw the green jeweled jars on the counter: I would always do what I had to to take care of Guy.

It's a choice I've never regretted.

But I also didn't understand, until I was sitting in that hospital hallway, how Aunt Clara had felt back then, the week of her sister's funeral. I remember thinking, while canning those green tomatoes, the acrid earthy smell of them filling my nose and finally my every pore, that Aunt Clara was silly for resisting being away from Guy for a few days. What could it hurt?

But now I understood that, too.

She didn't want to be away in case something happened to Guy. She understood just how vulnerable he would be if something went wrong, if his health failed or he was in an accident. And she wanted to be there to advocate for him.

That's what I wanted to do now for Guy. Don Richmond, Stillwater's director, told me that Guy had passed out that morning just before breakfast. In fact, he'd been having spells of being dizzy, not that he'd described it that way, because Guy has trouble communicating much of anything, let alone something subtle like fluctuations in how he's feeling. But several staff members had noticed him stumbling about a few times that week, clutching the back of a chair or the edge of a table to regain his balance.

Then that morning, he'd passed out in the dining hall. The staff hadn't been able to revive him. They'd called 911, and by the time the paramedics came, Guy had come to, and he was trying to talk, to say something, but no one was sure what.

He'd been taken to the hospital up in Masonville, and I needed to be there to sign paperwork for tests and to be with him. I'd seen him only briefly. He was sedated because he'd panicked when a nurse had tried to take blood samples from him, thrashing about and swinging his arms wildly. My eyes had pricked with tears when I heard that. Guy hated needles. Lots of people do. But Guy hadn't learned how to calm himself when it was necessary to get shots or have blood taken for testing.

I mentally cursed myself that I hadn't driven faster around the curving roads that lead from Paradise to Masonville. Maybe I could have kept him calm.

I was able to wait with him in one of the small rooms in the emergency wing, holding his hand, murmuring about nothing in particular to him, about the yellows and oranges of the trees as I'd driven there (which I hadn't, in truth, really noticed), about how I knew his pumpkins were going to be a big hit this year (Guy's in charge of growing the pumpkins for the annual fall harvest sale at Stillwater, a task he takes very seriously), even humming "I'm a Little Tea Pot." Aunt Clara had told me that was his favorite song as a toddler. She'd sung it to him over and over to keep him calm, until her throat hurt. That was before she and Uncle Horace learned Guy had severe autism.

In the emergency room, Guy just stared at me, his eyes wide and a bit watery. He moaned every now and then. I wasn't sure if he comprehended any of what I was saying, but a nurse told me my presence seemed to calm him.

Then, Guy had to go for an MRI. My heart sank at that news. Dr. Herlihy, the physician who attends the residents at Stillwater, wanted to ensure that Guy didn't have an underlying neurological problem that had caused the fainting spell. I could understand that, but I worried about how poor Guy would react. As much as he hated needles, he hated tightly enclosed spaces even more. He hated most the color red. At least that wasn't a factor in a hospital, where everything was an antiseptic white or gray.

A sedative helped him stay calm, though, as two attendants wheeled his gurney out of the emergency area and down toward the MRI lab. I'd trotted alongside his gurney, still holding his hand, hoping that maybe I could just trot on into the MRI testing area.

No such luck. The female attendant told me that I'd have to wait outside. Guy had grunted as I pulled my hand from his, but then his face fell back into expressionlessness.

My heart clutched as the attendants wheeled him through a double door labeled STAFF AND PATIENTS ONLY.

Then as the doors swung shut, I looked around. No one in the hallway but me. The waiting area was a trio of hard plastic chairs and a wooden end table, covered with magazines and a reading lamp. I sat down and stared at the wall in front of me for what felt like at least ten minutes of the hour and a half I knew I'd have to wait, resisting the stack of magazines. Leafing through them would somehow seem like giving in to the situation, admitting that I wasn't in control.

I glanced down the hall. Maybe someone I knew would come down it soon. Someone like — Owen. On the drive from Paradise, I'd dialed his number on my cell phone several times and was surprised that he didn't answer. Owen loves to sleep in late on a Saturday morning and then putz around his house.

Then I'd called my laundromat to apologize to Chip Beavy for my earlier abrupt manner, when I'd quickly told him about Guy and more or less ordered him to mind my laundromat for me. Chip had told me no apologies were necessary and that he'd stay until closing if necessary.

As I pulled into the hospital parking lot, Pastor Micah called me on my cell phone. Chip had called him to tell him about Guy. Pastor Micah offered to come up to sit with me. I assured him I was fine for the time being, but I let him say a little prayer with me over the phone.

Now, sitting in the hallway waiting area, still unable to reach Owen, I kind of wished I had agreed for Pastor to come up although I knew he was enjoying the gorgeous day with his wife and three young kids. After last night, he deserved it.

Besides, I told myself, the time would pass quickly.

I checked my watch.

A whole minute had passed since the attendants had wheeled Guy into the MRI area.

That's when I broke, and started perusing the magazines. I skipped the travel ones and focused on the cooking ones, then gave up, closed my eyes, and traveled in my memory to the night Aunt Clara came home from her sister's funeral and wept at the sight of my first batch of home-canned green tomato relish . . .

"Well, you've really made a mess of things now, haven't you?"

There she was, Mrs. Oglevee, wearing

paint-splattered overalls and a straw hat, and juggling green tomatoes.

"Long time, no see," I said. Mrs. Oglevee hadn't invaded my dreams for almost a month. It seemed more than a little unfair that she would interrupt my nap at the hospital.

"I've been busy," Mrs. Oglevee said. Her four green tomatoes somehow doubled to eight, but her hands just moved faster to keep up with them. She juggled effortlessly, even tossing a few behind her back.

"Such a fascinating skill you've learned," I said. "This would help you how in, uh, the afterlife?"

I'd never quite been able to figure out if Mrs. Oglevee had ended up in heaven or in hell.

"Juggling is a much underrated skill in our earthly life," Mrs. Oglevee said. Her green tomatoes had doubled again, but she still kept up easily. "You could use help juggling."

"I'm not planning to run off to the circus any time soon."

"There's juggling," Mrs. Oglevee said, her hands now such a blur that I couldn't tell if she still had sixteen tomatoes or had moved on to thirty-two. "Then there's juggling. Knowing the things that matter in life and making them all work together somehow."

"I'm not doing so badly," I said, cringing at my own voice. I sounded as defensive as I had back in junior high when I forgot my homework.

"Really?" Mrs. Oglevee put her hands on her hips. Suddenly, all the tomatoes — thirty-two? sixty-four? — hit the ground, turning from green to rotten red tomatoes. Mrs. Oglevee didn't even wince at the splatter.

"Really," I said, wincing at the acrid smell of the rotten tomatoes. "I have my work, Guy, Owen . . ."

Mrs. Oglevee shook her head in dismay, just as she had whenever I muffed up a multiple choice quiz yet again. "You don't have focus! You don't know what you want for your future! You just go day-to-day, never envisioning what you want!"

Suddenly, a big, red, oozing tomato appeared in Mrs. Oglevee's hand and she wound up like a baseball pitcher, about to throw it at me . . .

"Josie?"

I jolted awake and saw Dru Purcell standing before me. That I was relieved to see him and not Mrs. Oglevee is a powerful testament to the horror of my Oglevee-beset dreams.

Pastor Purcell was wearing a black suit and tie and a somber expression. I wanted to remind him that this was a hospital, not a funeral parlor, but I bit my tongue. Aunt Clara always told me if you can't say something nice, you shouldn't say anything. I hadn't always heeded Aunt Clara's admonition, but in this case, I did.

The silence made Dru uneasy. He shifted back and forth on his feet, ran his finger around his too-tight collar. His face glistened with sweat. I felt a momentary twinge of guilt, then hoped that Missy knew to pretreat his collars and cuffs with cheap shampoo to prevent ring-around-the-collar stains.

I was about to say it was nice of you to come, but really you shouldn't have — *really* — when Dru spoke again. "I see your own pastor isn't here, Josie, in this time of trouble."

There was a bit of glee in his voice. I sighed. I didn't need to explain that I'd already talked with my own pastor.

"What do you want? You didn't really come all this way to hound me at a weak moment that I didn't really see you with Ginny Proffitt. I did. You know it." I paused. Should I use the line I'd used on Missy? Sure. Why not. I was worried,

thirsty enough to drink a two-liter of Big
Fizz Diet Cola in one gulp, and butt-
numb. Aunt Clara, God rest her soul,
would understand. So I smiled and added
in my sweetest voice, "And God knows it."

Dru swayed a little and blinked. Then he
sat down in the seat next to me, hard. "I —
I don't know why you persist in spreading
that vicious rumor. I came here because I
heard that Guy was ill. Someone told
Missy that it might even be terminal."

I shook my head. Such is the way of
towns so small that the weekly cable TV
listings are thicker than the town's phone
book. Word travels faster than a naughty
virus on the Internet. Of course, I'd known
that when I let it drop that I'd seen Dru
and Ginny together at Serpent Mound,
hoping the rumor would force Dru to
admit the truth to Chief Worthy.

"Guy is going to be fine," I said. My
voice sounded a little shakier than I
wanted it to. Damn it. Guy *would* be fine.
"But thanks for going to the trouble to
check. You didn't have to do that."

I picked up *Home Town Cooking* again.
Maybe I'd find a zesty variation on sloppy
joes.

"I'd like to pray with you, anyway, Josie,"
Dru said, "about the state of Guy's soul,

just in case he is at death's door. Has he been saved?"

I looked back at Dru, incredulous. He really meant what he said. His concern was genuine even if, in my opinion, misguided. And ill timed.

"Pastor Purcell, I appreciate your concern. But not only does Guy have a while to go before he traipses through heaven's pearly gates, Guy wouldn't understand the concepts you're talking about. I think God knows that."

"But have you talked with him about it? If he would just say the words —"

This was getting wearisome. "Words aren't the way to God's favor," I snapped.

The set of Dru's face didn't change, yet his expression shifted dramatically, instantly, to an icy coldness. I shivered and thought of my aunt's expression . . . of her saying it, of Ginny writing it on the handkerchief that was still in my pocket. I squirmed uncomfortably. What kind of demons was old Dru wrestling with? What would he do if I whipped that handkerchief out and waved it at him?

"I had hoped and prayed, Josie, that you weren't as mule-headed as your Aunt Clara, that you'd see this time of trial as a message from God that you need to get both your heart and Guy's in the right place for the hereafter" — Dru's voice started quivering, rising dramatically — "that I could help you turn your heart to righteousness and away from evil —"

"Since when is being a coffee-hour and carry-in-supper-loving Methodist . . . evil?" I was proud of myself. I managed to suppress both laughter and eye rolling as I spoke.

Dru narrowed his eyes. "There are some Methodists who are fine with the Lord," he conceded.

Wow, I thought, I'd make an announcement at Sunday's services. Everyone would be so relieved.

"But you . . ." Dru's voice dropped dramatically. "You insist on consorting with those psychic demon worshippers —"

I held my hands up. "Please! One of those psychics is a Presbyterian, for pity's sake. Several of them are Wiccan, but that's not the same as demon worship. In fact it's as opposite to demon worship as Christianity or Judaism. I've researched it, you see, and —"

"You've been reading their texts, their lies?"

I put my head in my hands. "I give up."

A second later, I felt Dru's sweaty grasp

on my arm. "That's wonderful Josie! You give up believing as they do! You'll pray with me then . . ."

I jerked my arm from his grasp and glared at him. "No! I give up trying to have a reasonable discussion with you! What did you think? That I'd be in such an emotionally weakened state because of Guy that you could come up here and blither at me about our lost souls until I'd see things your way and condemn the psychics that are visiting our town for one tiny weekend?"

He returned my gaze.

"Wow," I breathed softly. "That is what you thought. And that if that happened, I'd drop this whole thing about seeing you and Ginny . . ."

He pulled out a handkerchief and wiped his brow. "You didn't see me and that Ginny Proffitt. Now, I'll admit, it is possible that one of those people might have bewitched you to think you saw us together, but —"

I groaned. "Pastor Purcell," I said, "go away."

He stood up. I reopened the *Home Town Cooking* magazine. Onward to a new and improved sloppy joe, a gourmet sloppy joe . . .

But Dru Purcell wasn't quite through with me.

"You know, it's really a shame your Aunt Clara left my church," Dru said. "Perhaps if she'd stayed, you'd be on the path of righteousness now instead of defending these lost souls. And possibly losing yours in the process."

I looked at him. He was smiling at me, smug, triumphant.

Why had she left his church? I'd never known. I just knew she'd never quite been the same after that, even though she'd seemed more relaxed at the Methodist church with Uncle Horace and me.

"Why did she leave?" I asked.

"You don't remember? I'd just started my ministry, taking over from my dad, kicking off my ministry with a tent revival." His chest puffed up proudly as he said it. "Your Aunt Clara came, and I asked her to let me pray with her about Guy."

Nothing odd about that, I thought. Aunt Clara prayed all the time about Guy.

But Dru's voice started to rise as he went on. "And so I prayed that whatever sins of her family — whatever demons might reside in Guy — be cast out —"

I didn't hear the rest of what he said. I stared at him in horror. I'd read everything I could find about autism and knew that well before the condition was identified for what it really is — a mental disability — there were descriptions written in the medieval times of both "saints" and the "demon possessed" that, in retrospect, described tics and actions and behavioral oddities that fit autism. But for someone in this age — even twenty years ago — to describe a mental disability as demon possession?

"Get out," I said.

Dru didn't hear me. I said it again. He stopped talking and looked at me. "I want you to leave now," I said, standing up, "or I will call security."

Slowly, a sad smile, that also hinted of satisfaction, widened Dru's mouth. "You're reacting just as your aunt did," he said, shaking his head. "I never knew that little lady could utter such words."

Aunt Clara's saying came to mind again. Had she used it on him? It would surely have been the perfect response. Guy was incapable of having figurative demons. His condition was not a choice or a supernatural punishment or the result of a soul gone wrong. His condition was just . . . his condition.

And Guy could not help his condition or the abilities it denied him.

But Dru had a choice. And he'd chosen to see other people less than generously . . .

sometimes as less than human if they didn't fit his narrow definition of "rightness." That surely sounded like a spiritual demon to me.

I narrowed my eyes at Dru, approximating the expression my Aunt Clara wore whenever she tossed out her saying. "That there is a devil, there is no doubt . . . but is he trying to get in? Or trying to get out?"

Dru recoiled as if I'd whopped him upside the head.

"Is that what Aunt Clara said to you?"

"I — I don't remember," Dru said. With a quivering hand, he ran the handkerchief over his pale, sweating brow again. Then he made an attempt at a laugh. "No, no, I'm sure I'd remember a clever saying like that. And I've never heard it before."

I narrowed my eyes further. Liar, I thought. Just like he'd lied about being with Ginny Proffitt at Serpent Mound. He'd heard that saying before — and it shook him up. It wasn't a common saying. And if he hadn't heard it from my aunt, had he heard it from Ginny? After all, she'd written it as a last message to me — in case of her death — on the handkerchief I had in my pocket. Was he shaken because the saying came from Ginny? Because she'd used it as a clue to her death, and he knew that?

I narrowed my eyes some more. "Which is it, Dru? Is he trying to get in? Or out?"

Dru flinched, then shook his head as if to clear it. "Now, Josie, I think you ought to reconsider praying with me —"

"And we think you ought to leave her alone."

Dru whipped around at the new voice, sing-song high and bubble-gum-popping sassy. Cherry's, in other words. I grinned. Coming down the hall with Cherry was Sally. An unlikely pair of rescuers, but I was glad for their arrival. I stood.

"Uh — maybe you would like to join hands in prayer?" He eyed Cherry, barely able to maintain his appreciation for how she looked. She wore three-inch-heel red pumps to complement her black leather skirt and red and white silk striped blouse, and plenty of the perfume and makeup he liked to preach against.

Cherry snorted and popped her bubble gum. "You wouldn't have a prayer of joining anything with me if we were the last two people on earth."

Sally crossed her arms. "She means beat it."

Dru shook his head and walked away. Quickly, I noticed.

"You know, you all are gonna burn for

talking that way to a preacher man," I said, barely keeping back both a laugh and the prick of tears. If they'd called and asked if I needed them to come, I would have said no. They knew that I'd say that, knew I did need them, hadn't called, and come anyway.

"Sounds like fun," Cherry said, waggling her eyebrows.

I laughed after all.

Sally hooked her arm through mine. "Come on. Bet there's a vending machine in the cafeteria stuffed with Big Fizzes."

I shook my head. "I need to stay. What if —"

"Guy will still be in testing for another forty-five minutes. We checked at the front desk."

Cherry hooked her arm through my other arm. "He'll be okay, sweetie," she said.

And I cried after all. But that was okay, because I had two friends to lead me to the Big Fizz machine.

10

At Suzy Fu's Chinese Buffet, Jell-O salad and pizza and lo mein all reside happily on the same buffet line. Crawfish, cashew chicken, and macaroons — like Sally was having? Fine. Egg drop soup, pork lo mein, and carrot-raisin salad — as on Cherry's plate? No problem. Or my choice — a plate piled with nothing but crab Rangoons and sweet-n-sour sauce? Okey-dokey.

Try ordering those combinations at a regular restaurant and see what looks the waiter gives you. But Suzy offered up a happy fusion of Chinese, Midwestern, and pizza. Occasionally, she clucked that, really, the hot and sour soup would be good for your sinuses, but other than that, her view was "to each his or her own." Ah . . . food free will. The world would be a better place if it applied Suzy Fu's Chinese Buffet's food philosophy to more than just food.

I happily ate one crab Rangoon after another, letting the goodness of comfort food and friendship renew my strength.

After we'd had our Big Fizz Diet Colas in the hospital cafeteria, we'd returned to the waiting area. Not long after that, Guy was brought back out of the MRI area. He was surprisingly calm, although he had a panicked look in his eyes. A nurse explained to me that he'd reacted badly to going into the MRI scanner and had been given another sedative. He'd probably be sleeping soon.

We went with him back to emergency. I stayed by Guy in the same small treatment room we'd waited in earlier, while Sally and Cherry waited for me out in the family waiting area, even though I'd told them I had no idea how long we'd be here. They told me to hush up, that of course they'd wait for me. Cherry'd put Lex in charge of her beauty salon, and Sally wasn't needed at the bar until 5:00 p.m. Sally's triplets — Harry, Barry, and Larry — were with their grandpa on a weekend fishing trip. Meanwhile, they told me, Winnie sent me hugs and was helping Chip make sure my laundromat customers were well tended, while gathering signatures for the petition we'd started.

An hour passed while I waited by Guy's side. He stared at me and I sang to him softly until he fell asleep. Dr. Herlihy came in and told me the good news was that the MRI had found nothing wrong. My heart soared at that. But Guy's symptoms suggested a hypoglycemic reaction, an effect of diabetes, and Dr. Herlihy wanted to give him a blood test on the coming Monday.

My heart fell. Aunt Clara's sister, Doreen, had had diabetes. Guy was a little overweight and in his midforties. He was just approaching the age where health risks start to go up for anyone. But for him, managing them would be trickier.

Dr. Herlihy assured me that the staff at Stillwater would call him immediately if Guy had any problems, but that probably Guy would sleep most of the afternoon. He wanted Guy to return to Stillwater, and me to go on back home and not worry.

Hah, I thought, but didn't say it.

Guy was groggy, but cleared to ride back with me to Stillwater. Cherry rode with us — just in case I needed help, she said — and Sally followed. Guy dozed during most of the fifteen-minute ride. We got him settled into his room, where I tucked him in for another nap. Then Cherry and Sally waited for me in the commons room while I talked with Don Richmond, who assured me that he and the rest of the staff would closely watch Guy.

I suggested that maybe I ought to spend the rest of the day and the night at Stillwater, but Don insisted that, no, Guy would be better served if he got back to his regular routine as soon as possible given that he'd have to follow the diet for the blood test the next day. They'd keep him busy and occupied and call me if there were any problems. On Monday morning, I'd come back up to take Guy to the doctor's office for the blood test. I'd either have to leave the laundromat open and unattended or see if I could hire Chip again.

And then we were done. Don smiled at me kindly, but it was clear he needed to get back to work. Suddenly, I felt exhausted. Guy didn't need me to be there until the coming Monday morning. The crisis had passed, at least for the time being.

I left Don's office and went back to the commons area, and found Sally in a checkers game with Emilio.

"How do you keep doing that?" she was asking in amazement.

Emilio guffawed and clapped his hands together. I grinned, feeling a bit of my energy come back. One of the wonders of autism is that people who have it can be developmentally delayed in most every area, and yet possess wondrous gifts in other ways. Emilio was the reigning checkers champion. No one could beat him. And Guy could repeat any music line on a harmonica and drew with almost photographic precision.

"He's beaten her five times already," said Cherry. I turned and saw her in a corner giving Dominique French-braided pigtails. Dominique normally wore her hair in a long ponytail.

I gasped. "How did you get her to let you do that?"

"What?" said Cherry, looking confused.

"Braid her hair. Dominique never lets anyone touch her hair," I responded.

"She's nice. Pretty. Looks like Lissy," Dominique said, and patted Cherry on the head.

"Who's Lissy?" asked Cherry, looking even more confused.

"I have no idea," I replied.

Emilio was not happy to lose Sally as his checkers partner, but by the time we left, he and Dominique were playing. That is, he was moving the checker for both himself (black) and for her (red), while she stared at the board and happily stroked her braids.

169

Then out in the parking lot I thanked Sally and Cherry. Sally said, "We're taking you to Suzy Fu's," and I said, "Thanks, but I have to get back to my laundromat," and Cherry said, "If I can play hooky from my salon, you can miss another hour at the laundromat," and so I ended up at Suzy Fu's, eating crab Rangoons to my heart's content, while filling them in on what was happening with Guy and how Dru Purcell swore he hadn't been with Ginny at Serpent Mound, even though I'd seen them.

"If you hadn't distracted everyone on the bus with your hickey," I said, dipping a crab Rangoon in sweet-n-sour sauce, "someone else might have seen them together and then Dru couldn't try to convince everyone I just thought I saw them because I'd been bewitched."

"It's not my fault I'm so fascinating," Cherry said, huffing a little.

"Besides, there are plenty of folks who would take Dru's word over even a busload of psychics," Sally said. "And over our word, too."

Too true. I'd already spoken up in support of the LeFevers and the psychics and against Pastor Purcell. Some folks didn't think a woman ought to be a bar owner, though no one had the nerve to tell Sally that to her face. And Cherry — well. In Paradise's dictionary, Cherry's picture was in full color next to "wild woman." Not that she minded. She played to the reputation.

"But I know they did meet out at Serpent Mound. And he was looking at her all tender," I said.

"Woo-hoo! You think Pastor Purcell's doing the hanky-panky with a witchy woman he just met?" Cherry waggled her eyebrows.

I shook my head. "It wasn't like that. It was too tender, at least the way he was re-acting to her. She looked like she was laughing at him. His look was the kind you can only have after you've known and cared about someone a long while."

"You sure did pick up a lot with just one glance out a bus window," Sally said.

"Josie is what psychics would call intuitive," Cherry replied, sounding like an expert.

"Lover boy tell you that — or did he pass along that insider tidbit through some nonverbal exchange?" Now Sally waggled her eyebrows. Cherry frowned primly.

I put a half-eaten crab Rangoon back down on my plate and looked at Cherry. "What?" I demanded.

She tried to look virtuous. Difficult, given the dreamy look that softened her shimmery-blue-lidded eyes and the slow way her tongue traced her fuchsia-glossed lips. "Sally's just jealous because Max and me were a bit cozy at the Bar-None last night."

Sally snorted. "Cozy? You and Max were so co-o-ozy that Bubba, Ronny, and Dewlap were taking bets on whether Max and you'd wait to get back to the Red Horse, or just hop on the pool table."

Cherry virtuously clasped the front of her low-cut, lime-green silk blouse. "Well, I never."

"Not what I heard. How do you keep your lipstick from smearing with all that smooching?"

"What do you care? You never wear anything more than Chapstick!"

"Puh-lease," I pled. "Suzy Fu's going to kick us out of here if you two get much louder. Nice, quiet families are staring." I eyed the remaining mound of crab Rangoons and mentally bemoaned the "100% no doggy bags, no exceptions!" policy. "Cherry, how did you hook up with Max last night, what with the psychic fair going on?"

"We went to the Bar-None after the psychic fair was over."

"You mean after you picked him up at

the psychic fair," Sally corrected.

"I went to the psychic fair for some advice," Cherry sniffed. "Max just happened to be the psychic I saw last before the fair ended."

"That was at what, 10:00 p.m.?" I asked.

"Yeah, that's right. Why?"

"Well, Owen and I stumbled across Ginny's body at about 8:15 last night. She should have been at the psychic fair. Did you pick up any gossip about why she left?"

Cherry looked virtuous. "I was there for advice. And I don't gossip." Sally snorted. I gave her a warning look.

"Cherry," I said, "Ginny was murdered. You do know that Max and Ginny were lovers not that long ago, right?"

Cherry gasped. "You're not saying that Maxy —"

Sally chortled. "Maxy? You've nicknamed that cowboy *Maxy?*"

"I'm just saying that Ginny was shot through the left side of her head." I shuddered, remembering. "So it would be real helpful if you could remember, say, seeing Ginny leave and someone —"

"— like Dru Purcell," Sally interjected.

"— like *anyone*," I said, trying to be fair, and thinking of all the psychics who had reason to hate Ginny, "following out after her. Preferably mad. Knowing what happened at the psychic fair before Ginny left might help us figure out what happened to her *after* she left, maybe even give us a clue about her murder."

Cherry forked up some carrot-raisin salad and chewed, looking thoughtful. "Well, I got there right at five, when the psychic fair opened —"

"You hung out at a psychic fair for five hours, just to pick up Max?" Sally groaned. "You've got it worse than I thought."

Cherry kept right on talking as if Sally hadn't spoken. "— because I'm seeking life wisdom and advice. The place was pretty crowded. I saw a lot of people I didn't know but also quite a few people I did know. A few of them surprised me." Cherry looked thoughtful again. "You know, I think I could really go for some of those steamed pork dumplings. With the soy sauce."

I pushed back a sigh. Cherry was the center of attention and had the information I wanted. "Sally, could you please go get Cherry some of those steamed pork dumplings?"

"With the soy sauce," Cherry added, smiling beatifically.

Sally grunted, but got up and headed for the buffet.

"So who'd you see there that surprised you?"

"Missy Purcell, for one. Oh, she was passing out Bible tracts, but I could tell she was real curious about what was going on. She kept staring at Ginny, too. She even had a Tarot reading at Skylar's table, I think so she could glare at Ginny. I overheard her witnessing to Skylar, to try to make it look like that's why she was really there, but I also saw from her facial expression that she was really taking in everything Skylar was saying." Sally chuckled. "When she started witnessing loudly, so everyone could hear, Skylar pointed to the cross she wears, but Missy kept going on. Until Skylar's mom appeared from out of nowhere and started giving Missy grief. Then Missy left, and Karen stayed behind the table with Skylar.

"The other big surprise appearance — well, the mayor was there and several business owners who'd said it would be so awful if the LeFevers opened their bookshop, all trying to act like they were just there to, you know, observe. Anyway, I was surprised to see Maureen Crowley there. I thought she was spending all of her time down at

Children's Hospital in Cincinnati?"

I frowned. "I thought so, too."

Sally came back with a heaping plate of steamed pork dumplings for Cherry, an egg roll for herself, and a bowl of banana pudding — the kind made with vanilla wafers — for me. I was full of crab Rangoons. So what. I picked up a spoon (Suzy Fu's is strictly a BYOC — bring your own chopsticks — kind of place) and dug in.

"What about Maureen Crowley?" Sally asked.

"She was at the psychic fair last night," Cherry said, around a mouthful of steamed pork dumpling. "And Josie and I thought she was spending most all of her time down at Children's in Cinci."

"She didn't want to come to the chilispaghetti fundraiser last weekend," I said. "But she did put in an appearance."

"Yeah. For about half an hour," Sally said. But all the sadness in her voice was for Maureen. I knew she was thinking about how awful she'd feel if Harry, Barry, or Larry became ill. And I knew all too well how I felt, knowing Guy might be ill. "Word that night was that Ricky's treatment isn't going nearly as well as the Crowleys had hoped."

"So why would she, a week later, take

time away from her son to go to the psychic fair?" I mused. It seemed beside the point of trying to figure out clues about Ginny Proffitt's murder, but I was still curious.

"She wanted to see Ginny Proffitt," Cherry said. "In fact, she cut into the front of the line. Several women at the front — not folks from around Paradise — were pretty unhappy about it. Maureen shouted at them to shut up, that she had a bigger need than them."

"That doesn't sound like Maureen. Not the psychic fair or the shouting," Sally said.

"Well, Ginny must have said something, because they settled down. Then Ginny and Maureen went off for a few minutes behind the curtained area. When they came back out, Maureen was a lot calmer, but by then Hugh Crowley was there wanting her to come home with him. I didn't hear what was said, but it's a good bet she wanted to stay and he wanted her to go, because when he took her by the arm, she pulled away from him. He looked unhappy, and kept looking nervously at Ginny. Finally, Ginny leaned forward and whispered something to Maureen, and Maureen left quietly with Hugh, but neither of them looked very happy."

"You saw all this, just standing around at the psychic fair?" Sally said.

"I wasn't just standing around," Cherry said, sounding a bit miffed. "I was in line to see Ginny Proffitt."

"She had a *line?*" I said.

"And you were *waiting* in it?" Sally said.

Cherry is notoriously impatient about line waiting. She's been known to go through the quickie checkout twice with eight items instead of going through the regular checkout with sixteen items just to save five minutes.

"Ginny Proffitt has — well, *had* — quite a great reputation as a seer," said Cherry, sounding even more miffed. Or at least, a little defensive. "I talked to one lady who lives in Pennsylvania and goes to see Ginny any chance she gets. Went all the way to Oregon once at a psychic fair there to see her. And I met some other folks from Michigan and Indiana and Tennessee. Ginny is a big draw because she's quite insightful. The lady from Pennsylvania said Ginny kind of goes into a half-trance as she stares into the crystal ball and then she gives the most amazing advice and predictions."

"So stuff appears in the crystal ball? Like flying monkeys?" Sally snorted with laughter, until I kicked her under the table.

Cherry rolled her eyes. "Gazing into the crystal ball's purity helped her clear her mind of distractions, then focus on the energy of the person she was reading."

"You get that out of some crystal ball 101 textbook?" Sally said. I kicked Sally again. This time Sally kicked back. Hard. I winced, and then ate the last bite of my banana pudding. It's comfort food, true, but my shin still throbbed.

"The lady from Pennsylvania told me," Cherry said.

"Please tell me you asked Ginny what the conference between her and Maureen was all about."

"That would be confidential. Just like between a doctor and patient. Or pastor and parishioner," Cherry said.

"C'mon, Cherry, Ginny has been murdered."

Sally's eyes widened. "You think Maureen killed Ginny over something she said?"

"Besides, I thought your theory was that Ginny's meeting with Dru Purcell had something to do with her death."

It was my turn to eye roll, but, virtuously, I resisted. "No. I think anything Ginny said or did" — like leave an ancient suitcase of dirty old overalls at my laundromat with a cryptic message on a handkerchief, but I hadn't shared that tidbit of info with them just yet — "might give us some clue about why she was killed."

"Us?" Cherry asked.

"We're investigating this death now?" Sally asked.

"Let's not call it investigating. I think, as concerned citizens, we could do a bit of poking around," I said. I could use the distraction until the coming Monday, when I'd take Guy to the doctor. Otherwise, I'd spend my time fretting about him. "If we turn up anything that might be useful, we can let Chief Worthy know. Unless you're not interested?"

"I'm in," Cherry said quickly.

"Me, too," said Sally. Then she laughed. Cherry and I gave her a look. "Sorry," she said. "Ginny's murder isn't funny, but I just remembered something about Josie."

I cocked an eyebrow. "Yeah?"

"Back in our junior high Sunday School class. Remember, we had Mrs. Trimbach. We had to draw each other's names and say what spiritual gift we thought the person had. So we said things about each other like, the gift of prayer, or the gift of witnessing, you know, stuff that sounded like what Mrs. Trimbach would want to hear," Sally said. "But we had an odd number of kids, so Mrs. Trimbach had to participate. She pulled Josie's name. She looked stumped, then finally stuttered out — 'Josie has the gift of questioning!' "

Cherry laughed.

I considered for a moment. "Yeah, I remember now. At the time, I felt horrible. The gift of questioning? That's not in the Bible, I recollect thinking. Now that sounds pretty good." I turned the idea over in my mind, then turned the phrase over again on my tongue, "The gift of questioning. Hmm. I like that."

Cherry looked at me. "You sure that's a spiritual gift?"

I shrugged. "One spirit, many gifts. Why not?" Plus, the gift of questioning sounded better than Nosey Josie.

"All right," I said, in the assured manner befitting my gift. "We know what we have to do. I'll get Winnie and Owen to help, too."

"Speaking of Owen —" Sally started.

"We weren't," I cut her off. "We were seeing if Cherry had asked Ginny about her conversation with Maureen."

Cherry shook her head, and her high-piled puff of blond swayed a little. "Right in the middle of her consultation with the lady from Pennsylvania, Ginny stood up abruptly and left."

"Just — left?"

"The Pennsylvania lady was sitting at Ginny's table. I was standing several feet back — my turn would have been next — so I couldn't hear what Ginny was saying. Damon LeFever had come by Ginny's table several times to make sure the line stayed back so Ginny and the current client would have privacy. But I could see Ginny's face. She had a serene expression as she stared into the ball, like a trance. Then all of a sudden, her face scrunched up something awful, as if she'd seen something just horrifying."

"But I thought you said she didn't see images in the ball?" Sally protested.

"Well, all I can tell you is that her face scrunched up, she went pale, and she screamed, 'Oh my God — no! No!' The poor Pennsylvania lady just about fell out of her chair."

Sally laughed. I bit my lip. Cherry frowned. "It's not funny. The poor lady was really scared. But then Ginny said — loudly enough that several of us could hear her — 'no, dear, you'll be fine and so will Henry —' "

"Who's Henry?" Sally asked.

"Just someone the Pennsylvania lady was concerned about, I guess. Anyway, Ginny said 'no, dear, you'll be fine and so will Henry, but I've flashed on something I must stop right away.' Then she grabbed Skylar's arm, taking her away from her client, too. They disappeared for about fifteen minutes in the curtained area. Then they came back out. Skylar went to her table — her client had left by then — and waited for someone else to come along. No lines for her table. And Karen looked plenty mad."

Mad enough to kill? I wondered.

"Then Ginny looked into her ball, gasped again, grabbed it, and walked out with it, still wearing her gold lamé robe. Several people in her line started calling to her, but she didn't respond — just walked out."

"She ignored their calls?" I asked.

"She didn't even hear them. She seemed upset."

"Like she'd seen her own death, maybe," Sally said in a low, thoughtful voice. We both stared at her for a moment. She shrugged, and then picked up a dumpling from Cherry's plate and popped it in her mouth.

We were all silent for a moment.

Then Cherry said, "Now what?"

I finally told them about the suitcase. "I'll take that to Chief Worthy when we're back in town," I said. "Then I'll ask Winnie to see what she can dig up about Ginny's background. She could use the distraction from her bookmobile woes." Just like I needed distraction.

"We can see what more we can learn from the other psychics," Cherry said. "I'll talk to Max."

"Like that's going to be tough duty for you," Sally said.

"It seems lots of the psychics didn't like Ginny," I added. "We need to find out if any of them left to take a break near the time Ginny left."

"I'll ask Max," Cherry repeated. Her voice had a dreamy quality to it.

"You ought to be more careful with your heart," I said.

"How's Owen?" Sally asked pointedly. "I'm surprised he wasn't at the hospital —"

"I called him. He wasn't home. I left a message. I'm sure he'll call me as soon as he hears it," I said tightly.

Sally opened her mouth to speak, but thank goodness Suzy Fu herself came over before she could. Yes, I've been to Suzy Fu's often enough that she knows me. I filled her in on Guy.

"Oh, my sweetie, I'm so sorry!" Suzy said. She gazed sadly at my plate of crab Rangoons. "I get you box. You need those. Comfort food." Suzy hurried off to get the box.

It's nice to know even rule makers sometimes break the rules for a friend. Suzy came back quickly with a box and three fortune cookies.

"Aren't these great?" Cherry said, plucking up a cookie. "I love reading them. I read my horoscope every day, you know."

"Me, too," Sally said, grabbing her own cookie. "And sometimes, when I'm really worried, I get out my old Magic 8 ball. Remember when those were the rage?"

"You still have yours?" Cherry asked, awe in her voice.

"Yeah," Sally said. "I love the simple answers. No. Yes."

"Reply hazy, try again later," I interjected, stunned by my friends. They didn't really think they were getting guidance from horoscopes and Magic 8-Balls, did they? I wondered, even as I snagged the last fortune cookie.

I grinned at myself as I pulled off the wrapper and cracked open the cookie. Sucker, I called myself. But I still felt a thrill of anticipation as I pulled out the white slip of paper.

" 'Do not confuse blessings for chaos,' " Sally read. "Wow. Whoever wrote this must have been by my trailer," she said, but with a smile. I knew she was thinking of her own little blessings, Harry, Barry, and Larry.

"Ooh, ooh," squealed Cherry. "Listen to mine — 'Love will find you when you least expect it.' "

"But you always expect it," Sally said, "And what Max expects from you ain't exactly love . . ."

While Sally and Cherry bickered, I read my fortune. "Where you look determines what you find."

I laughed and tossed the fortune down on the table, along with a generous tip for Suzy to more than cover my rule-breaking take-out box of Rangoons.

How was I to know that my fortune cookie would prove to be truly prophetic?

11

A traffic jam in Paradise usually means two drivers have stopped their cars or trucks in the middle of a street and rolled down their windows to have a chat, maybe to double check the Moose Lodge's bingo time. Or the deadline for entering baked goods at the county fair. Such traffic jams are easily cleared up with a tap of the horn and last at most three minutes. Even when all three of Paradise's traffic lights go out, traffic might slow, but it doesn't jam.

Today, traffic was stopped on the way into Paradise. But on the two-lane road, there was no traffic coming out of town.

"You reckon this is all from people going to the psychic fair?" Cherry asked, her tone incredulous. She'd ridden back with me because her salon is right next door to my laundromat, and the Bar-None was on the north outskirts of town. It was a

187

quarter to three o'clock as we sat in the traffic jam. The Red Horse Motel was on the south outskirt of town, so anyone coming down from Columbus would pass through town to get to the motel and the psychic fair.

"How crowded was it last night?"

"Not crowded enough to support a traffic jam," Cherry said.

"Maybe psychic fairs draw their biggest crowds on Saturday afternoons?"

"But no one's coming up the road away from Paradise," Cherry said. "That's definitely unusual."

True. Most Saturdays, while folks from the big cities of Cincinnati and Columbus and Dayton venture into Paradise to browse through old stuff at the antique shops, Paradisites leave to go to Cincinnati and Columbus and Dayton to browse through new stuff at the shopping malls. (Well, some Paradisites go fishing and boating, too, down at Licking Creek Lake.) You always want what's not in your own backyard, my Aunt Clara always said.

But there wasn't a bit of traffic coming out of Paradise.

A few miles later, we saw why. The main road into town, right by Elroy's Gas Station & Body Shop, was blocked off, and Officer

Dalton Hayes was directing traffic to detour to the right down Plum Street.

I rolled down the van window and hollered at Officer Hayes. "Hey, Dalton. What's going on?"

Dalton walked over and poked his head in my window. "Oh, hey, Josie. Cherry." He stared past me and gave Cherry a shy smile. Dalton's long had a crush on Cherry, but she's never done more than toy with the fact of his attraction. Which she did that afternoon by giving him a full-wattage grin and leaning so far toward him — which also meant into me — that he had a full view down her blouse if he wanted it. Her left boob squished into my shoulder. Dalton blushed. I elbowed Cherry's tummy. She winced, but moved back and kept grinning at Dalton. Cherry never has been one to let major hots for, say, a psychic named Max, get in the way of her flirtatiousness.

"What's happening here, Dalton?"

Dalton looked apologetic. "I hate to be the one to tell you this, but there's been a water main break, right on Main Street. In front of your salon, ma'am."

"Now Dalton, don't go callin' me ma'am; you'll make me feel old, and — *What?*" Cherry sat up straight so suddenly that she whapped her head into my van's interior light — a fitting symbol, I reckoned, for the figurative light bulb that had just gone off over her head.

"Any damage to our businesses?" I asked, my stomach curling at the thought.

Dalton looked at me, as if startled at my appearance. Note to self — if I should ever be insane enough to take a road trip with Sally and Cherry, Cherry's driving. No tickets that way. "That's right — your laundromat's right there by the salon."

Thanks for remembering, I thought. Dalton came in every Wednesday night to do his laundry. But he got his hair trimmed at Joe's, a one-chair barbershop at the other end of town. He'd probably pass out if he even entered Cherry's Chat N Curl.

"No damage that I know of," he was saying to me, while glancing at Cherry. "But the water's been shut off to your section of Main Street."

No water, no laundromat service. And no water in my apartment above the laundromat.

"I don't understand. It's a fairly warm day. The water lines couldn't have frozen," I said.

Dalton shrugged. "From what I heard,

it's the drought. After a drought this long, the ground shifts, and that caused a pipe to snap under Main and Orchard." That was just a block down from my laundromat. "Water was coming up fast through the sewer." He shook his head. "It's a mess. 'Bout a hundred thousand gallons of water before they shut it off, I heard. No water until next Monday afternoon — maybe Tuesday — when the crews get it fixed. The main's real old, anyway, and between the cold last winter and the drought since midsummer, it just couldn't hold."

I groaned. Not only was my business shut down, but also I wasn't going to be able to stay at my apartment without the use of the bathroom or kitchen. A hopeful thought glimmered — maybe I could stay with Owen?

"Can we get to our businesses to see if everything is okay?" Cherry asked, all the flirt gone from her voice.

"The fire department has shut off traffic from Main Street, but you might be able to get to them from Elm," Dalton said.

Elm was a residential street. My laundromat backed to a house, with a privacy fence between my tiny parking lot and the house's backyard. But I knew the people who lived on Elm; they wouldn't mind my crossing through their yards to work my way by foot to my laundromat. I at least wanted to get some clothes and a few other necessities from my apartment.

We thanked Dalton and turned left, working toward Elm.

"I sure hope my salon's okay," Cherry said, sounding tearful. "And your laundromat, too. I don't know what I'd do if I lost my business."

"You won't lose your business. You have insurance to cover any damage, right?"

Silence.

Oh Lord. Had Cherry done something silly and let her payments lapse?

"I'll be okay. I'll just go home and — oh, no. What are you going to do about where to stay?"

"I'll call Owen. Fish my cell phone from my purse," I said.

Cherry did as I asked, then repaired her mascara, turning my rearview mirror into a makeup mirror. Normally that would have annoyed me, but with everything going on, I let it slide.

I called Owen. No answer, unless I wanted to count the answering machine, which I didn't. But I left a message, anyway, for the sixth time, with my cell phone number. Where could Owen be? We had plans to get together that night, but I really wanted to talk to him right away.

"You could always stay with me," Cherry said. I glanced at her. She was smiling at me sweetly, her freshly mascara-ed eyes wide. We'd have killed each other before midnight.

I reckoned I could stay with Sally, but the thought of intruding on Sally in her tiny little mobile home — especially with Harry, Barry, and Larry returning the next afternoon — didn't make me happy.

Then there was Winnie, but she lived up in Masonville. That would put me closer to Guy, true, but farther from my laundromat. And I wanted to be nearby in case something happened to my business. Not that I could necessarily do anything about it. But still.

I sighed. I'd have to see if I could stay at the Red Horse Motel, with the psychics and psychic fair attendees.

My laundromat, Cherry's salon, Sandy's restaurant, and all the other businesses on a two-block strip on Main Street had been evacuated, as had the houses on the street behind me. It took a little begging, but the firemen finally let me through so I could cut through the backyard of the house that backed to my laundromat's parking lot. I shouldn't take long, the fireman warned me, and under no circumstances should I try to use the plumbing.

Chip had locked up my laundromat. I'd have to thank him later, I thought. Maybe buy him dinner at Sandy's, when she re-opened. When I was in a more thankful mood.

Which was not at all how I was feeling as I stood at the back of my empty laundromat, staring at the sheen of water at the front. Sitting on the counter were several boxes of supplies that had previously been under the counter. The boxes, I knew, held smaller sample-size boxes of detergent and fabric softener. I kept those available for sale at only a slight mark-up for customers who forgot to bring their own supplies. Even from the back of the store, I could see the wetness that had spread halfway up the boxes.

I went to the front of my laundromat and found the note Chip had taped to my cash register.

"Josie," it read, "sorry I didn't get the supply boxes up faster. But the water came in sudden and quick!" I blinked back a tear, sniffling. Damn it. I hated that my business, and the other Main Street businesses, were closed and maybe damaged.

"I closed up the front as fast as I could after me and Winnie got customers out the back," Chip's note went on. "Then we mopped up what we could. Hang in there. Chip."

I looked out my laundromat's front windowpane, past my logo — a grinning toad sitting in grass, rainbowed by the slogan: TOADFERN'S LAUNDROMAT: ALWAYS A LEAP AHEAD OF DIRT. Usually, the cute toad and slogan I'd created made me grin, but that afternoon I found no comfort in either.

The street was flooded and the water was about an inch over the sidewalk. Water seeped in under my front door. Already, some of the tiles around the door were curling up.

What if more water poured in, damaged the washers and dryers? My business insurance would mostly cover it, although the deductible would be hard to come up with, but it could be weeks before I could get back to business.

I could survive the business loss, but it wouldn't be easy. And what about Sandy and Cherry and the others? This kind of thing hits small businesses in small towns very hard.

I sat down on one of the white plastic chairs and put my head to my hands.

Fretting wouldn't set things right, though. I looked up, startled at the thought. It was something Mrs. Oglevee had always said, usually with a smile when she returned to me a homework paper marked with a C, or worse.

Mrs. Oglevee. Somehow Ginny Proffitt had known my dreams of her. I remembered Cherry saying that Ginny had suddenly gone pale at something she'd "seen" while gazing, trancelike, into her crystal ball.

Her own death, maybe?

And before I met Ginny Proffitt for those few minutes in the parking lot, a little more than twenty-four hours before, life had been good. Simple. Predictable. I was going to have a nice weekend with Owen at the corn maze, visit Guy on Sunday . . .

And then I met Ginny, who somehow knew about my dreams of Mrs. Oglevee, and everything went to hell.

Ginny murdered. Hugh wanting to quit tutoring. Winnie's bookmobile shut down. Guy ill. Owen off somewhere, not returning my calls. And now this, a water main break that could hurt my and other businesses in Paradise.

196

Why couldn't Ginny have predicted any of that and prevented it? Or had she seen something of her own death in her crystal ball, gone to try to prevent it, and failed?

And for pity's sake, I rented the apartment next to mine to two psychics. Couldn't they have predicted any of this? Warned Ginny to stay home? Called the city and warned them of the water main break? Realized someone would break into their store, and bought extra locks?

I sneezed in my cold laundromat. The electricity was off and no dryers were running.

At least, couldn't the LeFevers have told me to take extra Vitamin C pills to shore up my strength so I could better handle all of this?

I shook my head.

The fact was that a person could make plans, try to predict outcomes, believe she could see the future, maybe even actually see it, for all I knew — and every now and again, she'd still get broadsided, like I'd been. Or murdered, like Ginny.

I left through the back of my laundromat and went up the exterior staircase to my second-floor apartment to pack for a few nights at the Red Horse.

I packed clothes and dry sneakers (the

197

ones I'd worn into my laundromat were soaked) and toiletries and snacks, including a bag of tortilla chips and a jar of green tomato relish that I'd canned just a few weeks before. Then I locked up my apartment and left my suitcase just outside my door, while I used my master key to unlock the LeFevers' door. They were staying at the Red Horse during the psychic fair, I learned when I'd called and told them what had happened. They'd already heard, through the Paradise grapevine, but were grateful I'd called. Sienna had meant to come by that night to feed Eloise, Damon's and her black and white cat. Could I please go in, make sure she had dry food and a saucer of water? I could use the bottled water in the fridge, Sienna'd told me.

I smiled at that. My only "pet" is a pothos ivy, the sole plant I've managed to not kill in ten years of optimistically buying spider plants and jade plants and African violets and then killing them with kindness, too much water or fertilizer or something. I named my plant Rocky for its determination to survive despite my overwatering habit, and on that waterless Saturday in Paradise, poured the leftovers from my coffee maker on Rocky. Hey, the coffee was cool and besides, I'd read some-where once that some plants like a little caffeine.

Anyway, Sienna had also asked me to turn on the CD player in the bedroom so Eloise wouldn't feel lonely; she already had Eloise's favorite nature CD loaded in the player.

I wasn't sure whether to laugh at that, or feel touched. In any case, the LeFevers would make good parents.

I took a quick look around the apart-ment. It was neat and clean, decorated nicely with a new set of furniture, which surprised me, since the LeFevers had made comments about how tight money was since opening their New Age bookstore. Still, they'd always paid their rent on time and as their landlord, I was glad to see the apartment was nicely kept.

I filled the cat's food bowl, opened the fridge, and balked when I saw the bottled water: Perrier. Perrier for a cat? But that was the only bottled water in the fridge. With their money worries, what were the LeFevers doing buying Perrier instead of generic Kroger's bottled water? Or just drinking tap water, as I did? (I figured I could use the extra iron that Paradise's system provided.)

Not your business, Josie, I told myself. But I still cringed as I poured the Perrier in a bowl and carefully put the bowl on the floor.

Then I went in their bedroom. Most of the floor space was taken up with a new king-sized bed, covered with a rose-colored satin quilt, and numerous matching pillows. The bookcase headboard was filled with CDs and books with titles like *Wicca Through the Ages* and *Past Lives, Past Loves*. On top of the headboard were more CDs and books. I stared up at them, starting to read their titles, then told myself to stop. I didn't have time to snoop.

A small CD player was on a side table. I pressed the play button. A nature CD of birds chirping and wind rustling and a stream babbling started up. Suddenly, I realized I had to pee. I started back to my apartment, and then stopped. No using the plumbing.

I hurried toward the door again. I'd just have to get to Red Horse, fast. I stopped again as I realized I'd heard this CD before, through the wall that divided my bedroom from the LeFevers. Not that they'd played it loudly. It had been mostly a background hum I hadn't even really registered hearing — until I heard it again, now, in the LeFevers' bedroom. If I'd heard this, then the LeFevers could have heard me, say, hollering out in a nightmare about Mrs. Oglevee. Maybe I'd even hollered something like — "Mrs. Oglevee, shut up and go away!" Then they could have told that to Ginny Proffitt, and that's how Ginny could have known about Mrs. Oglevee and my dreams, and . . .

I shook my head. It didn't make sense. Why would the LeFevers bring that up, especially in the midst of pulling off the psychic fair and worrying about their financial woes?

I started to leave, but stopped yet again when I heard a shuffling sound under the bed. I knelt down, lifted the pink satin bed skirt.

"Eloise?"

Suddenly, it seemed, a black-and-white dust bunny sprang to life and streaked past me. Eloise. I yelped and then, when my heart stopped thudding, noticed the shoebox Eloise had knocked out from under the bed.

The shoebox's lid was missing, and credit card bills filled the box to the brim. I admit it. I looked at the top one. It was for a Visa . . . third notice . . . past due and over the $25,000 credit limit. I gasped. Below that, I saw an ATM slip. Okay, I looked at that, too. One of the LeFevers had tried to withdraw twenty dollars a few days before from a checking account, but the withdrawal had been denied, due to insufficient funds and an overdrawn overdraft protection. Try again later! the message at the bottom of the slip chirped cheerily.

But from what little I'd seen, the LeFevers were running out of financial options for trying again.

I pushed the shoebox back under the bed, knowing I'd seen more than I had any right to, even if I could blame Eloise — mostly. The LeFevers had talked about how tight things were financially for them, with the loans they'd taken out to open their shop. And yet they'd been reckless with their personal expenses. They had to be desperate for the psychic fair to go well and help build a regional customer base for them. And they'd been angry when Ginny had threatened to pull out of coming at the last minute. Had she done something else to anger them, to jeopardize the psychic fair after she arrived? Should I be suspecting them instead of Dru?

I got up and left the apartment quickly, waving my fingers at Eloise, lapping up her Perrier in the kitchenette. But she — as cats so often do — ignored me.

12

I was halfway down the metal stairs on the outside of my building when I lost my grasp on my heavy suitcase and it went tumbling, handle over wheels, down the steps.

"Damned suitcase," I muttered to myself.

That's when I remembered Ginny's luggage. The shock of the broken water main closing down my laundromat and rousting me from my apartment had pushed it from my mind until that morning.

Even though I was eager to get to the Red Horse, I knew I had to get Ginny's suitcase from the storage area of my laundromat and take it to Chief Worthy. The strange contents plus the handkerchief in my pocket might provide some clue that would help solve Ginny's murder.

I hoisted my own suitcase off the ground and let myself back in my laundromat to check under my desk for Ginny's bag.

It was gone.

Twenty minutes later, I rushed into the small building that serves as Paradise's mayoral and council chambers, prison (only two cells), and police station. I went in the section that houses the police station and prison and saw that Jeanine was dispatcher at the front desk that day. My heart fell.

Jeanine is fifty-something, raised four kids by herself, is one of Sandy's neighbors in the Happy Trails Motor Home Court, and has a thickly crusted battle-ax attitude. It's her way of coping, which I understand, but it also makes her hard to deal with.

Still, I rushed past her desk without saying a word.

"Josie! What the hell do you think you're —"

"Ladies' room," I said, rushing past Jeanine's desk to a tiny hallway to the left that led to the men's and women's rooms. Technically, I was supposed to sign in. But this was an emergency. Jeanine would understand, I was sure.

A few minutes later, I was back in front of Jeanine's desk, feeling much relieved. Plus I liked the freesia scent of the new bottle of hand sanitizer in the women's room. That had to be Jeanine's touch. None of the men, certainly not Chief Worthy, would think of such a thing. I told Jeanine as much.

"Want to fill out a comments form complimenting me on it?" Jeanine asked wryly, in her cigarette husky voice. "Maybe it'll get me a good evaluation and fifty cents more an hour."

I laughed. "Sure, I'll take a comment card. I'll fill it in later and drop it off."

Jeanine rolled her eyes. "That's what they all say."

"Fine. I'll do it now."

She pushed a card at me and watched, suspiciously, as I filled it out. When I finished, she plucked the card from me, and read my praise of her ingenuity and attention to detail that make living in Paradise a far more pleasant experience.

She looked at me, eyebrows lifted. But I could see a bit of softening in her eyes.

I smiled. "I need to see Chief Worthy."

"He's busy. If you got a complaint, you can fill out another form, then see Officer Trenton —"

I thought about asking for another comment card, but veiled threats would only harden poor Jeanine further, so instead I made puppy dog eyes. "Jeanine, c'mon, it's about the murder. Ginny Proffitt. Chief Worthy'd want me to talk with him."

Jeanine stared at me dubiously. Everyone knows Chief Worthy dislikes me so much that once a week he buys me a lottery ticket and leaves it on the front counter of my laundromat, hoping I'll win a million bucks and hightail it out of Paradise. Which I wouldn't, because of Guy, but Chief Worthy wouldn't understand that.

"I'll tell Sally to give you happy-hour prices at the Bar-None whenever you want, for a whole week," I said.

Jeanine sighed, but the hint of a smile slipped across her lips. "Go on. Don't take too much of his time."

I went, glancing back to see her carefully slipping my card into the comment box.

"You came to report a stolen suitcase that isn't even yours?" Chief Worthy glared at me.

I glared right back. "The suitcase that was stolen was Ginny Proffitt's. I think its contents might provide important clues to her murder."

Chief Worthy snorted. "You think dirty laundry could provide clues to solve a murder."

"Well, of course," I snapped. "How many people commit a crime in the nude? So if a killer is wearing clothes, the clothes are bound to have traces of the crime. Blood. Poison. Dirt or mud from burying the body."

Chief Worthy looked amused. "You found all that on the clothes in Ms. Proffitt's suitcase?"

"No! I'm speaking theoretically. The overalls in Ginny's suitcase were just paint spattered. But —"

Suddenly Chief Worthy lunged forward on his desk, waving a finger at me. I leaned back in my chair.

"But you just can't keep your nose out of things that are none of your business, Josie. So what if Ms. Proffitt dropped a suitcase with some dirty clothes at your laundromat? She probably just wanted some tips on paint-stain removal —"

"But she was murdered. So this could be relevant . . ."

Chief Worthy sighed. "You know, with the water main break, I'm real busy here."

I stared exaggeratedly all around the room. "Funny. I don't see any water seeping up through the floorboards. And last I saw, it was the fire department — plus most of your staff — who was busy on

Main Street." I turned a sharp gaze on Chief Worthy. "So why don't you want to hear about something a murder victim did in the last few hours of her life — even if it was something as mundane as dropping off at my laundromat filthy clothes that are way too large for her and years old? Even if you don't like the idea I might actually have a clue, you ought to listen. You're usually not this mule-headed."

Chief Worthy slapped his hands on the edge of his desk. "All right, since it will probably hit the news by tonight anyway, I'll tell you why I'm not interested in your clue. Because Ginny Proffitt wasn't murdered. She committed suicide."

"I don't believe that. Ginny wasn't suicidal. She —"

"You knew her well?" Chief Worthy demanded.

I thought about Ginny in her brightly colored warm-up suit, bounding across the Red Horse Motel's parking lot just yesterday morning. Her jolly insistence on reading my palm. Her eerie ability to divine my dreams of Mrs. Oglevee. Her sly gaze in the Serpent Mound parking lot. Her odd note that echoed my Aunt Clara's devil saying. All the things I'd heard about her over the past day.

Did I know her well? No. But I did know human nature fairly well. And people who are by turns pushy and conniving and clever and even jolly are not suicidal.

"No," I said, "but —"

"She left a note, Josie. We found it in her pocket," Chief Worthy said.

"Notes can be faked by killers," I said.

He rolled his eyes.

"What did it say?"

He shook his head.

"Why not tell me if it's going to be in the news anyway?"

He shrugged.

"I'll go to the press. I'll tell 'em you ignored evidence."

He looked amused. "About a suitcase of dirty clothes you can't even produce?"

I crossed my arms. "It might make me look crazy, but it won't make you look good. And I might mention how you tend to look the other way every third Saturday night in the backroom poker games at the Bar-None."

"What — that's not — how do you —" he sputtered.

It was my turn to lift my eyebrows.

"You wouldn't do that to Sally," he said, finally.

Of course I wouldn't. For one thing, she

gets 10 percent of the illegal gambling take, which she's putting away for Harry, Larry, and Barry's eventual college educations. The money's sacred to her. Even on weeks when she has to serve boxed mac-n-cheese as dinner three nights in a row, she doesn't touch that money. No way I'd betray Sally on that score.

Plus she'd probably pummel me.

But Chief Worthy didn't know that. So I just grinned at Chief Worthy. Hey — I've never played in the poker games. But I've heard Kenny Rogers croon, "You gotta know when to hold 'em" enough on the Bar-None jukebox to, well, know when to hold 'em.

Amusement changed swiftly to anger on Chief Worthy's face. "Fine. Here's everything I know. Ginny Proffitt killed herself with a .22-caliber pistol, one bullet through the left temple. We found the pistol just a few feet away from her body, in the corn rows. The pistol could have flown from her hand and landed there as she fell. The pistol had only her prints on it and was registered to her name."

"But, she could have had it with her, argued with someone, and that someone could have taken it away from her, shot her —"

"You're thinking Dru Purcell?"

I was. But I didn't say anything.

"All Pastor Purcell is guilty of is having a different belief system than yours."

"And lying about meeting Ginny at Serpent Mound yesterday —"

Chief Worthy held up a hand to stop me. "There was a note in her pocket, Josie. It was very simple but clear. It just said, 'I only have a little time left. I'd rather go fast than slow.' And her signature. We also searched her rental car that was parked at the back of the field the Crowleys cleared for parking for the corn maze. There was no evidence that she was forced to drive to the corn maze. Everything points to a simple scenario: she drove herself to the corn maze of her own free will, went to the back corner of the corn maze, and killed herself. Simple as that."

I thought of the other note she'd left for me in the suitcase. Even without that note, this case was anything but simple. Why would Ginny kill herself in the corn maze instead of, say, in her motel room? Or in the woods? Or, for that matter, since the place held spiritual significance, at Serpent Mound? Did mazes represent something that would make it a symbolic place, particularly for a psychic, for suicide? Maybe the location was for irony — Ginny had spent her life trying to help others unravel the convoluted twists and turns life often throws us, and then finally killed herself at the end of a maze.

I shook my head at that. I just couldn't believe Ginny had committed suicide. Should I pull out the note she'd left me, show it to Chief Worthy, I wondered? Well, yes. But since it wasn't signed he could say the note was a prank, maybe put in Ginny's suitcase by one of the "crazy" psychics. Or he could say she'd changed her mind after leaving the suitcase and the bizarre note with me, and killed herself after all. No, if I left him with that hanky, he'd just file it away somewhere. He wouldn't take it seriously as a clue of what I still believed was Ginny's murder. Ginny wouldn't have killed herself, not the full-of-life, headstrong Ginny I'd met . . .

"Ms. Proffitt's note referred to the fact she had cancer. We checked with her neighbor back in Chicago. Melanoma. She'd had several tumors removed, but additional tumors appeared, and she just learned the cancer spread to her lymph nodes. The neighbor said Ms. Proffitt still felt okay but she refused chemo and was interested in alternate treatments, including psychic healing," Chief Worthy said. To his credit, his voice had lost his edge. I knew he'd lost his mama to breast cancer a year before.

I stood up. "Well," I said. "You've told me more than you had to. I guess Ginny wasn't murdered after all. She must have, as you say, committed suicide."

Chief Worthy lifted his eyebrows at me. "You're nosey, Josie, not a liar. I know you don't believe me."

I turned and left. Quickly. Besides knowing when to hold 'em, I know when to run.

Plus, I wanted to get to the Red Horse, get a room, and start investigating Ginny Proffitt's murder. Someone had to.

13

For the first time in at least my twenty-nine-year life, and in probably a good deal longer than that, the NO was lit beside the VACANCY on the Red Horse Motel sign. The NO flickered, as if it couldn't believe its own resurrection, or that the neon gas was really flowing through its glass tube body, or that it wouldn't be snuffed out, soon.

I was happy for the NO, for the Rhinegolds, and for the LeFevers. Unless that NO had taken on a life of its own, the fact that the Rhinegolds had flicked it on meant that they were doing more business this weekend than they had the entire year. And that meant the LeFevers' psychic fair was a hit.

But the NO didn't portend well for me. I leaned against my van, staring at the sign as I tried Owen again on my cell phone. No answer; just his answering machine.

I decided to find the Rhinegolds and see

if they knew of someone checking out later. If not, and if I didn't track down Owen, I could always sleep in my van, I guessed. Or at Sally's trailer.

The van sounded good. Maybe the Rhinegolds could at least loan me a pillow and a blanket. I envisioned myself, curled up in the dark van, fetal-style, all alone with my certainty that Ginny had been murdered, under a thin blanket that smelled of moth balls, nibbling on crab Rangoons from my take-out box. The Rangoons, which had already nicely perfumed the inside of my van, would be my only comfort in a cruel world that had, in just one day, dished out a disappearing boyfriend, a beloved cousin with health issues, and a closed, water-damaged business. All the while, inside the Red Horse throngs of much happier people would receive glorious predictions of health, wealth, and super sex lives.

Meanwhile, Ginny's killers would learn I alone questioned the verdict of suicide and attack me in my own van. I envisioned Dru and Missy pummeling me to death with packets of super-sized eternal-life tracts. My last meal — a semistale crab Rangoon. My last thought — they'll all be sorry now!

I shook my head. At this rate of self-pity,

I would likely eat the Rangoons right then, plus a big chocolate bar from the vending machine that stood to the left of the motel's front door, if I could get the machine to work. Then I'd be in a sugar stupor all the rest of the day. Instead of investigating Ginny's murder, I'd stew and worry about Guy's upcoming medical tests.

I butted away from the van and went into the motel.

Sure enough, the motel dining room was filled with throngs of people, although they didn't look as happy as they had in my parking-lot vision. I walked through, looking for the Rhinegolds, but taking in the minidramas that were being acted out at the psychics' tables and in the lines.

At Samantha Mulligan's table, a woman sat weeping while Samantha, the pet psychic, chirped back and forth with a cockatiel in a cage. The cockatiel's chirps were weak and pitiful while Samantha's seemed more questioning. Then Samantha said something to the woman, who gasped, bowed her head, then finally stood up and walked over to another younger woman who was standing near me.

"What'd she say, Mama?" the younger woman asked.

"That Pepper says I need to stop taking him to the vet every few days. It's time for him to go."

"Can you handle that?"

"I think I can. Now."

The younger woman wrapped an arm around the pet owner, who was still crying, but calmer now. Whatever Samantha told her comforted her enough to let her beloved cockatiel go.

"Have you had a consultation yet with Max Whitstone?"

I turned at the voice, which belonged to Mrs. Beavy, the eighty-something, delightful lady who was one of my regular customers until she finally got her own washer and dryer. Chip, her great-grandson, had helped me out earlier that day.

"Mrs. Beavy! It's good to see you." I leaned forward to give her an enthusiastic but gentle hug. She returned it with a forceful hug of her own. I grinned even as I gasped for a breath. Mrs. Beavy may be aging, but she's lost little strength and none of her savvy. I deeply admire and respect her.

"What are you doing here?" I asked.

"Well, I was evacuated from my house because of the water main break —"

Of course, I thought, sorry I hadn't checked on her. She lived just one street over from Main Street.

"— and so Chip brought me over here," Mrs. Beavy said.

"Here? But I wouldn't think . . . I mean . . ."

"That I'd go for this kind of thing?" Mrs. Beavy cackled, then waggled a finger for me to lean down again so she could say quietly in my ear, "Chip was going to take me to Marla's."

Mrs. Beavy shuddered. Marla is her granddaughter, whom Mrs. Beavy loves very much, but Marla, Mrs. Beavy says, always fusses over her too much and talks too loudly and slowly, as if she thinks Mrs. Beavy is slow and deaf and ready to keel over dead any moment. To use Mrs. Beavy's words, it drives her nuts.

"Staying overnight will be a test enough," Mrs. Beavy was saying. "I didn't like the thought of spending all afternoon, there, too. So I thought I'd come see this psychic fair that's created such a fuss in town."

I glanced around at all the people — just ordinary-looking people. There *had* been quite a fuss about them coming, though.

"You don't think all of this is — well — silly? Or sinful?"

"Just because I'm old doesn't mean I'm stodgy," Mrs. Beavy said, a hint of admonition in her voice. "I love history but I love thinking about the future, too. And maybe this fair is silly or sinful, depending on how you approach it. Anything can be, though, if you go at it with the wrong attitude.

"But I'm old enough to know that we don't know everything there is to know about the universe. Maybe there's something to all this." Mrs. Beavy waved a hand around. "It's fun to think about anyway. And I hear that Max Whitstone channels communication with the dearly departed."

I stared at Mrs. Beavy, horrified. She wasn't really thinking of trying to conjure up Mr. Beavy, was she?

She stared off in the distance, a dreamy look on her face. "I do so miss Harold. I can't wait to talk with him again . . ." And then she refocused on me, with a glint in her eye. "You know, Harold as a young man kind of looked like Max Whitstone. Except for the cowboy hat. He'd never have worn that."

And then she laughed at my stunned expression. She waggled her slightly arthritic fingers at me as she wobbled off, leaning on her cane. "Remember, be open-minded, Josie."

That was good advice, I thought. Mrs. Beavy: the anti-Mrs. Oglevee.

And I'd try to follow it, soon, when I found Skylar and talked with her. But at that moment, I noticed, Skylar had a short line of customers. Her mother was nowhere in sight. Maybe that was partially why her business was building. Who'd want a reading while a psychic fair stage mama hovered in the background? I was glad for Skylar. I could check with her later; right now, she didn't need me to create a distraction of a different kind.

And I did need a room. I needed to find the Rhinegolds, or I really was going to get stuck in my makeshift Rangoon B&B for the night.

Luke Rhinegold was behind the bar, serving up soft drinks, chips, hot dogs, and grilled sandwiches. He looked thrilled.

"Josie, this is the best day of business we've had in a decade," he said quietly, grinning, taking a break to wipe down the top of the bar, while Lenny Longman — the "Dracula" from the Methodist church youth group — took over serving. "Greta's cookin' grilled cheese and hot dogs as fast as she can. Back in the kitchen singin'. She couldn't be happier."

"Let me know if anyone wants a beer," Luke had told him, before moving down to the end of the bar to chat with me and wipe at the one space that wasn't filled — a space that didn't need wiping, but the Rhinegolds love to be busy. The last few years of fewer and fewer customers had been tough on them both emotionally and financially.

I'd ordered a cola. It tasted good and sweet. Just what I needed to take the edge off my thirst and my tension. Somehow, knowing my laundromat was closed for the weekend, my home unavailable, and my ideas about Ginny's death laughable to Chief Worthy, had made my throat dry and tight.

People were lounging at the bar or at the few tables that had been left set up for dining. Others were wandering outside to the courtyard, as Greta called it, formed by the four sides of the motel. The courtyard was really the old swimming pool, filled-in and planted with a few annuals and perennials. A birdbath in the middle of the plantings was the only reminder of the pool. Plastic white deck chairs and tables had been arranged around the filled-in pool turned flowerbed. For Paradise, that was as close to a courtyard as we were likely to get.

And on such a gorgeous autumn day, it worked.

"Is everyone here because of the psychic fair?"

"Mostly. Some attendees are staying in motels up in Masonville. We sold out our last few rooms because of the water main break in town." Luke's joy at a business bonanza turned to a look of concern. "Is your business okay? I haven't heard exactly where the break happened."

I shook my head. "My laundromat's closed and I'm evacuated from my apartment for the next few days." I smiled at Luke, wanting to soften the sound of my next statement. I knew he'd be upset if he couldn't help me. "I was hoping to stay here. I saw the no vacancy sign out front, but I was hoping you knew of someone checking out later this evening?"

Sure enough, Luke looked worried for me. "Sorry, Josie. We're booked up through tomorrow night." Then his face brightened. "But if you don't mind sleeping on a couch, you could stay in our apartment." The Rhinegolds have a second-story apartment over the motel's lobby and office.

I glanced at all the people milling around, then looked back at Luke and saw the tired lines in his face. I knew I'd see the same lines in Greta's face. And as gracious as they'd be to me, I knew they didn't need a guest that night, when they finally did get to retire to their private quarters.

"That's right sweet of you to offer," I said. "But I don't want to put you out." I held up a hand when Luke started to protest. "How about loaning me a blanket and a pillow and I'll just sleep in my van in the parking lot tonight if —" I was about to say, if I can't get ahold of Owen, "— if I can't think of something else?"

Luke scowled. "Aw, Josie, I'd hate for you to have to — wait!" His face brightened a bit. "There is one room — but I don't know how comfortable you'd be with it if Chief Worthy says it's okay to use again. Ginny Proffitt's room is empty. It still has the yellow police tape over the door."

I took another sip of cola, and then asked casually, as if I didn't really care but was politely interested, "Did the police officers say what they were looking for? I mean, she died elsewhere."

"I guess for anything that would give them a clue as to her murderer. But they sure didn't search long."

"Well, not much to search, right?" I kept

my tone casual, fishing an ice cube out of the top of my glass. I popped it in my mouth, and then squirreled it back into my cheek. "I mean, just a suitcase and maybe an overnight bag."

Luke laughed. "Josie, you never change, do you? Always the curious one."

I sighed. Was I really that transparent? Yep, I reckoned I was. "I have a personal need to know. This is strictly confidential, what I'm about to tell you." I knew I could trust Luke. He and Greta, after all, checked in Paradise couples by night who weren't necessarily allied by day, but never gossiped about who'd come with who, who'd left brokenhearted, or who'd come to retrieve who.

I leaned forward, lowered my voice. "Ginny Proffitt dropped off a suitcase at my laundromat just hours before she was murdered. One of those old-fashioned, hard-sided ones, caramel colored, you remember the style?"

Luke nodded. "Sure I do. The kind popular in the fifties and sixties." He frowned. "Come to think of it, I had Lenny here help her in with her luggage, seeing as how she was the guest of honor and all. The LeFevers had told me to give her extra-special treatment — not that I don't treat all my guests special. But usually at a motel, people carry their own luggage to the room. I thought maybe she was frail. So I arranged for Lenny here to carry in her luggage." Luke chuckled. "God rest her soul, she was anything but frail. Hale and hearty, from the one time I met her."

I'd thought so, too. Yet, Chief Worthy had just told me that Ginny had melanoma and a bad prognosis.

"She came screeching up to the entry in a sporty number — had to cost a pretty penny to rent that instead of the usual compact model," Luke went on. "Stopped at the last minute — I thought she was going to plow the car right into the lobby!

"Then she hopped out of the car, wearing that bright athletic suit and the hot-pink high-tops. Not the image of frailty. But I had Lenny waiting and ready to carry in her luggage. So after I checked her in, he asked her, polite as can be, if he could carry her bags to room 23.

"She looked like she was going to punch him! Hollered at him — what do you think I am, some frail old woman? He stuttered no, ma'am, and she hollered at him not to call her ma'am, so he said, okay, miss."

I sucked in my breath at that.

Luke chuckled. "Oh, he said it all polite,

not at all sassy. All of a sudden she laughed and said sure, he could carry in her luggage if he'd let her give him a big tip. Then they went outside to her car."

Luke shook his head. "Bizarre, how her moods changed on the snap like that."

Maybe she'd always enjoyed great health, I thought. Maybe knowing that not only was she sick, but might die soon, had made her act so bizarrely. Could it also have something to do with why she'd met with Dru?

Luke was motioning to Lenny to come over to our end of the bar. As Lenny moved over to us, Luke told me he'd go give Chief Worthy a call to see if Ginny's room could be released. I suggested he might not want to mention he needed the room for me. Luke just smiled at that as he went over to the phone behind the bar.

"Luke tells me you carried Ginny Proffitt's luggage to her room?" I said to Lenny.

"Yes, ma'am."

I cringed at Lenny's politeness, understanding how Ginny felt — although she was old enough to be his grandma. At twenty-nine, I was just old enough to be his big sis, only twelve years older than him. Sheesh.

"She didn't like me helping her at first," Lenny said. "But then she somehow found the whole thing funny and let me carry in her luggage."

"You remember anything about what her luggage looked like?"

Lenny lifted his eyebrows at the question, no doubt wondering why a dead woman's luggage would be of any interest to me. But he didn't question my interest. He'd been raised to respect his elders, after all. I cringed again at the thought, and then refocused on the issue at hand.

"I'm not likely to forget anytime soon," Lenny said. "She tipped me fifty dollars — a real fifty dollar bill! Just to carry two bags to her room. One was just a regular black suitcase — you know, one of the wheeled kind that has a pop-up handle. But she'd tied a hot-pink bandanna to the handle, I guess so she could pick it out from all the other black suitcases at the Columbus airport."

Lenny said this with an air of worldly knowledge meant to show he'd been places besides Paradise, Ohio. And I knew he had. To Columbus, for the state basketball championship a year before.

"The other one was this weird kind of small square case, with this little handle. It was hard and brown."

Like Aunt Clara's makeup case, I reckoned.

"She told me to take care not to drop it, that it had a mirrored inside."

"My Aunt Clara always said that kind of thing about her makeup case," I muttered.

"What?" Lenny looked confused.

"Never mind. What else did she have you carry in?"

I expected him to name the matching large caramel suitcase, but he just shrugged. "Just the two bags. She had a large tote purse thing she carried herself," he said. You gotta love how males describe women's purses. "And there was a big brown suitcase that matched the little boxy suitcase —"

"The makeup case."

"Yeah, that. Anyway, the big brown suitcase was in the trunk, too, but she kind of snapped at me when I went to get it out — told me just to leave it there. And then she got out the fifty and gave it to me. And that was the last I saw of her." Lenny shook his head. "Sad and creepy how she died at the corn maze. She seemed kind of nice, in a nutty sort of way. You know, like someone's lovably crazy grandma."

I didn't know. My own nutty grandma,

on my daddy's side, my Mamaw Toadfern, wasn't exactly lovable. She hadn't talked to me since my childhood, blaming my mama as she did on my daddy's disappearance from town when I was just three. I still fail to see why I should share the blame for that, but there you have it. Nutty grandma.

"Are you sure you didn't see Ginny Proffitt after that — maybe at the corn maze? You were working there when she was found."

Lenny shook his head. "No, ma'am. I left here, went home for dinner, got my Dracula outfit, went straight to the Crowleys' to meet with Mr. Crowley and Pastor Micah and the others in the barn. We met there to get organized. Then I got on my costume and went out to my spot at the corn maze."

"You never saw Ginny Proffitt come through?"

Lenny shook his head again, started again with the "no, ma'am," but I held a hand up to cut him off on the first mmmm.

"Lenny, I am old enough to be your big sister. Or an older cousin. Maybe even, possibly, in a large family in which I would have a much — and I mean a *much* — older sibling, your aunt. I am not enough older than you for you to call me ma'am. So stop it."

Lenny grinned. "Yes, m— I mean, Josie."

I exhaled slowly, feeling better. "Thank you. You're sure you didn't see Ginny in the maze? This is really important."

He squinched his eyes closed, concentrating. Then he looked at me confidently. "I did not see her come through. Even with all the people passing by, if she'd have come through in that bright warm-up suit, I'd have noticed her."

I believed that. Lenny had sharp eyes and a good memory.

"And you didn't hear or see anything odd around the maze when you first got there?"

Lenny shook his head. "No. I got there at seven o'clock. By then it was well after dark. Me and all the others who were dressing up to haunt the maze met in the barn, just like Mr. Crowley had asked us to."

The barn, I recalled from my few visits out to the Crowley place, was a good bit away from the corn maze. Anything could have been happening in that corn maze, and no one would have had to see or hear a thing.

"We got our instructions from Mr. Crowley — he was real particular about us not breaking down any of the corn stalks, because he wants the maze to last another few weeks, and he was real proud of that maze, I gotta say. We were all dressed in our costumes and in our spots by 7:45."

"That was fifteen minutes before opening?"

"That's right," Lenny said.

"Thanks, Lenny." I held up my glass, shook the ice cubes. "Refill on cola?"

He got the cola for me quickly, and then moved on to help other customers clamoring for hot dogs or burgers and chips and sodas.

I sipped on my cola, waiting for Luke to come back and tell me the verdict on getting Ginny's old room, and thought about what I'd learned.

According to Lenny, no one was out at the maze until 7:45. Darkness would have fallen at about six o'clock and in the countryside, darkness gave a complete cover. And Ginny had been seen leaving the psychic fair at about six o'clock. The corn maze workers arrived at seven but didn't go to the maze until 7:45. It should only have taken her fifteen minutes to get to the maze. So, she had to have been murdered

231

between 6:15 and 7:45. The sound of a shot could be shrugged off as someone hunting in the nearby woods — it was deer season, after all. True, hunting after dark is prohibited, even in season, but hunters don't always follow the rules.

But why would she go to the maze to meet someone? Why would someone kill her there, knowing she'd so easily be found? The murder must have been an unplanned act of passion at the maze.

Killing her elsewhere, say, in the nearby woods, and moving her to the maze would have been difficult and surely left telltale signs on her body. And the way the corn was bent, where we found the body, made it look as if Ginny had fallen there. Then been pushed out by her feet, headfirst through the corn.

I shuddered. Took another drink of cola. Worked through the most likely murder scenario: Ginny had met someone at the corn maze. They'd gone to the farthest corner to talk. They'd argued. Ginny pulled her gun out, maybe to threaten the other person. The other person had snagged the gun from her, shot her, then shoved her body through the corn, wiping the gun clean of his or her own prints . . . but, no. Ginny's fingerprints, and hers alone, had been found on the gun.

I shook my head. My scenario made a certain amount of sense — but it also left a lot unexplained.

Like the suicide note.

And why the killer would leave Ginny's body at the corn maze, knowing that the corn maze would be open that night.

Maybe the killer had planned to come back later, after the maze closed, to move the body, thinking the remoteness of that particular corner and the dark would be enough of a mask for the body.

Except Dru Purcell had ruined that by creating a ruckus that grabbed Owen's and my attention, enough to make us come through the corn maze. Then Owen had found the body.

Then a horrible idea hit me . . . what if the killer was angry enough at Owen and me for finding the body that he or she would try to hurt us, for revenge? Fearful that Owen or I might remember something that would disprove suicide, despite the cheesy note and the evidence?

I'd been on the go all day and in the company of other people, except while driving to Stillwater, at my laundromat and apartment, then driving to the Red Horse.

But Owen lived out in the countryside.

My heart was pounding as I tried his number again on my cell phone. Still no answer — this time just a busy signal.

I shook my head. No. Surely I was just being paranoid. But as soon as Luke told me whether or not I had a room, I would drive out to Owen's house. Just to be sure, I told myself. Not because I really missed him, or anything like that.

To distract myself, I pulled a pen out of my purse and jotted a few notes and questions on my bar paper napkin:

1. What did Ginny hear from Skylar — and see in her crystal ball — that made her leave suddenly at six o'clock? Why did Ginny take her ball with her? Where's the ball?
2. What happened to the little case that Lenny carried in?
3. Why the corn maze? Privacy?
4. Who doesn't have an alibi for between 6:15 and 7:45? Dru? Other psychics? Who else?
5. How explain only Ginny's fingerprints on the gun?
6. Why had Ginny and Dru met in the first place?

I shook my head. How would I ever find

out now what that meeting was all about?

"You ever answer yourself back?"

I startled, and looked up at Luke, who was smiling at me.

"You were mumbling to yourself," he said.

"Oh." I pulled the napkin — now covered with my scribbled questions — into my lap, and started folding it.

"Just got off the phone with Chief Worthy," Luke said. His grin broadened. "I'm happy to say I now have one vacancy — for you, rent free."

"That's good news." No crab Rangoon B&B for me. "But I'm planning on paying you."

I stood up, followed Luke toward the front office. "Now, Josie, I can't charge someone who's been evacuated . . ."

"Luke, come on, you have any number of customers who'd be glad to pay you for the room . . ."

We squabbled like that, all the way to Room 23.

14

Luke won out, of course. As he pulled the yellow POLICE ONLY tape off the front door of Room 23 and handed me the room key, he gave me a scowl, trying to look stern, and said, "I'm pretty sure your Aunt Clara and Uncle Horace taught you not to sass your elders."

He had me there.

But I'd find a way to repay him, sooner or later. Maybe not charging for doing the linens for a few weeks. I could call it a frequent customer appreciation special. Tell Greta that. I always dealt with her about the weekly motel laundry.

I carried my one bag of luggage and my container of crab Rangoons, my green tomato relish and the other provisions I'd grabbed from my fridge, making several trips. The foodstuff I put in the minifridge. I put my clothes in the dresser, my grooming supplies in the tiny but clean bathroom.

Then I sat down on the end of the bed and looked around.

I'd never stayed in the Red Horse before, unlike several fellow Paradisites were rumored to do . . . and not with the partners they should be sharing motel rooms with.

This room was small but neat and tidy, the bedspread a pale blue chenille, the one picture in the room a painting of Tecumseh, the legendary Shawnee leader who defended his people and homeland in what would later become southern Ohio in the 1700s. (There's even an outdoor drama about his life — called *Tecumseh* — every summer at an amphitheatre, built just for the show, near Masonville.)

There was a dresser holding a TV and an ice bucket and a laminated card with local businesses and their phone numbers, mine included.

Now, I'm not a believer in ghosts, usually. But still. Here I was, in the room whose last guest was murdered. Maybe it was the effect — the karma? — of being at a psychic fair, but I found myself wondering, even though this was not my usual practical way of thinking, that even though Ginny had died elsewhere, maybe something of her spirit was still here.

After all, Ginny herself had somehow known about my dreams of Mrs. Oglevee — even though she hadn't named her by name — and even called Mrs. Oglevee my spiritual advisor.

Spiritual advisor? Hmmph. More like exactly what I'd always thought of her, both when she was living and now: a bad dream. But still, if it was possible that I could tap into some spiritual beyond while dreaming, why not while I was awake? It would sure be easier to just ask Ginny herself for the answers to all the questions I'd jotted down on the paper napkin.

Of course, my Aunt Clara believed that people who died terrible deaths lingered near the place of their deaths. Still, this had been the last place Ginny had slept before her death. Plus I was at a motel hosting a psychic fair, so it seemed reasonable to expect that the karma of the place might heighten my chances of tapping into Ginny, whatever part of her spirit might still be on this earth.

But how to go about tapping into the great beyond?

At Serpent Mound, the psychics had sat in a circle, legs crossed, and looked very peaceful. I wasn't really sure what else they had done; up in the observation tower, I'd been too far away to hear the specifics of their chanting. And I wasn't sure how sitting positions would enhance a person's ability to tap into anything beyond the here and now.

But I was also a woman of faith. I went to the Methodist Church most Sundays, and didn't totally understand everything we said we believed. Who did? So that was a leap of faith.

Why not take a somewhat different leap of faith? After all, Mrs. Beavy had advised me to be open-minded.

I criss-crossed my legs and winced at the pull in the backs of my thighs. I really had to make good on that promise to myself to start working out. Stretching in the mornings, at least.

I rolled my shoulders a few times and tried to relax. Recalled a yoga class I took up at the Masonville YMCA about five years before. I never finished it because I kept falling asleep in the middle of the lotus position.

Still, maybe some of the techniques would be useful for tapping into spirits. I put my hands palms up on my knees. I inhaled slowly, then exhaled, while glancing around the room.

But there were no shadows other than the ones that should be there, no flickers of movement other than the hem of the curtain fluttering from the warm air huffing out of the heating unit. I didn't sense a thing as I looked around the room. The room was just . . . the room.

I closed my eyes, inhaled and exhaled slowly again. Maybe I could tap into some connection if I weren't distracted by mundane shadows and flutters. Inhale, exhale. Inhale, exhale.

The back of my left calf started to itch. Attending to the physical wouldn't necessarily get in the way of tapping into the spiritual, would it? Especially if I kept my eyes closed and left my hands palms up.

I wiggled my left leg. My calf still itched. I wiggled again. Tried to refocus. Wiggled again. And again. And —

Thud. My butt jolted into my spine, my spine into my neck, my neck into my jaw. My eyes opened wide and I looked around.

Room was the same. The only difference was that now I was off the bed, on the floor, and hurting. And my calf still itched. I gave it a good long scratch.

Just before her sister in Florida died, my Aunt Clara had the chill bumps one hot night as we sat out on the front porch, she and Uncle Horace on the porch swing, Uncle Horace snoring softly as Aunt Clara rocked them back and forth and fanned herself with her Rothchild's Funeral Parlor fan in rhythm to the rocking. (The fan was free, and so fit nicely into her frugality plan.) I sat on the front porch steps, staring into the darkness of Plum Street.

All at once, Aunt Clara gave a shiver that was far more of a reaction than the funeral home fan could have generated.

"Lord-a-mercy," she said. "The chill bumps. I've a mind to go call Jeanne. Something tells me that if I don't, I'll never have a chance to talk with her again. Leastways, in this life."

"Well, what tells you that?" I asked impatiently.

Aunt Clara sighed. "You just don't have a lick of the sight, do you child?" Though Aunt Clara didn't care much for my daddy's family — ignoring me as they did — she still revered my Great-Aunt Cora Lee's gift of the sight, through her dreams. And she believed it ran in her own family, through sudden thoughts that seemed to come from nowhere.

I reckoned my efforts to tap into Ginny's spirit — which resulted only in my butt thumping to the motel room floor —

proved Aunt Clara's observation. Fine with me. Back to the practical.

First, I called Stillwater and talked briefly to Don Richmond, who assured me that Guy was doing just fine — he was back into his regular routine — and that the staff was watching him closely for any symptoms of stress. I felt only mildly reassured, though. It wasn't that I didn't trust the Stillwater staff. It was just that I was really worried about Guy.

My own voice hitched up as I relayed the fact that I was temporarily staying at the Red Horse, and why, and gave Don the Red Horse phone number and my room number.

Next, I called Winnie and was lucky enough to reach her at home. Before the water main broke, she told me, she'd been able to collect thirty-seven signatures on her bookmobile petition. Would I help circulate the petition when everything was back to normal on Main Street? Of course, I told her.

Then I asked her for a favor I knew she'd delight in fulfilling: researching Ginny Proffitt's background. I brought Winnie up to date on what all had happened since I'd last seen her that morning in my laundromat — she was worried about Guy, too, and said she'd pray for him — and I made arrangements to meet her and Martin at the Bar-None. They went there on Saturday nights for line dancing, anyway, and while taking breaks, Winnie could fill me in on what she'd learn about Ginny.

And I had every bit of faith that between the Internet and a few phone calls, she'd learn a lot. Winnie is like a coonhound on a scent when it comes to research questions. She won't rest until she's explored every possibility. I'd learn way more than I needed to know about Ginny, but somewhere in all the facts Winnie would uncover, would be something that would help me solve Ginny's murder.

The Bar-None would also be the best place to go over the details, away from the other psychics, who along with Dru were my top suspects (Dru being my favorite). Of course, Dru wouldn't haunt the Bar-None's door. He and his followers counted drinking and dancing as sins. If he hadn't been so preoccupied these past few months with trying to run the LeFevers out of business, to put a stop to the psychic fair, and to protest Halloween celebrations, he'd probably be arranging a protest demonstration at the Bar-None.

After I finished with Winnie, I tried

Owen's number again. Still busy. It was time to go see for myself that he was okay.

"Now, take a look at this one, Josie. Doesn't he look great in his uniform?"

I looked at the picture of the twelve-year-old boy on Owen's computer screen.

The boy had Owen's offbeat but somehow charming good looks: the slight bend to the nose, the roguish grin, the wide-eyed expression, as if in amazement or anticipation.

The boy's face also carried other qualities that I reckoned came from his mama: clear green eyes, a firmness to the chin, a spattering of sandy freckles.

The boy's hair I couldn't judge. He wore a red baseball cap and his hair was cropped so short that only a fine burr of light brown showed above his ears. The cap matched his red and blue baseball uniform, which boasted his high school team name: PANTHERS. Eagerness showed in how he held the bat, poised as if about to swing.

"He's a pitcher. I was a pretty decent pitcher in my day," Owen said. "Had a mean slider I liked to throw, you know."

No, I thought, I hadn't known that. I hadn't even known that Owen played baseball in high school. Or that he had an athletic bone in his body. The past summer, when we'd gone riding on the bike trail that winds just past Paradise (one of the many bike and hike trails created from the old railroad lines and canal towpaths in Ohio), Owen kept losing his balance.

We'd played putt-putt golf, one of my favorite summer to-do's, and he scored 202 to my 88 (two strokes under par.)

We'd gone to the park and played sand volleyball — I was an ace volleyball player in high school — and Owen kept serving the ball into the net.

So no, I had no idea he was in any way athletic. He'd never mentioned it.

But then, until the previous July, he'd never mentioned key elements of his past to me. Like the fact he'd been married. Fathered a child. Divorced. And on a trip to his troubled home for his brother's funeral, gone into a bar, gotten into a fight with an old high school enemy, and in self-defense had knocked his knife-wielding foe to the floor, accidentally causing the other man to hit his head hard enough on a table corner that he died. Owen had then served time in prison for involuntary manslaughter and, upon his release, moved to Paradise, buying a house out in the countryside and taking a teaching position at

Masonville Community College.

I'd learned all this only because I'd caught Owen in a lie about where he'd grown up. Then the truth came out. I'd often wondered whether Owen would have avoided telling me about his real past for-ever, if possible.

He'd added little to the story since then, except that Tori, his ex-wife, had gained total custody, including control of visiting rights, after Owen went to prison. And she'd denied him any contact with their son, Zachariah.

Until, it seemed, this past September. For the past month and a half, Owen had been corresponding with Tori through e-mail, he told me after I got to his house.

And just that morning, he said, after I'd left to go to work at my laundromat, he'd checked his e-mail and found a message from Tori. Their son had been asking more and more about his father. And after talking with her counselor, she'd decided to allow Owen to come visit them in Kansas City. He'd been on the Internet all day, shopping for the best air fare prices, or on the phone, arranging for other in-structors to substitute in his classes, get-ting permission from his dean to take off. He didn't want to risk waiting until

Christmas break to go to Kansas City. What if by then Tori had changed her mind?

He hadn't left his house all day, hadn't communicated with anyone other than Tori and his community college colleagues.

Which meant he hadn't heard about Guy being in the hospital. I wanted to tell him about Guy, to seek comfort from him, but a coldness welled up within me, tightening my throat, and instead I found myself asking, "When were you going to tell me about all this, Owen?"

He looked confused. "I am telling you about this. It just came up this morning. I'm stunned by the turn of events myself."

I shook my head. He just didn't get it. The man had multiple PhDs, and at times he was still as dumb as a box of rocks when it came to practical matters of human relationships.

"When were you going to tell me you and Tori had started e-mailing each other? You've been in contact for almost two months, and it never occurred to you to tell me?"

Owen sighed. "Oh, come on, Josie. It's not like I'm having some seamy cyber affair with someone I met in a chat room." He studied me, then said, very slowly, "Tori is my ex-wife."

I jumped up from the rocker, turned around — that was as much angry pacing as I could manage in the overstuffed spare bedroom he called an office — and glared down at Owen, who had pushed back from the sloppy desk and his computer. He was looking up at me, completely mystified. Which irritated me further.

"Don't patronize me!" I hollered. "I know Tori is your ex-wife. But only because you were more or less forced to tell me last summer about her and about your son and about — about —"

"Careful," Owen said quietly. Something passed across his face, something that warned that he'd withdraw from ever connecting with me again if I didn't choose my words carefully.

The fact he'd killed another human being, even in an act of self-defense for which none of the witnesses could fault him, had burdened him for life. The depth of his feeling about that had increased my tenderness toward him. More deeply than most, he knew from the central tragedy of his life — as I knew from tending to Guy — that life is precious and fragile and not to be taken for granted. It was a shared knowledge, born of different experiences, which had bonded us together.

But not, I thought bitterly, closely enough that he would open up to me about the essentials.

I took a deep breath, sank down into the rocker. I picked up the glass of sweet tea Owen had given me — I'd taught him the proper way to make sweet tea and knowing that it was one of my favorite beverages, right up there with Big Fizz Diet Cola, he kept a pitcher for me in his fridge. I took a sip. He'd made it well. He'd made it just for me. I tried to cling to that fact as I spoke carefully.

"I am happy for you that you will finally get to see Zachariah. I truly am. I am happy for you that you and Tori are able to communicate with each other. I truly am. I think that is best for you and for her and for Zachariah," I said. "But you have been e-mailing with Tori for almost two months and you haven't even once mentioned this to me."

Owen groaned. "Oh, Josie, don't tell me you're jealous. My marriage to Tori was never good. The only good that came out of it was Zachariah. There's nothing to be jealous of." He gave me a big, goofy grin that I normally found endearing.

At that moment, I wanted to slap it off his face.

He held his arms open to me.

And I was supposed to put down my sweet tea, and accept his comfort, let him think I'd suddenly realized that I was being a silly little jealous thing, that we could just laugh all this off. That would be an easier game to play than not playing any game at all and facing the truth.

I wasn't playing that game.

I sat, still, sipping the sweet tea, which suddenly seemed just a mite too sweet, and stared dead evenly at him.

Slowly his arms sank down to his sides. His grin started to fade. I waited until it disappeared completely before I spoke my final piece.

"I am not jealous, Owen, and you know that. If you don't, then you've been dating some image of me — not the real me. What I am is angry. Something important has been developing in your life the past two months — a chance for a relationship with your son. And you haven't shared a bit of that with me. I've been trying to trust — to believe — that you would always be open with me about your thoughts and feelings, about anything important to you, ever since this past summer.

"You'd tell me in great detail about a great antiquarian book find. How could you not tell me something like this?"

He stared at me for a long moment, bewilderment radiating from his gaze. My heart sank. He didn't get it.

Finally he said, "I guess I just thought this was from my personal life and I'd tell you about it if something came of it. I was going to tell you when I'd confirmed my flight."

I felt as if I'd been hit so hard my solar plexus had turned inside out.

I stood up. "Owen, do me a favor. Have a good trip and enjoy visiting your son. But find a few minutes to think about this — if you want a relationship with someone, you share your personal life with him or her. In fact, that's the point of a relationship. Whether it's with your son. Or with me. I don't want just fun times, Owen."

My heart panged as an image or two of the fun times from the night before — after we'd come back here, after finding Ginny's body, needing to laugh and love to purge the sadness and horror from our hearts and minds — flashed across my mind.

"I want a close relationship with only the silences being comfortable ones," I said. Like the sweet, comfortable silences Aunt Clara and Uncle Horace had shared on their front porch swing. I realized how much I wanted that with someone — with Owen? — myself. "Think about what I've said and if you want to talk about it, call me when you're back."

I walked out of Owen's study, then out of his house.

I got in my van, taking care not to slam the door, taking care to pull out of his gravel drive casually and slowly.

I was almost back to Paradise before I realized that I had not told him a thing about Guy, or about the water main break, or about Ginny's suitcase or anything else I'd learned.

Then I remembered something else, too.

The night before, he'd asked me about the dream I'd told Ginny about. And I'd told him the same little white lie I'd told Sally and Cherry — that I'd dreamed about drowning.

Maybe a small thing, compared to him withholding his renewed e-mail relationship with his ex-wife.

But, somehow, it made me feel worse, about both of us.

15

I love the names of apples. I have no idea who came up with them or how they chose them, but there's something so poetic and earthy about them: Winesap. Rome Beauty. Red Delicious, Golden Delicious, Jonathan. Even Granny Smith.

At Beeker's Orchard, across from the Red Horse Motel, I took comfort in the apple names, pausing before each bin to carefully read the handwritten placards as if this were the first time I'd ever encountered appledom's glorious variety.

The Red Horse Motel's parking lot was full and overflow parking had been set up in the fields in front of Beeker's Orchard. I'd parked my van on a grassy rise, being careful to set the parking brake.

The orchard was also busier than usual, even for a glorious Saturday afternoon in autumn. I selected two Winesaps — they would be good for a midnight snack in my motel room — and got in line and breathed in the sweet hay and apple air of the old barn.

The Beeker Orchard sells unpastuerized cider, impossible to get, except at a few roadside stands. Some folks worry that they'll get sick if they drink unpasteurized cider, but generations of Paradisites and Masonvillians and folks from other villages and forks in the road in the county had grown up sipping the tasty beverage every fall, and I never knew of anyone to fall sick as a result.

Sometimes I think we just worry too much. You can't protect yourself from every possibility of ill health or disaster. After all, say you're in line at a convenience store to get the pasteurized cider, which is as bland in comparison to the real stuff, as flat soda is to fizzy. A nut ball could come in and decide to rob the place and shoot you dead.

You just can't predict everything, I thought. Owen couldn't have predicted that walking into that bar years ago, just wanting a cold brew to help him past the hurting of losing his brother, would lead to a tragic outcome that would take his attacker's life, and change his own forever.

The day before, I would have predicted that the weekend would be busy but pleasant. I'd never have foreseen Guy needing emergency medical help, Ginny's murder, the water main break, my decision to investigate Ginny's death, and Owen and I having a relationship-threatening fallout. If I had, I'd have crawled down between my field-of-flowers-fabric-softener-scented sheets and stayed there.

And maybe if any of these good folks knew what might await them in the next month . . . the next week . . . the next hour . . . they'd have stayed at home, too, also trying to avoid it. Maybe there was a good reason we couldn't see into the future.

And yet it had always been part of human nature to try. As much as Dru might protest such "witchery," it was part of the Bible, too: Joseph with his dream interpretations for the Pharaoh; the Old Testament high priests with their Urim and Thummin for getting "yes" and "no" answers about God's will. Not that much different from flipping a coin, or jiggling a Magic 8 ball, or reading from a crystal ball or a pack of tarot cards. Who's to say one is heavenly inspired, or directed by some psychic gift, and the other is not?

As I shuffled forward in the line, I refocused on the sights, taking comfort in the good scents from the barn, and in watching families pick out their fall goodies — bags of apples, cider, pots of mums, gourds, pumpkins, caramel apples, home-canned jellies and jams and relishes, apple pies.

Out front, kids clamored for the pony rides, one buck to go around the large flaming red maple tree three times on one of the four ponies, named Big Bird, Cookie Monster, Ernie, and Oscar the Grouch. Sonya Beeker Woods, who ran the orchard with her parents, had played with me on the volleyball team in high school. She had two kids now, ages three and four.

My eyes stung, and I realized I'd been crying for a few minutes now, quietly, my face slicked with tears. I glanced around. The couple in front of me was preoccupied with their two toddlers and a baby. I glanced over my shoulder. No one was behind me yet, but I saw a teenaged couple smooching over by the Winesaps, taking guilty pleasure from quick little pecks on each other's lips.

The line shuffled forward. Sonya was serving the family in front of me. I dug through my purse, pulled out a tissue and wiped my face, then stuffed the crumpled tissue into my pocket.

The family moved on, and Sonya's grin upon seeing me quickly shifted to a look of concern. "You okay, Josie? I heard about Guy taking ill."

"You heard, huh?"

"Ella Withers heard about it from Naomi Crider who heard about it from Mrs. Beavy. Naomi was in your laundromat this morning and then ran into Ella up at the Pick-N-Save. Ella stopped by here on her way back from Masonville and told me about it. Said she'd already put Guy and you on the prayer chain."

I smiled at that. Ella's the head of the prayer chain at the Paradise United Methodist Church. I wasn't sure I believed that the chain really made that much difference in the outcomes of whatever the chain members prayed over, but it made me feel better knowing that many people would be thinking of me and Guy and caring about us. Maybe that was the real power of such things.

"Ella said she wasn't sure, but she thought Guy has . . ." Sonya dropped her voice to a whisper, as if that would take away from the power of whatever dread disease she was about to name. ". . . well, she heard he has leukemia."

I shook my head. "God willing, not that. The doctors at the hospital tested him for all kinds of things. They think he has diabetes. I'm taking him in Monday for more testing."

Sonya exhaled in relief, which made fresh tears well up in my eyes. "Well, diabetes is bad enough — my mama's had high sugar for several years now — but that's easier to deal with than the other. Do you mind if I get you on our prayer chain, too?"

I smiled. "That'd be fine." I'd take good thoughts from everyone who wanted to spare a synapse generating them. Did Wiccans have prayer chains? I might ask, later, when I got back to the psychic fair. "Thanks. How about a pint of the regular?"

Sonya laughed when I said that. Beeker Orchard only sells one liquid refreshment, their homemade cider. It's not like you can get it in decaf, or low-carb/sugar-free. That's one of the beauties of cider.

"Just a pint?" she said, knowing I usually got a gallon, which lasted a week, as long as I portioned out a glass in the morning, another in the evening, making sure to savor it. You can only get Beeker's cider for a scant eight weeks out of the year. Then you can buy pints or quarts and freeze it (after pouring a bit off the top, to keep the plastic jug from bursting), but I've just got a regular freezer, and only freeze two quarts at the end of the season. One I thaw at Thanksgiving, the other in February, on some particularly gray and gloomy and heartbreaking day.

"I'm staying at the Red Horse," I said. "My place was evacuated because of the water main break. I just have a minifridge in my room."

Sonya looked concerned. "I'm sorry to hear that. I heard there was a water main break, but not specifically where. You need anything?"

"Thanks, but I'm fine. I was able to get in my apartment long enough to get the essentials for a few days — clothes, toiletries, and such." And green tomato relish to try with the crab Rangoons, tortilla chips, and a bottle of wine . . . but I didn't mention those things.

I heard some people get in line behind me. Sonya walked over to the large glass-fronted refrigerator unit behind her. "Well, now, you give us a holler if you need anything while you're over there," she said over her shoulder.

She came back with a pint of cider and an apple covered in gooey melted caramel and chopped peanuts. I eyed the caramel apple.

"It's on us," Sonya said.

I accepted her generosity gratefully and took comfort in the accepting. There are a few good things about living in a small town, after all.

"What do you want to know about?" Skylar Temple asked gently.

What I wanted to know was what Skylar had told Ginny that had made her dash out of the psychic fair to the dismay of all the people waiting in her line.

But I knew she'd shut down cold if I asked directly like that, even without her mama hovering in the background.

"Your mama's not here," I said.

"What?" Skylar looked startled by the question, then annoyed. "Oh. Well, she went to take a rest. Headache." Skylar laughed, but without mirth. "She's tense because now that Ginny's gone, she says the lighting where we're sitting is poor, and that's why people are avoiding my table."

"You had a line earlier," I said.

"My mother says that's because Ginny wasn't here to hog all the clients. Maybe. But whatever advantage that gave me, my mother ruined by hovering nearby while I worked. I keep telling her it makes people nervous." Skylar looked around as if she were afraid that her mother might suddenly reappear and take offense at the comment. "Talking to a psychic is a private affair."

I glanced around. On the surface, it didn't seem all that private. Just a few feet away, Samantha Mulligan, the pet psychic, was talking to a man holding his guinea pig. On the other side, Max Whitstone was holding the hand of a middle-aged woman, and stroking her palm slowly as she stared at his cowboy-hat-shadowed face in fascination.

But I couldn't hear anything anyone was saying at the other tables. Everything was conducted in soft murmurs. And I could understand that if Karen, Skylar's mother, was usually insistent on hovering behind the table, that would drive away potential clients. When I'd returned to the psychic fair, after putting away my cider and apples (including the luscious caramel one), I'd noticed that Skylar was the only psychic with no clients. The crowd had thinned. It was 6:30, the heart of the heartland's dinner hour, but the other psychics, those who hadn't left for dinner themselves, all had clients.

Skylar had brightened when I'd walked up to her table, then looked serious as she asked, "What do you want to know about?" as she did now, repeating the question.

Maybe after I got a reading from her, I could convince her to take a break, tell me about what happened between her and Ginny before she took off for the corn maze.

I definitely wanted to know about that.

But what did I want to know about personally?

If Guy would be okay, for starters. How soon I could get back to my laundromat and home. My future with Owen . . .

"I want to know about my future love life."

"What kind of future are you hoping for?"

My mind went immediately to the families I'd watched at the Beeker Orchard. "Marriage. Children."

The words stunned me. Did I want that? Really? I'd never thought so. Back in high school, when I had sat out on Aunt Clara and Uncle Horace's porch on too-hot nights, I'd dreamed of traveling to faraway places — Greece, Nepal, Arizona — anywhere I'd read about in the books and magazines from the bookmobile.

Then I'd taken on the laundromat and Guy's care and found a steady, peaceful fulfillment in those things. I was so focused on making sure I was a good caretaker for Guy that I hadn't really thought about marriage or children for me. At least not on the surface of my mind. But maybe deep down . . .

Could my future really be found in a pack of cards? Could Skylar really have some kind of gift that maybe the cards nudged into action, the cards being just a tool for her true gift of sensing the future . . . my future?

Skylar sensed my hesitation and spent some time giving me a general introduction to tarot, since I'd never had a reading done before. She explained that she did not view tarot reading as going to an oracle and getting an exact prediction. Ginny, she said, had tended in that direction, at least in her later years, but Skylar's view was that what a tarot reading did was help the person getting the reading to tap into insights already in their subconscious; the tarot reader's psychic gift was to intuitively guide the person toward those insights.

Skylar told me no one really was sure where tarot cards, or even the word tarot, came from, although many thought tarot cards were developed in medieval Italy, and the word "tarot" might come from the medieval Italian game *tarocco.*

Hmm, I thought, at that bit of information. The same people who gave the world pasta and cannoli may have developed tarot. Well, then, tarot couldn't be all bad. I relaxed a little.

Skylar went on to tell me that there were many designs available and that readers picked sets based on anything from intuition to carefully researching the imagery. She herself used a Celtic tarot for her own readings and for regular customers, and a classic set for psychic fairs.

In any case, she told me, the tarot deck has seventy-eight cards, fifty-six of them in the minor (or lesser) "arcana," and the rest in the major (or greater) "arcana." The minor cards are divided into four suits — swords, wands, cups, and pentacles, each representing a different element or idea — and into cards numbered Ace (or one) through ten, plus a King, Queen, Knight, and Page.

Skylar's cards were lushly illustrated with some pictures that I liked — "Temperance," for example, or "the Lovers." But some of them were just as frightening as they were beautiful, like "the Hanged

Man," and "Devil," and "Death," which also happened to be the thirteenth card of the major arcana.

Skylar smiled at my reaction to that one. "Most people don't like seeing this one," she said, "but it doesn't mean you'll get hit by a bus, any more than the 'Devil' means the evil one is lurking around the corner. That one represents people who aren't good for you, or unhealthy or unwise behaviors. Like eating cheese puffs when you know you should have carrots."

I had to laugh at her lighthearted explanation.

"The 'Death' card is symbolic — like all the others. It can mean that some aspect of your current life has to die before something new, something you really want, can emerge, for example." Skylar gathered up the tarot cards and began shuffling them. "You said you wanted guidance about your future relationships — marriage, children."

I nodded, suddenly feeling a lump in my throat take the place of laughter.

"Let's focus the reading a bit, maybe on a current relationship. You have a boyfriend?"

"Yes, I do," I said. "Owen."

She nodded. "All right. Let's see what kind of insight we can gain about your relationship with him."

Truth be told, I don't remember all the details of the reading Skylar gave me. It was a complicated affair — Skylar said she was using a "Celtic spread," one of any number of spreads, or arrangements, of cards that could be used.

She had me pick one card to represent me — I chose "Temperance" — and then she had me shuffle the remaining cards. Then she laid out the top twelve cards. By the time she was done, I was looking down at a funny shaped *H*, with the twelfth and thirteenth cards making a little hook off the top right of the *H*.

The cards represented my current situation, my past, and my future. Skylar pointed out that the future is always open, its unfolding subject to the choices we make in the present and influences from the past.

Still, I listened carefully, torn between what I thought I wanted to hear — that everything would work out fine between Owen and me — and being open to however Skylar's interpretation might resonate in my mind.

The "Two of Pentacles" took the spot of the current situation, and signified restless-

ness. The "Five of Swords" suggested part-
ings, or someone leaving. Similarly, the
"Hermit" suggested that in the near future,
I might need to withdraw or pull back, perhaps, Skylar said, working on personal development first or being sure of what I
wanted, before rushing to commitment
with someone else.

Despite Skylar's earlier comments, I
shuddered at the "Death" card, which fell
into the "turning point" spot. This signified a need for change before being able to
move forward, possibly a change in my
current relationship or a change of my own
heart. Did that mean, I wondered, that
Owen and I should develop a way to communicate that we'd both be comfortable
with? Or did it mean that our relationship
would end?

But the "Ace of Cups," the true card of
love, Skylar said, fell in the "outcome"
place. That meant, she said, that things
looked promising for a new — or renewed
— long-term relationship.

By the time Skylar was done, my head
was spinning. How could she keep all
those cards, and their meanings, and the
significance of the positions in the spread,
straight?

And as for the significance of the reading

to me . . . well, it looked as though I was in for some difficult times, relationshipwise, which I already knew. But that things would eventually work out well. Which I already hoped for. Still. I have to say that somehow the reading made me feel better.

At the end of the reading, I said as much to Skylar, then added, "You know, it would have been simpler if you'd just said, don't worry Josie, things will work out with you and Owen, or Josie, give up now."

Skylar laughed, then looked serious again. "It's not that straightforward. The path is never clearly given for any of us. Through this art," she waved her hand over her cards, "we can only know of possible obstacles or helps that may come along our path. Knowing that can help us choose our path carefully."

I studied her somber face. Skylar was only twenty-three and yet she had the conviction of someone twice her age. There was something very consoling about her complete seriousness.

Her gaze wandered a bit, and her look brightened. I glanced back over my shoulder. In fact, someone was coming up to her table. I started to say "thanks" and leave — maybe I could catch her later to ask questions about Ginny — but then I saw Skylar's mother trotting from the bar area over to us, ready to hover just behind her daughter.

Skylar's expression fell in disappointment, and then hardened. I didn't have to glance over my shoulder again to know what had happened. The potential client, having seen Skylar's infamous mother, was detouring to another psychic's table.

"My mother's back," Skylar said stonily.

"Coming right up behind you," I said. "Hey — I think I'll grab a bite over at the bar. I know the owners. Greta makes the best grilled cheese sandwich on earth. Want to join me?"

Skylar was standing up before I even finished the question. "I'd love to."

"Yoo hoo, Skylar, dear!" Karen trilled. "My headache's much better now. Where are you going?"

Skylar tensed, said through gritted teeth without turning around, "Just to get a bite of dinner, mother."

"Oh, okay, I'll come with you, then —"

Skylar turned, faced her mother who was now standing right behind Skylar's chair. "No, mother. You stay here. Just in case anyone comes along wanting a reading. Tell them I'll be back in forty-five minutes or so."

For just a second, Karen looked crest-fallen. Then, as Skylar edged around the table toward me — I was standing now — Karen's face brightened again. She sat down in Skylar's chair. "Good idea, sweetie," Karen said. "And while I'm here, I'll just straighten up these brochures."

I don't think Skylar heard her, though. She was already heading toward the bar.

16

"How do I tell my mother that it's time she had her own life? I've got to be the only psychic who has a stage mama," Skylar moaned. "How is it that I can give other people readings about their future but mine is totally foggy?"

Then Skylar bit into her grilled cheese sandwich — her first bite, and golden cheese oozed out of the other side. I'd already eaten half of mine. We'd ordered Big Fizz colas to go with our sandwiches, which came with chips and pickles, and I'd asked Greta to see if she had an item I'd need later. It was something that might help me solve Ginny's murder, but I didn't tell her that.

Skylar moaned again, this time in appreciation of the grilled cheese. "My Lord, this is divine."

I grinned. "Isn't it though? Greta

Rhinegold is magic with a grill. I think she misses the days when this was a full service restaurant, but this event will have her sleeping for a week."

"Hard times around here?" Skylar said, relieved to be focusing on someone else's problems again.

"Always," I said. But I wasn't about to let her off that easily. "Tell me about how you became a psychic."

"You sure you want to hear about that?"

Of course, I thought, especially if it meant I could eventually ask Skylar about her conversation with Ginny.

I gave a casual shrug. "I'm not gifted in the psychic arts. But I'm a good listener and I'm pretty good with everyday common-sense advice. And it looks to me like you could use some of that about how to handle your mama."

Skylar sighed and nodded, pushing back her plate of grilled cheese and pickles. The thought of her troubles had stolen her appetite for even Greta's fare.

"I was sick as a kid. Nothing too serious — but always catching whatever went around and staying sick longer than everyone else. Too skinny. My mother was divorced, my father living in Texas. He sent plenty of money, visited twice a year, called once a week, but it was my mother who got the worrying part of parenthood," Skylar said. "And she was plenty good at that. She took me to every doctor she could find, who gave me every test, it seemed, to see why I was always sick. Was it allergies? Anemia? Something worse? Nope, nope, and nope. I always got a clean bill of health, but I was always run down and sick anyway.

"Finally, my mom took me to Ginny. Mom had been seeing her about once a month for a few years and Ginny had let it slip that she had been a psychic healer, a long time ago."

I swallowed my bite of sandwich. "A psychic healer? What does that mean?"

Skylar took a long drink of her Big Fizz Cola. "You know how in some religions, there's faith healing — a laying on of hands?"

I nodded.

"Well, psychic healing is just a psychic's version of that. Harnessing psychic energy and directing it to the person's diseased or broken spots," Skylar said. She lifted her eyebrows. "A bunch of hokum, you think?"

I shrugged.

"Just as with prayer or faith healing, it can help the patient get calmer, more centered, and that can help medical treatment work better," Skylar said.

I thought about that, and then nodded. "I reckon that makes sense. If a person is overly tense, then maybe traditional treatment wouldn't work as well."

"It's more than just being calm," Skylar started, "it's also directing karmic energy —" She stopped, shook her head. "Never mind. The point is, psychic healing can be a good boost to traditional healing, in my view. I don't see it as a complete alternative."

"Some folks do?" I wasn't sure how this information would allow me to learn anything that could help me solve Ginny's murder, but I figured the more we talked, the more open Skylar might be to the question I really wanted to ask.

"A few do," Skylar said. "Including Ginny. She even had a psychic healing practice, out in California, along with someone else — I don't know who. But she told my mother she'd retired from psychic healing, although she still believed fervently in it. In fact, she was quite opposed to traditional medicine. Not the balanced view I've come to adopt."

I lifted my eyebrows at that. Ginny was a New Age fundamentalist, I thought. On the surface, it was a strange concept. But the truth is, anyone can be fundamentalist in his or her beliefs — have the view that those beliefs are the only ones that work. And from what Skylar was saying, Ginny, in her way, was as much a fundamentalist as Dru.

"If she believed so strongly in psychic healing, why didn't she still practice it?"

"She told my mother that, after some experiences in California, she realized her greatest gift was in orb reading and dream interpretation. She said she'd be glad to recommend us to another psychic healer she knew. But you know my mother."

"She insisted Ginny treat you."

"Yes. My mother trusted Ginny completely. And finally Ginny agreed to see me. I was about thirteen. I went into the room at the back of her house where she did her readings — just her and me. She made us chamomile tea.

"Then we started talking. About the weather. Then about school. Then about ideas about things — like what did I think of psychic phenomena and life after death and that kind of thing."

Tears welled up in Skylar's eyes. "You know, it was the first time an adult really talked to me about anything other than me feeling poorly, or having the sniffles, or whatever.

"Finally, Ginny just looked at me and said that I was fine. That I was just reacting to my mother's nervousness over me. That my mother loved me a lot but the only way she could show it was through worry, and I was picking up on all that, and making myself sick, and that I just needed to focus on knowing I was a smart, pretty, funny girl and I'd be fine."

Skylar stared down at her plate and started picking the crust off of her sandwich.

"Wow," I said. "That was pretty good advice."

"Yeah. I didn't tell my mother that's what Ginny said, though. I just told her what Ginny told me to tell her, that Ginny had used meditation to direct healing energy to me."

"And you were fine after that."

"I'm allergic to fall pollen and I've had two sinus infections and one sprained wrist since then," Skylar said. "Anyway, my mother was so happy that I didn't get sick all week after seeing Ginny that first time, that she started taking me to see her every two weeks for psychic healing treatments. Ginny and I just talked at first, and then I expressed an interest in what she did.

"The orb and some of the other methods she showed me didn't excite me, but somehow, when she showed me the tarot — that was not a gift for her, but she did know the basics — something inside clicked. It just somehow made sense to me, kind of like tumblers in a lock falling in place so a door could open. And Ginny became like a second mother to me.

"When I was fifteen, Ginny finally told my mom the truth, that she'd been teaching me tarot, and that she thought I had a gift. A real calling."

"Ahhh," I said. "So that's why your mother didn't like Ginny. She felt tricked. Or maybe that Ginny held a special place in your life that she couldn't, or —"

"Are you kidding?" Skylar said. She took a sudden, large bite out of her sandwich, chewed angrily, and swallowed. "She was ecstatic! Suddenly, her average kid has a gift. A calling. I was a psychic child protégé! She started having me do readings for her friends.

"Ginny was appalled. She said a young gift like mine needed to be protected, developed. My mother thought otherwise. They argued. I kept doing readings for my mom's friends, who just thought it was delightful.

"I felt, though, like I was doing cheap parlor tricks. When I turned seventeen, I announced to my mom that I had somehow lost my sight. That laying out the tarot was about as inspiring to me now as a game of solitaire. She was heartbroken.

"I graduated from high school, moved out with a friend, went to night school at a community college while working as a waitress. I finished up an Associate's in computer technology, got a good job, a better apartment . . . and was miserable. I finally realized it was because I missed tarot so much, that it really was my true calling. So I started up again and started building a business about the same time my mother retired and in a moment of weakness I said, sure, she could be my manager and now here we are. You see what's happening."

We munched our cheese sandwiches in silence, while Skylar stewed in her misery and I thought about what to say to her.

Finally, I said, "You know, Ginny gave you some great advice years ago. You are a funny, smart, pretty young lady with a gift and a calling. Now, I'm not sure what I really believe about the psychic arts, but I do know I believe this: God put us each here with our own unique gifts."

Skylar fingered the cross she wore around her neck. "Yes," she said, "I believe that, too."

"And it's our job to do the best we can with the gifts we're given," I went on. "Even if we have to tell our mamas that we need to do that alone." Of course, my mama had run off when I was a young girl, so I'd never had to have any such conversation. But Skylar didn't need to know that.

Skylar sighed.

"Her feelings will be hurt, but she'll get over it more quickly than you think. She loves you."

A look of pain flashed across Skylar's face. "How do you know that?"

I didn't, I thought, any more than Skylar really knew what choices I'd have to face. But she trusted in her gift of intuition, and every now and again, I trusted in mine. "I just believe that," I said.

A look of relief crossed Skylar's face. "You're right. I need to talk to my mother. I knew that. I was just putting it off." She started to stand up.

"Wait," I said. "I want to ask you something now."

Skylar sat back down. "For you, Josie, it's complimentary."

That was good, I thought, since she'd charged me twenty bucks for my reading.

"Several people noticed that last night, Ginny saw something in her crystal ball that upset her. Then she got your attention and both of you went to the break area. When you came back out, Ginny looked upset, gazed into her crystal ball, grabbed it, and then left. What happened, Skylar?"

Skylar's face closed again. "She asked me for a tarot reading. I gave it to her. She was distraught over the results."

Interesting, I thought. For some reason, Ginny sought out her former pupil for guidance. Didn't she trust her own abilities to, as Skylar put it, find her path? Or had she seen something so awful on her path that she found it unbelievable? Had she even been concerned about herself, or could it be someone else's path that worried her?

More questions. And I hadn't come any closer to answering the ones I'd already written out.

"What was she asking about?"

Skylar frowned at me. "That's confidential. Clients come to us with problems that they don't want anyone else to know about."

"I can appreciate that," I said. "But Ginny was murdered."

Skylar flinched at that, but held my gaze and didn't say anything.

I leaned forward. "This is confidential, too, but I'm going to tell you anyway. In a few days, it will be ruled that Ginny committed suicide."

At that, Skylar gasped. "No, no, she wouldn't — she wanted —" she stopped, put her hand over her mouth. Her hand was trembling.

"I don't believe she would commit suicide, either," I said. I sucked in my breath sharply at a thought that hit me all at once. I wasn't sure if I should share it, though. It might get her to tell me why Ginny had come to her. But it also might make her and her mama run. Karen was still on my list of suspects for killing Ginny. After all, Karen had been angry that Ginny took clients away from Skylar. As crazy as it seemed, it was possible that Karen had killed Ginny with the notion that somehow getting rid of Ginny would help Skylar's career.

I studied Skylar for a moment. Would Skylar have helped her mama with a scheme like that? No, I didn't think she'd plan out something like that, but she might protect her mama.

There was only one way to shake information loose from Skylar. Scare her a little.

"Skylar, I heard about your and Ginny's private meeting from my friend earlier today. She'd been at the psychic fair yesterday, and saw you and Ginny go off, saw how Ginny looked when you two came out of the break area. If she remembers you two, and noticed Ginny's expression, then lots of people could have, too."

Skylar shrugged as she ate her grilled cheese.

"My friend assumed you gave Ginny a reading. She assumed the reading was based on something Ginny told you or asked you, something important. If she saw all that and assumed all those things, then the killer could have, too. Or heard about it from someone who did."

Skylar's eyes widened as she peered nervously around the dining area. She dropped the last crust of the cheese sandwich back to her plate.

"You really think Ginny's killer could have picked up the fact that Ginny — that she —" Skylar's voice trailed off.

I was right! I thought. Ginny had told Skylar something important just before rushing off to the corn maze — and her death.

"If Ginny told you something or asked you something that relates to why she ran out of the psychic fair last night, you need to tell the police," I said. "It might help them figure out why she was killed."

"But you said the police believe she committed suicide."

"True." I paused. "But I don't believe that."

Skylar glanced around again, and then leaned toward me. "All right. I'll tell you what I know, and then you tell me if you think I should go to the police. Ginny was ill. Very ill."

I'd learned that from Chief Worthy, but I lifted my eyebrows in an effort to look surprised.

"She had cancer, melanoma," Skylar said. "She was in the early stages of the disease, so she still had most of her energy, still could look and act as she normally did. She hadn't started any traditional medical treatments, although she was doing things with her diet and herbs to fight the illness. She'd started psychic healing on herself, saying she'd refound her gift. In fact, it had worked so well on her, that she was thinking of again practicing psychic healing for others. And I know she wanted to go to Tijuana, Mexico, for a radical alternative cancer treatment, but didn't have the money, yet."

"She told you all this yesterday."

Skylar shook her head. "No. She called me about two weeks ago. She was excited about the treatment as a complement to the psychic healing and diet changes she'd already started. She described the treatment as including organic supplements, lymphatic massage, coffee enemas . . ."

I shuddered.

"My mother doesn't know anything about the conversation I had with Ginny."

Really, I thought. Could Skylar be so sure? What if Karen had found out about the contact and killed Ginny in a fit of maternal jealousy? Skylar had said moments before that Ginny had been, at one point, like a second mother to her. I didn't think Karen would handle that very well. She might even feel betrayed by Skylar's contact with her daughter and take it out on Ginny.

"Ginny and I met several times," Skylar was saying. "I gave her tarot readings around the question of her health and her decisions to seek radical treatment." Skylar paused, chewed on her lip. "I always told her, after the readings, that she should keep talking to her traditional doctor, whatever she decided.

"But she was adamant that she had no faith in traditional medicine. That she'd seen someone young and important to her die in its care."

"Did she say who?" I asked. Winnie was researching Ginny's background that afternoon. This would be important information to her. "Was it a relative, a child?"

Skylar shook her head. "Ginny never married, never had kids. I didn't press for information."

"Was this what she was asking you about last night, then? More guidance on her illness?"

Skylar stared off, her expression distant and troubled, as if seeking guidance from some other place about just how much to tell me. I kept silent. There was no point in pushing her.

Finally, Skylar looked at me. She spoke quietly, evenly. "She did not ask about her health last night. She told me she had an important meeting to go to. She had to give advice as well as seek it, she said, and she wanted to know what probable obstacles or outcomes to expect.

"So I did a simple one-card tarot reading around that question, having Ginny shuffle the cards until she was ready for me to pull the top one. It was the Death card. I interpreted it to mean that a distinct change in action was needed — either for her, or for the person she was meeting with." Skylar shook her head. "But Ginny took it more literally. The word in the psychic community is that she's been telling her clients specific outcomes, not potential paths or changes that might be considered. I guess she's been doing that with her personal readings, too. Dangerous territory."

I sucked in my breath at that. "So Ginny interpreted what you saw as being about her death?" And yet Ginny had run out of the psychic fair, with her crystal ball, to her death.

But Skylar was shaking her head. "I don't think so. She kind of went into a momentary trance, and said something to herself at the end of the reading, something like, 'no, not again,' then snapped out of it and thanked me and ran out of the break area."

At which point, I thought, lots of people — and possibly her killer — saw Ginny emerge from her conversation with Skylar, looking distraught, saw her look into her crystal ball, look even more distraught at whatever she saw there, then run out of the psychic fair, abandoning her many fans and clients.

"Do you think I should talk to the police about this?" Skylar asked.

"Yes. But I'd keep it simple and say that Ginny mentioned to you that she had an important meeting just before she ran out of the psychic fair. Tell them you're concerned that Ginny's killer might have seen that Ginny was talking to you and assumed Ginny told you about the meeting — she didn't tell you more than what you've already told me, did she?"

Skylar shook her head. She looked terrified. If she had known more, she would have told me.

"The suicide ruling won't be public for a few days, so the police should listen to you. The fact Ginny was planning a meeting — not something someone about to commit suicide would do — might get them to take another look at her case." I thought about Chief Worthy and doubted it. "At least, you might get some protection from them, if they know you're scared."

Skylar shook her head. "This whole fair has been a bust for me. I'm going to head home."

"When do you think you'll go talk to the police?" I asked.

"Right away!" said Skylar. "Then my mother and I are going to stay put in the motel room and leave first thing in the morning."

"You'll want to avoid mentioning to the police that you're talking to them as a result of having first talked with me," I added.

Skylar lifted her eyebrows at that.

I grinned sheepishly. "Long story. Short version is that the chief and I have known each other all our lives. We dated for a while in high school, broke up, and he's never quite forgiven me since I was the one who did the breaking up."

"Ah. You damaged his male ego," Skylar said. "You must really watch your speedometer carefully when you're wheeling through town."

I laughed, both at the truth of her comment and in relief at her being able to make a joke. She'd be all right, I told myself.

"You two doing okay?"

I looked up at the gruff voice of Greta, who had materialized at our booth, hands on her aproned hips. Greta looked worn out but happy. She'd always loved running the motel's restaurant until it no longer made sense to keep the restaurant open for anything other than a limited menu. Well, this weekend's menu was still pretty limited, but at least she had enough customers to cook for that it seemed like the good old days to her.

"Doing fine," I said. "I told Skylar here

you make the best grilled cheese sandwiches in the world."

Skylar, despite her worries, didn't miss a beat. "And she was right, Mrs. Rhinegold."

Greta beamed. "Well, I'm right glad to hear that. Josie, I found what you were asking for."

She pulled a brown bottle labeled HYDROGEN PEROXIDE out of her front apron pocket and put the bottle on the table. Skylar stared at it curiously.

"For a cut on my toe. It's a great disinfectant," I said.

"Yep," said Greta. "My mama swore by it for cuts and I do, too. It was in my medicine cabinet."

"I'll return the bottle tonight," I said.

"No hurry," said Greta. "I don't plan on any cuts any time soon." Then she cackled in glee at her joke. Skylar and I both smiled as she hurried back toward the kitchen.

"In a way, this motel gives service as good as a four star," Skylar said. "Not that I've stayed at that many." She eyed the bottle of hydrogen peroxide again. "For a cut, huh?"

"On my foot," I said brightly.

I didn't want to tell Skylar — or anyone just yet — that the hydrogen peroxide might help me figure out why Ginny had been killed.

17

I admit it; I didn't have a cut on my foot. But if the hydrogen peroxide helped me figure out why Ginny'd been killed, I was pretty sure the Almighty would forgive my fib. At least, back in my motel room, as I carefully opened the bottle to do my little experiment, I prayed that He (or She) would.

See, on the drive back to Red Horse from Owen's, I'd started thinking again about the now-stolen suitcase that Ginny had left with me, filled with the overalls that appeared to be paint spattered, as well as the handkerchief and its odd message. I turned my thoughts to the puzzle of the suitcase mostly as a way to distract myself from my worries over my relationship with Owen.

Ginny had left me a message that if anything happened to her, I should start at the end and work back to the beginning.

And I was trying to do that. Winnie was

putting her fantastic skills as a researcher to use to find out more about Ginny's background. And I was talking to people to find out as much as I could about her. We were, basically, starting at the end — Ginny's death — and working back to the beginning of her life, as much as we could. Would something emerge from her life story to give us a clue about her death?

But Ginny had left me another clue besides the strange note. The white men's-size overalls, that I'd assumed to be covered in paint. Why would she want me to have the overalls of some man who painted walls in shades of brown and blue and emerald green and yellow and purple and red?

Unless, it struck me on that drive back from Owen's, there wasn't just paint on the overalls and on the handkerchief.

What, I'd asked myself, was odd about the overalls and the handkerchief? Besides the fact Ginny'd left them with me . . . and written the odd note I was trying to obey on the handkerchief . . . and that someone had stolen the suitcase.

And what, I'd also asked myself, did the thief think when he, or she, opened the suitcase and discovered the handkerchief was missing, if he or she even knew it was in there? If the thief — who, I reckoned, was also Ginny's killer or involved in her murder — knew the handkerchief was supposed to be in there, and saw it was missing, then that person would think that I still had it. That thought made me so uncomfortable that I'd been careful to not be alone all afternoon since arriving at Beeker's Orchard, until I returned to my motel room after dinner with Skylar. And then I double-checked the locks on my motel room door.

Why would someone want paint-streaked old overalls and a handkerchief back?

What was odd about them?

And then, as I'd driven along, looked at the bright jeweled colors of the gorgeous afternoon — the reds and yellows and oranges — I'd realized what was wrong about the coveralls was the brown streaks.

If I remembered correctly, the brighter colors looked as if they could come from a wayward brush of a painter tired of laboring over other people's walls all day.

But the dull brown was in much broader streaks, as if the painter had gotten that color on his hands, then wiped them off on the pants.

And, I'd remembered, there'd been the faint smell of earth about the pants and handkerchief, the tinge of dirt to them, mud around the frayed hems of the coveralls. Mud that had dried brown, but not the same shade of brown as the streaks I'd at first thought were dried paint.

And on my car ride, I'd wondered if they were something else. Like streaks of dried blood.

Blood dries to a dull reddish brown, and over time, loses the red cast.

But one thing gets out blood better than anything else.

Hydrogen peroxide.

Which is why, after my dinner with Skylar, I stood with the handkerchief and the bottle of hydrogen peroxide over the bathroom sink.

I studied the handkerchief in the bathroom light, glad for its garish glare, which made every speck on the handkerchief stand out. I didn't want to harm any of the writing on the handkerchief. And I only wanted to test one of the stains, one near the edge.

I turned the handkerchief in my hand until I saw the perfect brown blotch to test, one in the corner, away from the writing.

I placed the handkerchief over the edge of the sink. Then I opened the hydrogen peroxide bottle and poured a little into the cap, willing my hands to be steady. They trembled anyway, and I sloshed some of the hydrogen peroxide into the sink, but none of it splashed onto the handkerchief.

Then I held the cap in my right hand, while picking up the handkerchief just below the corner of the stain I wanted to test. I draped most of the handkerchief over the sink's edge, pinching the cloth just below the stain, so that all that peeked above my thumb and forefinger was the stain. Then I carefully poured the hydrogen peroxide from the cap over the brown splotch.

And watched the hydrogen peroxide start to fizz just a bit on the brown spot, and then begin to fade.

The exact chemical reaction of hydrogen peroxide to blood.

My heart tightened. Blood — old, dried blood from some long-ago accident . . . or, I wondered, from another murder? . . . was on the handkerchief and the overalls that Ginny had wanted me to have in case something happened to her.

I carefully folded up the handkerchief in a washcloth and put it in my tote bag and headed for the motel door. I was going straight to the police department with the handkerchief, and handing it over, whether Chief Worthy liked it or not. Just as I should have done on my first visit.

Of course, this time I had additional information that ought to get even Chief Worthy's attention. At least, I hoped the fact of blood on the handkerchief and the stolen overalls would make him think again about his deduction that Ginny's death was a suicide.

I had also written down on the Red Horse Motel scratch pad, word for word, the message from the handkerchief. I wanted to be able to read the message again, to see if any new interpretations came to mind about what Ginny meant about starting at the end and working to the beginning. After all, I'd made an assumption about the paint on the coveralls that hadn't turned out to be right, as in the fact that the brown paint was really old, dried blood.

I shuddered as I let myself out of the motel room. Just whose old blood was I carrying around in my tote bag? Truth be told, I couldn't wait to turn over the handkerchief to Chief Worthy.

My grim thoughts were interrupted by a delighted giggle that, I swear, came out as a definite "tee hee hee hee!"

I turned, and saw Cherry and Max Whitstone at the door of the room next to mine. Cherry saw me, waved, and "tee hee hee hee-ed" again. Max lifted his Stetson in brief acknowledgement that was, I reckoned, supposed to be gentlemanly. Or maybe just manly. In any case, it set off another round of Cherry's "tee hee hees."

I made sure my motel room was locked, put my motel room key in my purse, and went over to the duo, wondering as I walked just how thin the Red Horse walls were. I supposed I could always stuff toilet paper in my ears.

"Why, hello, there," I said brightly. "Cherry, I wish I'd known your home as well as your business had been evacuated. You could stay with me!"

Not that I really relished an overnight with Cherry. But I could see it in her eyes. She was sure she'd finally speared the great white hunk who'd make her happy. And I could see the truth in the glint of his eyes. Bottom-feeding mud sucker.

Cherry's voice faded in mid tee hee. She cleared her throat, glared at me as she fluffed her hair with her fingertips. "Why yes, as it turns out, since my home's on Plum Street, right behind Main, I've been turned out for the night. I came over here to see if there were any rooms but the Rhinegolds told me they were sold out. You must have gotten the last one."

Cherry could have spent the night with

one of the other hair stylists, especially with Lex or Danny. They wouldn't turn out their boss, and they liked her, anyway. She'd come over here on the pretense of looking for a room, knowing in the primal depths of her mind — somewhere in the brain stem at the spot labeled "lust" — and in the depths of her misguided, lonely heart, that she'd hook up with Max.

She knew it. I knew it. Max, who'd left his room key dangling from the lock and who was now picking his teeth with a toothpick, probably knew it. (Ugh. Maybe Owen's sin of poor communication wasn't so bad, after all.) Max watched us in fascination. No doubt hoping for a full-scale, hair-pulling, nail-scratching chick fight.

"It was actually Ginny Proffitt's room," I said. "The Rhinegolds had to call the police to have it released."

"Ew," Cherry said, wrinkling up her pert nose cutely. Max grinned at her around his toothpick. "How can you sleep in a dead woman's room?"

I started to make some comment about why my sleeping arrangements were better than hers, and then took a deep breath. No cat fights. It would please Max too much.

I looked at him. "Ginny left the psychic fair suddenly last night. Did she say anything to you about why?"

"Nope," Max said. "We weren't exactly on speaking terms."

"You didn't speak at all yesterday, coming and going to your rooms?"

"Nope."

Cherry grinned up at him admiringly. I wasn't sure why. She couldn't want him for his masterful command of language. Then he flashed a grin at her, flexed his muscles under his cowboy shirt as he resettled his hat, and I thought, oh yeah. Cherry was only interested in Max's body language.

Which didn't translate for me, but there you have it. No accounting for taste.

"Did you see anyone come to Ginny's room yesterday afternoon, before the psychic fair? Either while she was here, or while she wasn't?"

"Nope," Max said. But this time his eyes slid away from mine and his shoulder slumped, just a little. Aha. Maybe his body language did translate for me, after all. This message I was clearly getting was: "I'm lying."

"I need to talk to Cherry. Alone," I said.

"Oh, uh, sure," Max replied, and opened his motel room. He stepped in, leaving the door ajar.

I grabbed Cherry's arm and pulled her

back toward my room. She jerked away. She was glaring at me, I could tell, even though night had mostly fallen and the only light we had came from the parking lot.

"Just what do you think you're doing?" Cherry hissed.

"Trying to save you from some heartache!" I said. "If you really need a place to stay, just share the motel room with me."

"No!" Cherry snapped. "Max offered for me to stay the night with him. He's being a real gentleman about it. Got a rollaway cot from the Rhinegolds."

"Oh, like you're really going to sleep all night on a cot. How thoughtful of him."

"No, he's going to spend the night on the cot," Cherry huffed. "I get the bed. At most, we'll just smooch."

"Cherry, you really expect me to think you're gonna spend the night on the bed, and he's gonna stay on the rollaway cot?"

Silence. Then Cherry grinned. "Well, we'll start in those positions. Who knows what position we'll end up in. Tee hee . . ."

I groaned. Her tee hees ceased. "Josie, you are such a prude," she pouted.

"That's one way of looking at it. Listen, I can tell you right now, this guy's trouble. He just now lied to me about not seeing anyone come to Ginny's motel room."

"How do you know he lied?"

"I just could tell," I said exasperated. "Kinda like the way you can tell a rattler's dangerous when it starts rattling."

"Josie, there are no rattlers in southern Ohio. You've only ever seen them in the Cincinnati Zoo, like on the field trip we took with Mrs. Oglevee back in Junior High."

"What?" I shook my head. Cherry could upset a line of logic faster than a broken track line could derail a freight train.

"Come to think of it, you tried to ruin my fun then, too, telling Mrs. O about me and Fredo at the back of the bus."

"Yeah," I said, "Wasn't his nickname Fredo Feel-up? He's probably working in some boring job now, sweating in tacky business suits, still trying to feel-up all the females."

"Oh, so now you're trying to ruin my memories of the first time I ever —"

I put my hand over her mouth. I absolutely, totally, completely did not want to know what she did the first time with Fredo Feel-up.

Cherry bit my palm.

"Ouch," I said, jerking my hand away. I looked at my palm. At least she hadn't drawn blood. Amazing, what with her tiny little raccoon teeth. "Look, you're a

300

grownup now, so whatever you do is your business."

"Why, thank you," Cherry said with exaggerated politeness.

"Just do me two favors."

"What?" She stared back at Max's room, as if she were afraid he might leave without her. Which, eventually, he would — but there was no point in telling her that.

"One, find out if you can who Max saw come to Ginny's room, if Ginny was there, if he overheard anything —"

"I got it, I got it. What else?"

"If you need to, just come to my room, okay?"

Cherry didn't say anything. She looked at me for a moment, and then headed back toward Max's room. But just before she turned, I caught a glimpse of her expression turning just a little sad, and a little grateful.

I was fuming to myself as I crossed the interior courtyard, a shortcut to the road I'd have to cross to retrieve my van from the grassy parking area in front of Beeker's Orchard. I was so lost in my own thoughts, I almost didn't hear the quiet sobbing, but then I caught it, soft and almost lost under the waning fall chorus of bugs.

The lampposts that had lit the pool for night swimming were still there, now lighting the courtyard. Near one, just out of reach of its direct light, I could see a figure sitting in one of the plastic chairs, hunched forward over its knees. The crying was steady, rhythmic, as if born up from a deep well in the person's soul.

I wavered. This person was caught up in an intensely personal moment. Something overwhelming must have caused such a reaction, maybe a reading at the psychic fair that was frightening or disappointing. But no, I didn't think so. I noticed most of the people leaving their readings feeling upbeat or thoughtful, but not distraught.

Except for Ginny.

And except for this person.

Whatever the person was keening over was none of my business, but still. I couldn't just walk past without at least trying to offer some concern, some comfort.

I started over, and as I got closer, realized I recognized the person: Maureen Crowley.

"Maureen?" I said softly.

The crying didn't end at once, but tapered off slowly as Maureen looked up at me. "Josie Toadfern?" she said.

"Yes." We'd met each other just a few

times, in the course of her Uncle Hugh's tutoring and the fundraisers for her son, Ricky. "Are you okay?"

"I just wanted to find a healer . . . a healer . . ." Maureen said quietly. She started rocking back and forth in her chair. I knelt down beside her.

"Are you sick? Do you need me to get help?" I glanced around. A brisk wind sharpened the night air. Maureen and I were the only people in the courtyard. I didn't want to leave her alone. Maybe she could come with me to find help. I gently took ahold of her elbow. "Come on, let's go inside —"

She jerked away from me and kept rocking. "I just wanted a healer for him, someone who could really help him . . ."

I realized two things: that she was talking about finding a healer for her son and that she wasn't really talking to me. She was lost in a trance of her own worries and fears about Ricky. My heart clenched. I felt both sorrow and understanding for her as my thoughts turned briefly to Guy and my own mixed sense of hope and helplessness.

"Maureen, let's get inside where it's warmer. It'll be okay, you'll see —"

Maureen stood up suddenly. I lost my balance and almost plunged from kneeling to sprawling. Then I stood up, too. Maureen glared at me.

"It'll be okay? Okay?" she said in a mocking, angry tone. "That's what I've been hearing for nearly seven months now. That Ricky will be okay. That things will work out. But he's getting worse, worse damn it! Prayer chains, second opinions, this treatment and that, and he's still sick!"

Maureen put her hands to her face, covering eyes, nose, and mouth. I could barely make out her next words. "But she was a healer. A healer with special powers . . ."

I realized who she must have been talking about. None of the other psychics at the fair claimed to be healers . . . only Ginny, long ago. And again, recently, but just for her own illness.

Still, I ventured her name. "Ginny Proffitt? Is that who you're talking about, Maureen?" I asked gently.

"She said she was returning to her roots, getting back to her true God-given talent, that she should never have abandoned that in the first place," Maureen moaned. "But now she's gone and I need to find another healer —"

"Maureen!"

The deep voice snapped suddenly from the other side of the courtyard, startling both of us. We looked up in its direction and watched the man walking toward us. Then he came into the light. It was Hugh Crowley.

"Maureen," he said again, more gently as he stopped beside us. Like me, he knelt down by Maureen's chair. "Your mama wants you to come home, honey," he said. "She needs you to come home. She's worried about Ricky, too. We all are. She wants you to come back to the house. We can pray together —"

"Prayers! Hopes! Doctors! None of it's doing a bit of good," Maureen said. Her voice was a thin, high-pitched moan. Tears pricked my eyes. Her pain was so strong, so desperate that it thickened the night around us.

"You know this fool's errand you're on won't do a bit of good, either," Hugh snapped. "And you know what we think of this." He threw out an arm, taking in the courtyard, but meaning, I understood at once, the psychic fair that was going on inside the Red Horse Motel.

Maureen laughed bitterly. "Oh, I know, all right. Psychic healing, foretelling, all of this is of the devil. But mama turned to it quick enough for Little Ed's sake, didn't she?"

What? I thought. I'd never heard of Little Ed. Who was Maureen talking about? I looked quizzically at Hugh, but his gaze was intent on Maureen. I wasn't even sure he was aware of my presence.

"That's history," said Hugh. "Best forgotten."

"Like Ricky will be forgotten, if he dies? Because God knows, we can't talk about pain in our family, we can only just pray for deliverance —"

Hugh stood swiftly, grabbing Maureen's arm as he did so, pulling her up so hard that she gasped, and I gasped, too. I'd never known Hugh to be anything but gentle.

"No one's going to forget Ricky," Hugh said. "And medicine has made a lot of progress since —" he swallowed, hard. "— since Little Ed died."

For a long moment, Hugh and Maureen stared at each other. Hugh still held Maureen's arm, at an uncomfortable angle. Truth be told, I wasn't sure what to do. I didn't know Hugh to be a violent man, but he clearly was intent on forcing Maureen to go home, and she seemed just as intent on staying at the psychic fair. And Maureen was a grown woman. Whatever her mama and her uncle thought of the fair, she had every right to choose to stay. Or go.

But then Maureen let out a long sigh. "Oh, Uncle Hugh," she said simply.

Hugh let go of her arm, and Maureen put her head to his chest. Hugh put his arms around her and Maureen finally released the sobs that had been building up in her.

I stood up, walked away from them. Maureen would be okay with her Uncle Hugh. And they needed no witnesses to their private conflict, to the pain that the Crowleys all masked behind tense smiles and tight nods of appreciation in public, at fundraisers and church services and even just coming into my laundromat.

And I needed to deliver to the police department the handkerchief as well as my knowledge that it and the pants in Ginny's stolen suitcase were stained with blood.

So I walked away from Hugh and Maureen Crowley, toward the break in the row of motel rooms that opened to the parking lot, moving at a fast pace.

Until I heard loud, angry shouts coming from the parking lot, and suddenly became aware of the smell of something — leaves? paper? — burning.

Then I took off running toward the motel parking lot.

18

Dru and Missy Purcell were backlit by the Red Horse Motel sign, and its flickering neon red NO.

Near them were gathered about twenty of their faithful followers, carrying signs as they had before, but this time their placards read NO WITCHES IN PARADISE! and PSYCHIC DEVILS, BACK TO HELL!

Before them the fire's flickering flames cast dancing shadows on the faces of Dru and Missy and their protestors, its primal light at odds with the harsh neon behind them.

As I pushed to the front of the crowd, to the edge of the fire, I gasped.

Someone had made a fire ring, a circle of stones, in front of the Red Horse Motel sign, then laid the kindling and logs for a fire, which now crackled and leapt, feeding itself on books. My stomach turned. I swallowed hard to keep myself from being sick.

I grabbed a stick on the edge of the fire circle, and used it to prod toward me two books that lay just outside the fire. I knelt. The edges of the books were smoking. But their titles were still readable: *A History of and Some Speculations about Serpent Mound.* And: *Magick and Healing.*

I had to swallow again. These were titles I'd seen at the LeFevers' bookstore. Which had been broken into just the day before.

I stood up, stared across the fire at Dru.

"These tomes of the devil burn tonight just as those who follow their evil teaching will also surely burn," Dru chanted.

"Amen!" shouted one of his followers. I heard a less certain "Amen" echo from the crowd and saw it came from Elroy, who owned the gas station just outside of town. Sickness gripped my stomach. Elroy was a good man. A man who was fair to his customers, who was sincerely concerned about the future of Paradise and shared that concern at every Paradise Chamber of Commerce meeting. A man who put his goodness into action at every chance. Such as helping with the chili-spaghetti fundraiser for the Crowleys the previous weekend.

He wanted to do, and be, right. But I could see in his face that while he wasn't sure that going along with Dru was right, he wasn't sure that not going along was right, either.

The problem with wanting to be right, wanting to see things as either absolutely right or absolutely wrong, is that the impulse to be right can make even people like Elroy forget the value of tolerating a different view, of knowing that faith means trusting in the ultimate rightness of the universe even though you don't have — can't possibly have — all of the answers.

I could see that conflict in Elroy's face. I looked at the fire, at the two books I'd rescued. I didn't know if I would agree with their contents. In fact, I didn't buy into much of what the psychics and their devotees believed. But then, I didn't buy into everything that my church taught, either.

I did know that tolerating an amount of not knowing in my own soul made me more than human. It made me humane. I did know that trying to stomp out another's belief with the certainty of one's own only led to destruction and hatred and hurt.

I looked back across the fire at Dru. Despite the heat, my aunt's saying coursed through my thoughts again, chilling me inside and out: That there is a devil, there is no doubt. But is he trying to get in, or trying to get out?

Which is it, Dru? I wondered, as he droned on and the chorus of Amens grew.

Suddenly, the ranks of the crowd broke as Damon Lefever and Luke Rhinegold stumbled through to the edge of the fire circle. In the light from the fire and the neon sign, I could see the strain in their faces.

"What do you think you're doing?" Damon interrupted. "You don't have to like our event, but what gives you the right?"

Dru pointed upward. "The Almighty gives me the right."

But Luke was in no mood for religious or philosophical discussion. Suddenly, a dash of water slapped the fire, which sizzled, but then kept burning.

"Well, the Almighty doesn't give you the right to trespass on private property," hollered Luke.

The crowd shuffled as Greta herself broke through, armed with two buckets. Luke took one and threw its water on the fire, which sputtered.

So did Dru. "We're protesting in the name of the Almighty, burning these evil tomes —"

"And how did you get them?" I called. "These are titles I've seen at the LeFevers' shop." I was furious. Dru and his followers, destroying books, precious pages of others' thoughts. Never mind if they did or didn't agree with those thoughts. The loss of books, any books, was a sin.

"We bought them for the purposes of destroying them," called one of Dru's followers. "We can do anything we want with things we've purchased."

"Hey, Damon, you got the records for the sales of books to these fine folks?" I hollered to him.

His stricken face answered me before his words. "Our computer was destroyed in the break-in. No records are left —"

"We are good citizens. We bought these books for this very purpose, to do the Almighty's bidding —" Dru started.

Greta took aim with her second bucket of water, but skipped the fire and threw it at Dru, who sputtered. A few folks — hangers-on, watching the spectacle as entertainment — laughed.

"Don't care how you got 'em," Greta shouted. "You're trespassin'." She pushed forward to Dru and faced him, her head reaching the middle of his chest, which she poked hard with her finger. "And you're creating a public disturbance —"

Poke.

". . . and a fire hazard, and destroying

private property . . ."

Poke, poke.

". . . and we're filing a police complaint on all accounts."

"The laws of the land are important to me, dear lady, but the laws of the Almighty reign supreme. In the Bible it says —"

Greta ran out of pokes and patience. She swung her empty bucket back, then up, then down on Dru's head. Dru stumbled back into Missy. They barely kept from falling over.

"Don't lecture me on the Bible! I read it every damned morning, even before my first cup a coffee," Greta hollered. "And I taught fourth-grade Sunday School for thirty-two years. The Bible doesn't say a thing about burning books to worship the good Lord."

Sirens cut over the crowd noise. I exhaled, relieved. Thank, well, the good Lord, that the Rhinegolds had called the police before coming out to the crowd.

But Dru was incensed. He poked at the red horse on the sign behind him. "When filth like what smolders before us fills our land, the riders of Armageddon shall come forth, as in the book of Revelation, seven riders on seven horses . . ."

"Stop!"

The voice was high, harsh, and unmistakable. Missy.

"Stop," she cried again at her husband.

He did stop and blinked as if suddenly confused. He turned and looked at her. "Missy?" he said.

"Enough," she said, her voice softer now. "Let's go." She looked past him to their followers. "It's over now. We've made our point. Let's go home before there's more trouble."

The placard carriers looked confused, but did as she bid and started wandering off. So did some of the spectators.

Dru rubbed his eyes, still looking mystified. I was confused, too. What was Missy up to? She'd always stood by in silent but proud support of her husband's fiery protests and revivals, speaking up only to defend him, as she had earlier that day at my laundromat, when I'd dropped the barb about seeing Dru with Ginny.

But now she was quieting him down, and hurrying him toward the parking lot. Almost as if she were protecting him. And he accepted her taking charge. Almost meekly, I realized in surprise. And I knew Greta hadn't beaned him that hard. What was going on with Dru and Missy?

Greta followed after them, though.

"Don't think you're going anywhere! The police are here and when we tell them what you've done to our property . . ."

Luke followed after her. "Greta, come on, we'll go talk to the police now, let them handle it."

The crowd was mostly gone. "I'm going to get more water to put this out," Damon announced wearily, "before it can do any more damage to the Rhinegolds' property. Anyone want to help me?" He picked up two of the buckets the Rhinegolds had dropped.

"I'll help," a soft voice said, cutting across the now quiet night.

I looked over. It was Hugh, staring sadly at the fire that licked about the remains of books, books that he couldn't yet read, that probably he wouldn't want to read anyway.

But still.

Maureen took his arm in a comforting gesture. Hugh's and my gaze met across the fire.

I knew and understood his pain, what he was thinking.

I nodded gently, so he'd know I understood.

He turned, then, without another glance at the fire, and picked up a bucket and followed after Damon.

19

I was late getting to the Bar-None for my meeting with Winnie, but truth be told, she didn't notice. She was too busy happily kicking up her heels with Martin on the parquet dance floor in a line dance to the local band, the Shoo Flies, playing "Prop Me Up Beside the Jukebox If I Die."

I sat at the bar, watching the dancing in wonderment. The transformation of Winnie, from Super Librarian who wears retro 1960s' peasant shirts and skirts, to a denim-clad line-dancing fool, never ceases to amaze me. But I reckon we all have multiple sides to our personalities. I'd sure observed that just an hour or so before in Maureen and Hugh. And in Dru and Missy, for that matter.

On the way to the Bar-None, I'd stopped by the Paradise Police Department, catching Jeanine just before she was about to leave work and make way for the third shift dispatcher. I told her I'd been at the Red Horse Motel when the police and sheriff had arrived to break up Dru's protest and illegal bonfire. She grunted at that. I tried to pry from her the name of who'd called in the complaint, but got nothing. My guess was the Rhinegolds, but I'd just wanted to be sure.

Then Jeanine sent me back to talk to night lieutenant Tammy Holladay — Chief Worthy was gone for the night — and I indulged in a little white lie by saying I'd forgotten the handkerchief in my pocket. Then I indulged in yet another little white lie saying I'd gotten it out while changing clothes, then accidentally spilled hydrogen peroxide on it in the course of sterilizing a new set of pierced earrings. Officer Holladay looked perplexed by that. You always sterilize your earrings the first time you wear them? she'd asked, staring at my left ear lobe which, like my right ear lobe, sported a simple silver loop. Oh yes, I'd said brightly.

Well, I couldn't very well say the truth, or use the white lie that I'd been cleaning a cut on my own person, or the officer (and later Chief Worthy) was likely to dismiss the report of blood on the handkerchief as just being from me. I explained that I saw

317

the brown stain fizz and start to disappear and realized, from my stain-expertise background, that the brown stains on the handkerchief were in fact blood.

Officer Holladay bagged the handkerchief carefully and filled out her report, assuring me the evidence baggy would be checked in with the other evidence in Ginny's case, and that I should be available in case I was needed to answer more questions about the handkerchief.

A half hour later, I found myself slumping on my stool, my elbows propped on the beaten-up wooden bar in the Bar-None, while I nursed a bourbon and water as well as a Diet Big Fizz Cola, sipping first from one, then the other.

"Want to tell the bartender your troubles?" Sally asked, wiping a glass.

I looked up at her. She looked tired, dark circles under her eyes. In about an hour, the Bar-None would close. She'd go home to her tiny two-bedroom trailer in the Happy Trails Motor Home Court, spend a bit of time missing her three little ones who were off on their fishing trip with their grandpa, then probably tackle something else, like mending some clothes or trying to figure out which bills to pay and which she could put off.

And yet, she sincerely wanted to hear about my troubles. I smiled at her. "You don't have all night," I said. "And I wouldn't know where to begin."

Sally lifted her eyebrows at that. "And yet your weekend started out so perfectly. Come to think of it, as of yesterday morning, your life was pretty much just the way you wanted it."

"Just goes to show there's no predicting how things might change. Or how fast," I said.

"Don't tell the folks over at psychic fair," Sally said.

I laughed, took another sip of my bourbon and water.

" 'Course, things might change again, for the better," Sally added, helpfully.

"You never know," I said. Although, truth be told, I felt that I did know. Things had gone sour on every front and weren't likely to get better, I thought. I wasn't in a mood to be easily cheered up.

"How'd I get here, anyway?"

"You drove, I thought," said Sally, suddenly looking worried. "You have a nip at the Red Horse before you got here?"

I shook my head, a bit hurt at the question. "You know that's not like me."

"I know. But it's not like you to not

know how you got to where you are."

"I meant how did I get to this point in my life? Alone. Not wanting to be."

"You're with Owen."

I didn't say anything.

"I thought you liked being single. Fancy free."

I took another sip and still didn't say anything.

"Well, I reckon there's no predicting how what you want might change, either," Sally said. She patted my hand. "You'll be okay."

"That's your prediction?"

Sally grinned. "Yep. And I'm sticking to it."

I grinned back, and then held up my glass. "Here's to the best damned prediction I've heard all weekend."

Sally finished wiping up her last glass and went over to help another customer. A few minutes later, I felt a tap on my shoulder and whirled around on my stool. Winnie was standing behind me, huffing from her exertion but glowing with happiness. I was glad to see her looking like that, especially after how miserable she'd seemed that morning with her news about the bookmobile.

"We have a booth," Winnie said. "Come on over while the band's breaking, and I'll tell you what I've learned. Martin is off talking to Jimmy Dobbs about a possible deer hunting trip." She rolled her eyes. She wasn't thrilled about her husband's hunting hobby, but it was a topic they'd agreed to disagree on.

I left my empty bourbon and water glass on the bar and took my Big Fizz Diet Cola with me, following Winnie to the booth.

We settled in, across from each other. "How are you doing?" I asked. With the band on break, I didn't have to yell to be heard.

Winnie knew just what I meant, that my question wasn't general politeness. Her expression turned serious. "I'm still upset about the bookmobile," she said. "But I'm calmer about it, now that I'm taking action. We have more than fifty signatures already. I think by midweek, I'll have well over two hundred, because quite a few folks agreed to gather signatures, too." Winnie gave me a grateful look. "Thanks, Josie, for understanding this morning and suggesting the petition idea."

"I'm glad the petition's working out," I said. "You know I'll do anything I can to help get the bookmobile back."

Winnie shook her head. "I'm still stunned. I knew we were having financial problems because of the state budget cuts, but I'd never have predicted . . ." she stopped and shook her head again.

I had to smile at how her comments echoed my own.

"Tell me what's happened since we talked, and then I'll tell you what I've learned," Winnie said.

I filled her in on the events of the day. I hesitated before telling her about the book burning that Dru had tried to start, and that Luke and Greta had ended. I knew how passionately she felt about books and freedom of expression, and after the bookmobile's closure, this news might be emotionally overwhelming to her.

But Winnie is a strong woman. So I told her about the book burning. She glowered as I described the fire and the books that were tossed on the bonfire.

"Dru Purcell is desperate to have everyone focused on the psychics and how awful they supposedly are because of more than just his religious beliefs," Winnie said. "I found out today why he didn't want the LeFevers here, or the psychic fair at the Red Horse, or in particular, Ginny Proffitt here."

She smiled triumphantly. I wanted her to just spill the facts, but I knew I had to praise her first. Winnie takes great (and justifiable) pride in her research skills.

"Winnie, how did you find out all of that?" I asked, then sipped on my Big Fizz, and settled against the booth back.

"I started by digging into Ginny's background — news clippings, mostly, about her business in Chicago. Some of the earlier ones mentioned she'd had her first business, a psychic healing practice, in Randsburg, California, which is a tiny town in the Mojave Desert, about eighty miles east of Los Angeles. There's not much out there, except a Naval weapons-testing and development facility.

"So then I started looking for articles about Ginny in the *L.A. Times* online archives. And I found one — just one. But I hit pay dirt."

Winnie opened up her quilted cloth handbag and pulled out a manila envelope and handed it to me. I took the envelope, opened it up, pulled out a printout, and started reading.

When I finished, I looked up at Winnie. "Oh my Lord."

Winnie grinned and nodded.

The Shoo Flies started warming up for their next set. Martin came over. "Hey, Josie!" he said to me. Then he grinned at his wife, beaming as he always did in Winnie's presence. Twenty-five years of marriage later, they still acted like newly-weds. As they went back to the dance floor to wiggle to the Shoo Flies' version of "Let's Give 'Em Something to Talk About," I scanned the article again.

Twenty-five years ago, when Winnie and Martin really were newlyweds, Ginny Proffitt, who had claimed that she'd never married, had in fact been married for three years . . . to Dru Purcell.

The article was a feature about Crystal Visions, a psychic reading and healing program run by Ginny and Dru Purcell. People from all over southern California had flocked to their program, swearing by the results. "Amazing!" and "Miraculous!" patrons were quoted as exclaiming.

The article went on to explain that Ginny and Dru had first met each other at Serpent Mound, when they'd each been on group trips from their separate high schools to the site. Then, Ginny had moved out west to pursue her interest in the "psychic arts." Dru had enlisted in the Army with his good friend Ed Crowley (that made sense, I thought . . . I knew they'd been friends). Dru and Ed had been stationed out at Edwards Air Force Base.

Dru and Ginny met again at a psychic fair in Bakersfield. Ginny was working at the fair and Dru was attending it. The couple fell in love and married and Dru did not re-enlist. Dru moved to Randsburg with Ginny to help her with her business and to pursue his real love, painting landscapes. (My eyebrows shot up at that. Dru, a fine artist? And then I thought of the paint-spattered overalls in the suitcase. The paints were artists', not housepainters', as I'd assumed. The overalls, with their paint . . . and their blood stains . . . had to be Dru's.)

Then, the article went on, Dru discovered he, too, had an ability in psychic healing. (Just how does someone discover an ability like that? I wondered. Ginny says, damn, cut my thumb opening the tuna fish can, and Dru, instead of grabbing a Band-Aid for her, starts meditating over her thumb and it heals?) So he became her partner in the psychic-healing portion of her business, although she was the only one who did readings.

And that was it. The article was an upbeat feature, just a little patronizing in tone in places (I could sympathize with the skeptical reporter on that), laced with quotes from the Purcells' large following,

325

and a few quotes from a Christian fundamentalist preacher in Bakersfield (the nearest city to Randsburg) condemning the Purcells for their "dabbling in devil's arts."

Wasn't that ironic? I thought, crunching on an ice cube. The Shoo Flies had moved on to another song, but I wasn't sure what it was. The music and laughter and chatter whirled around me as I thought over what I'd just learned.

No wonder Dru hadn't wanted the LeFevers opening a psychic/New Age bookstore in town; the young couple reminded him too much of when he'd been married to Ginny.

And no wonder Dru hadn't wanted the psychic fair — especially with Ginny as the star attraction — at the Red Horse.

What would his flock think if they knew of his past as a psychic healer and husband to Ginny? What would Missy think? Would Dru kill Ginny just to hide his history with her?

Or what if Missy knew? Would she kill Ginny out of jealousy?

I shook my head at myself while crunching another ice cube. Nope. Those theories were too simple. They didn't explain a lot of things, like why Ginny wanted to come here in the first place to meet Dru again after all those years. Why she'd left me with a suitcase that contained only the handkerchief with the annoyingly cryptic note and the overalls, which I was reckoning (but couldn't know for sure) had belonged to Dru. Overalls and a hand-kerchief that also held old bloodstains.

Those simple theories also didn't tell me whose blood was on the overalls and hand-kerchief, or who Ginny had met at the corn maze and why, or who had come to her Red Horse room and why Max wouldn't tell me about the visit, or what she'd thought her tarot reading with Skylar really meant, or what she'd seen in her own crystal ball right after that reading, or why she'd run out after the two readings, or what role, if any, her illness and her return to psychic healing and alternative medi-cines played in her decision to come here to Paradise.

I'd run out of ice cubes, so I started chewing on my lip. I remembered Skylar telling me that Ginny had planned on going to Mexico to try a radical alternate cancer treatment to supplement the psy-chic healing she'd been self-administering, when she got more money.

Could Ginny have been hoping to black-

mail Dru with their past and with whatever
knowledge those stained overalls represented? So she could get the cash she
needed to go to Mexico?

Possibly. I could believe that. But that
still left a lot of questions unanswered. I
was bothered by what she'd seen in her
readings that made her rush out in a hurry,
apparently unplanned. I was also bothered
by why and how she'd known about my
Mrs. Oglevee dreams and why and how
she'd homed in on me as the person to
figure things out if something happened to
her.

The circumstantial evidence pointed to
Dru and Missy, and I wanted to believe it,
but, somehow, even as angry as I was at
Dru and Missy for all the havoc they'd created over the weekend with their protest at
the corn maze and the book burning, for as
annoyed as their self-righteousness made
me, I suddenly felt uneasy with the idea of
either Dru or Missy as Ginny's murderers.
Maybe it was because I hadn't had time
yet to investigate the other suspects.

True, Winnie had uncovered fascinating
information about Dru, but something was
niggling at the back of my mind, something that didn't feel quite right about all
I'd learned of Ginny's life and the circum-

stances surrounding her death . . .

"Hey, pretty lady, want this dance?"

"Huh?" I said. Not the most elegant response to a dance request, but the question had jolted me out of my reverie.

I looked up at the source of the question, a tall, dark-haired man, with blazing azure eyes and a sexy, confident grin that made me grin right back. He had a fit, muscled body that filled out a denim shirt and jeans nicely. Even the silly cowboy hat didn't look silly on him.

His was the sort of physique and style that usually quickened my pulse, and set my desires to humming. In fact, gazing back at Mr. Azure Eyes, I felt that hum start up, a pleasant little buzzing just under my skin that revved up quickly.

Before Owen, I'd have said yes to that dance request in a red-hot minute, never mind the fact that with this kind of man there was no future. That had always been the point.

But this was after Owen. Or maybe during Owen. I wasn't sure. All I knew for sure was that this wasn't before Owen and that, even though part of me envied Cherry's good times back at the Red Horse, I didn't really want that for myself. I wanted Owen. Didn't I?

I sighed. Confused and lonely are not good states of mind in which to accept dances with handsome strangers, even at a friendly bar where the bartender's your cousin and will willingly whap upside the head anyone who gets too fresh, too fast. Or send Junior, the bouncer, to do the whapping.

"Thanks," I said, "but I'm not fit for company right now. In fact, I'm heading home." Or to the Red Horse, anyway. But explaining that, I thought, would probably sound like an invitation of some sort.

Mr. Azure Eyes tipped his hat. "I can take no for an answer. But maybe the next time our paths cross, you'll feel like company. Or at least a dance."

He glided off, and I had to smile. The ego he wore on his shirtsleeve was at least genuine. A little thing like "no, thanks," wasn't going to make him pouty or demanding. I didn't know who he was. Probably he lived in Masonville or maybe he was from one of the Columbus suburbs and liked to get out to the "real" country bars away from the slick, themed ones. I'd heard that line before, too. Before Owen.

I blinked back tears. Damn it, I wished I knew what was going on with Owen, why he hadn't talked openly with me, what was going to become of our relationship.

Hard times and a difficult choice . . .

Skylar's words from her tarot reading for me flitted across my mind. She could have been talking about selecting between a mutual fund and an annuity. Or picking out a comfortable, well-fitting bra.

But it seemed her words also fit my relationship with Owen. I stood up, pulled a pen from my handbag, scrawled a quick note across the manila envelope — "Thanks. I've got the printout. Josie." — and left it beside Winnie's drink. I folded up the printout and put it and my pen back in my handbag.

Then I left the Bar-None. In the last thirty-six or so hours, I'd had an eerie psychic reading foisted on me, found a murdered body, gotten myself tangled up in investigating the murder, discovered my beloved cousin might be quite ill, sort-of broken up with my boyfriend, or at the very least had a doozy of a fight with him, been evicted from my business and my home, witnessed the sickening sight of a book burning, and turned away Mr. Azure Eyes.

I was weary. All I wanted to do was get back to Room 23 at the Red Horse and collapse into blissful sleep.

20

Half an hour later, I'd had a nice, hot shower and put on my comfy Tweety Bird jammies and my thick white socks, and gotten into bed in my room at the Red Horse.

And I was wide-awake.

I couldn't think about anything. My head was buzzing — no thoughts, just buzzing. My whole body felt awake, vital, poised to spring. This was not the effect I'd hoped the earlier bourbon and then the hot shower and the comfy jammies and socks would have on me.

So, of course, being wide-awake but unable to focus on anything, I was eating crab Rangoons, which I'd nuked to gooey warmness in the motel microwave in the lobby. I used my green tomato relish as a dipping sauce. It was a combo that was much tastier than it probably sounds.

And I had on the TV. A Mary Tyler

Moore rerun, on TV Land. (The Rhinegolds got a satellite dish the previous Christmas, and as a result, all the Red Horse room TVs have access to just about any cable station available.) I was a newborn at the time the show was a hit its first time around.

I wasn't the demographic, agewise at least, that the show in its second time around was aimed at, but I didn't care. Mary Richards, as played by Mary Tyler Moore, was more pulled together as a single woman than I'd ever be. And her apartment was cooler. I won't even go into how much better her sense of style was, which anyone could figure out given that my big fashion inspiration for the year had been pairing the ancient Tweety Bird T-shirt with the kitten-print PJ pants I'd picked up at Big Sam's in Masonville.

I watched Mary deftly handle Lou Grant's rant and ate another crab Rangoon with green tomato relish. Then Mary had a sensitive conversation with Rhoda about Rhoda's nagging mother.

Where was my Rhoda? I thought. I wanted a Rhoda to talk to . . .

I heard a bang and a fit of giggles from room 23. My Rhoda was next door, in the form of Cherry, doing God only knew what — well, I could guess — with Max. No, I thought, munching another crab-Rangoon-in-green-tomato-relish. The analogy just didn't work. Cherry was no Rhoda. I was surely no Mary.

A few minutes later, I jolted awake, disoriented. It took me a few seconds to realize where I was and why. Then I moaned. My tummy hurt. I looked at the crab Rangoon box. Empty, except for a few dollops of green tomato relish. I glanced at the TV. Still on, but Mary had given way to *Miami Vice*. Ugh. I felt around, found the remote, and clicked the TV off.

I'd finished my snack and drifted off, I realized, to a dreamless sleep. Lucky me — but not for long. Something had jolted me awake. What?

There was a banging on my door. Ah. I swung my legs around, hopped out of the bed, went to the door, and peered out the peephole. I couldn't see a thing. Still peering out the peephole, I felt along the wall until I found a switch. I flicked it up and the light outside by the door popped on. A figure jumped back.

I caught the outline of a cowboy hat first. Mr. Azure Eyes? Maybe I was still dreaming. Hmmm. This could be good. Then the figure leaned forward to knock on the door again. Max Whitstone.

I opened the door.

Max looked worried. "We're in a terrible fix next door and Cherry asked me to come get you."

I eyed Max suspiciously and started to shut the door. "I'm not interested in your weird games. Go knock on another door."

Max stuck out his hand to keep the door from shutting. "Look, Cherry's in trouble and she said she needed your help."

That was pretty unbelievable, Cherry specifically asking for my help. But Max looked distraught. And I heard a wailed "Damn it!" from their room.

"All right. Just a minute," I said. I popped back into my room long enough to grab my room key, attached to a big plastic red horse, then stepped outside and shut my room door.

I followed Max for the five or six steps it took to get to his room. He opened the door, stepped in and then to the side, and I stepped in, too.

The bed was a jumble of sheets and pillows. Cherry, in a bright red lacy nightie, sat on the floor in the midst of chip bags and pop cans and the ice bucket, which was empty, open, and on its side. She was next to the minifridge, her head smack against its door just above the handle, as if she and the fridge had fused into a weird variation of Siamese twins. Then I realized that Cherry was sitting like that because a large shank of her hair was stuck inside the fridge. And that she was crying.

Cherry pointed at Max. "It was his idea! He wanted to use the Silly Putty! At first I said no, but then he described what we could do, and so I said, s-s-sure, and it was fun — k-k-kinda — but then the Silly Putty got in my hair . . ."

Max tried to sound calm even though his voice trembled. "Now, Josie, it's like this. I read in a book called *Advanced Sex Tricks* that you can enhance foreplay with Silly Putty by —"

I didn't hear the rest. I'd stuck my fingers in my ears and scrunched my eyes closed in a hear-no-evil, see-no-evil pose. It wasn't that I didn't want folks to have-no-fun. I just didn't want to hear about it. Long after Max was gone from Paradise, Cherry'd be running the Chat N Curl next to my laundromat, and we'd be hanging out with Sally, and squabbling, and there were just certain images, I was sure, that I didn't want randomly popping into my head. The one of Cherry fused to the minifridge and sobbing was bad enough.

I opened one eye, then the other. Max was still looking embarrassed, Cherry still sobbing by the minifridge. Both of them had their mouths shut, though, so I slowly removed my fingers from my ears.

I looked at Cherry. "You have Silly Putty in your hair. And you want my help in getting it out."

Cherry half sobbed, half hiccupped. "I remembered that if you get Silly Putty on your clothes you put them in the freezer and then scrape off the putty, so I thought if I stuck my hair in the minifridge that would help, but it's not working —"

"I thought if she waited a little longer . . ." Max put in.

"Shut up," Cherry and I told him in unison.

"Then I remembered you had some trick for Sally when Harry ground Silly Putty into his new jeans. She told me about it because she was so amazed but now I can't remember what it was, and oh, Josie, do you think it could work on hair?" she stopped in a fit of hiccups and sniffles.

"I take it that the Silly Putty is not just on the tips of your hair?" If it were, Cherry could have just trimmed the ends and avoided this entire embarrassing scene.

"It is," she said with as much dignity as

she could muster, "embedded all the way to my scalp. In places."

I really, really did not want to know how that had happened. But there was something else I did want to know.

Folks think having stain expertise just qualifies you for rescuing clothes or linens that would otherwise have to become cleaning rags. But truth be told, a little bit of stain expertise can go a long way in helping you solve puzzles and gathering information.

Sometimes, that expertise helps directly, as in my figuring out the pants and handkerchief Ginny had left me were stained with not just paint, but also old blood.

Sometimes, that expertise helps indirectly, as in the situation with Max and Cherry and the Silly Putty and the fact that I knew someone had visited Ginny's room, and Max had seen the visitor, but for some reason refused to say who the visitor was. Cherry wanted the Silly Putty out of her hair, Max wanted Cherry to stop being hysterical, and I wanted Max's information.

Time to barter.

"Well," I said carefully, "I do in fact know how to remove Silly Putty from hair. But before I share that tidbit of knowledge —" I paused, and turned to glare at Max,

"— first Max is going to tell me who he saw visiting Ginny's room earlier and what he heard."

Max looked worried. "Now, Josie, now, really, I don't think it's that important —"

"For pity's sake, just tell her, Max!"

"And with Cherry here being your best friend and all, surely you're not going to just leave her with her hair stuck in the minifridge —"

I crossed my arms. "I still owe her payback for the time she scared me to death at Ranger Girl camp by telling me she'd switched the shampoo with Nair hair-removal gel — right after I'd lathered up in the sink —"

"But I hadn't really made the switch!" Cherry wailed.

I glared at her. "I had to sleep on the floor all night as punishment for screaming so loudly that I scared the younger girls in the next cabin."

"But, Josie —" Cherry pled. Then her eyes narrowed. "All of that was just payback for what you said about my finger back in junior high. Remember that? You still owe me for that."

I blanched, remembering.

Only once did Aunt Clara ever turn her devil saying on me, when she got a call from my Junior High teacher, Mrs. Oglevee, that poor Cherry Feinster had been crying in history class because I'd teased her at lunch when she'd bragged that John Worthy had given her a ring, a diamond set in gold. The truth was she'd waved her hand over our plates of beef-a-roni, showing off. All the other girls oohed and ahhed, but I said it was a dumb glass-and-tin gumball-machine ring sure to make her finger turn a nasty green and fall off.

Sure enough, during the next period (history, Mrs. Oglevee's class), Cherry's finger turned green. But it stayed firmly attached as she pointed it accusingly at me.

When Aunt Clara confronted me with Mrs. Oglevee's report, I defiantly said Cherry was uppity and had deserved the scare. Aunt Clara went into her bun-quivering stillness, let her eyes go icy blue as she gazed at me, and intoned her scary adage in the slow whisper she always used just for saying it.

Now, I looked at Cherry in dismay. "I can't believe you're still bringing that up after all these years."

She pointed her finger — the same one that had turned green all those years ago — at me and hollered, "Just help me, Josie!"

Max had backed against the wall. He was staring at us with a terrified look on his face. I reckon he thought we were nuts. I didn't care. I crossed my arms, pressed my lips together, and glared into space. After all, Aunt Clara was no longer around, God rest her soul, to guilt me out with her devil saying.

"For pity's sake, just tell her whatever she wants to know!" Cherry screamed.

"All right, all right," Max said. "I don't know the name of whoever came to visit Ginny. But it was an older woman. Frumpy. Baggy kind of dress, hair twisted up on her head in a bun, no makeup. I assume the woman is from around here. She wasn't one of the psychics."

Max's description, I thought, fit Missy Purcell.

"And they were arguing," Max added. "The woman was shouting at Ginny to stay away from her family, to leave them alone, that they didn't need any trouble from her. Ginny was trying to calm her down. They seemed to know each other. That's it, Josie, that's all I heard."

"Could you identify the woman if you saw her again, or a picture of her?" I asked.

"Maybe. I — I was hurrying from my own room."

I lifted my eyebrows. "Why the hurry?"

"I just wanted to get to the psychic fair, that's all."

"That's all, huh? You know, you just gave a pretty straightforward description of what you saw. Doesn't make you look bad at all. So why the reluctance to share?"

Cherry had stopped sniffling — though her hiccups continued — and she glared at Max suspiciously. "Yeah, why the reluctance?"

Max stared down at the floor.

"There's only one trick for getting out Silly Putty," I said. "And I'm the only one who knows it."

"Max!" shrieked Cherry.

"Okay, look, I was with Skylar, and both Ginny and the woman saw us coming out of the room, and I really don't want this to get back to Karen, because she's so over-protective that she'd probably claw my eyes out and —"

Cherry grabbed the ice bucket and threw it at him, yanking her own hair as she did so, which caused her to yelp. It was a good throw, though. Cherry beaned him right on the temple.

"You were with Skylar earlier?" Cherry shrieked.

I'd gone over to the phone and dialed up

the Rhinegolds' private number. I glanced at the digital clock on the nightstand. 11:30 p.m. Poor things. I hated to wake them up.

"Now, Cherry," Max was saying.

"After we made our plans at Serpent Mound?" Cherry's voice went up a notch, to nails-on-chalkboard level. I winced and tried to focus on listening to the Rhinegolds' phone ring.

"Hello?" Greta answered the telephone, not sounding at all sleepy. Maybe a little out of breath. Hmmm. Was everyone in the world snuggling with someone tonight . . . except Owen and me?

"Hi, it's Josie," I said.

"And you were more concerned about Skylar's mama finding out than about me finding out?" Cherry was yelling, wincing every third word as her hair tugged in the mini fridge.

"You okay, Josie?" Greta asked.

"I'm fine. I just wondered if you happened to have any rubbing alcohol handy."

"You'd have to know Skylar's mama to understand," Max said, ducking as the lid from the ice bucket whirled, discus-fashion, at his head.

"You're a creep and a fraud, you know that? I've heard some of the others talking

343

and they say you couldn't predict the weather with a tornado on the horizon!" Cherry shouted.

"Now, Cherry, that truly hurts," Max protested, looking, truly, hurt.

"I take it you're not in your own room, needing this rubbing alcohol," Greta said.

I sighed. "No. The room next door. Max Whitstone's room. He has a . . . guest . . . who got Silly Putty in her hair, and —"

"I'll find the rubbing alcohol," Greta snapped, and I could just see her making the hear-no-evil, see-no-evil gestures.

21

Amazingly, rubbing alcohol really is the secret to getting Silly Putty out of clothes. Or hair.

Truth be told, though, I'd never tried it in hair before that night. I just hoped it would work.

I convinced Cherry to release herself from the minifridge and did my best not to gasp when I saw the bright green Silly Putty mashed into the right side of her hair, thoroughly entangled up to her scalp. Then I gave Cherry my room key and told her to gather up her things and to sit on my bed and leave my room door ajar.

I waited outside my door for Greta, who soon brought a bottle of rubbing alcohol from her own medicine cabinet.

Max had shut the door to his room. But after Greta handed the rubbing alcohol to me, she banged on his door. He answered and I paused — just for a moment — on the threshold to my room and heard Greta say something about "extra charges if Silly Putty was found ground into the sheets or carpet."

She turned and marched off, ignoring Max as he stood in the door, calling, "it's not my fault."

He looked at me as Greta rounded the corner, his expression pleading. "Tell Cherry I'm sorry and she can come back over here after you take care of the Silly Putty."

I snorted. "Not likely," I said.

Then I went into my room and had Cherry bend over the sink, while I alternated pouring rubbing alcohol onto the Silly Putty in her hair, and working it out as it turned crumbly and lost its stickiness. It's harder to get Silly Putty out of hair than cloth, so every now and then I pulled a little too hard, and Cherry moaned and sniffled.

By and by I got all of the Silly Putty out of Cherry's hair. While she took a shower, I straightened up the room, tossing out the crab Rangoon container and chip bags. My stomach hurt and I wished for antacid, but I wasn't about to call poor Greta and Luke to have them raid their medicine cabinet on my behalf for yet a third time that night.

By the time Cherry finished showering, it was past midnight. I assumed she'd just spend the rest of the night with me and was all set to divvy up the bed covers, but she got dressed, grabbed her overnight bag, thanked me for helping her with her hair, and said she was going to Sally's because there was no way she was going to sleep in a room next to that two-timing, no-good Max.

As she left, I shook my head, not sure who to feel sorrier for, Sally or Cherry. (I had no sympathy for Max.) On the one hand, Sally was about to be awakened by a distraught Cherry. On the other, Sally wouldn't hold back a bit in letting Cherry know how silly she thought she was for hooking up with Max in the first place.

I crawled into bed, this time with no doubt that I would fall asleep easily, even though my hands still reeked of rubbing alcohol, despite the fact I'd thoroughly washed them with freesia-scented soap. Sure enough, soon the smell of the rubbing alcohol faded as I drifted off to sleep . . . lovely sleep . . .

Sleep that was doomed because it wasn't dreamless. I'd been drifting in gray nothingness for mere moments when Mrs. Oglevee sauntered into my sleep world.

I moaned, looking at her. She was playing with a cornhusk doll from hell. The doll had a red nub where its head and bonnet should have been. Mrs. Oglevee — who wore a mauve cornhusk apron that matched the doll's — was talking to the gory-headed doll.

"It's amazing," Mrs. Oglevee was saying, "how frequently Josie can just plain miss the point. She was like that in school, too. Why, I recall one time, on an assignment about Ohio history, she —"

"If you have something to say, why don't you share it with the whole class?" I asked sarcastically.

Mrs. Oglevee looked up from the doll, with a glare that withered my momentary bravado. "You've got your nose stuck in this murder and you're too goofy to follow the main clue the victim herself gave you." She turned the headless cornhusk doll to face me. Ugh, I thought. "Little Ginny here just finds that appalling," Mrs. Oglevee added.

I was trying to think of some snappy comeback when a new head bubbled out of the top of the cornhusk doll. "Truly. I did give you very specific directions," a little voice squeaked.

I gasped, then recovered my wits and realized that the new cornhusk doll face had a little "oh" of a mouth, but thankfully, it was perfectly still.

I glared at Mrs. Oglevee. "Nice trick with ventriloquism."

She grinned at me. "Thanks. I've been taking classes."

There were classes in . . . wherever? "Summer school?" I asked. I couldn't resist.

"Don't be impertinent," Mrs. Oglevee snapped. "You're the one who needs to go to summer school. Or maybe pick up the Cliffs Notes to *Detecting for Dummies.* I doubt you could handle the real book."

Now, that was an uncalled for insult. Mrs. Oglevee knew perfectly well that I never used Cliffs Notes. I always read the whole book for all my assignments. I'd always loved reading.

"Look," I said. "I'm worn out and I could use some peaceful sleep. I know the note you're talking about —"

"Recitation! What does the note say?"

I sighed. She'd just nag me until I quoted the note back to her, word for word. " *'In case anything happens to me, know this: That there is a devil, there is no* doubt. *But is he trying to get in . . . or trying to get out? Mrs. O will help, If you start from the end, And go to the beginning, to find out.'*

"And that's exactly what I've done. Winnie traced Ginny's background all the way back to when she was married to Dru Purcell —" I was a little disappointed that Mrs. Oglevee didn't look shocked by this news. She'd been known to go to Dru's tent revivals every August, pray and swoon and find Jesus all over again, and swear she'd be sweet and nice. That always lasted a few weeks, until the school year started.

But Mrs. Oglevee didn't look stunned at all. I guess there really are no secrets from those in the hereafter.

I went on. "And I've run down every lead I can find, working back from what had to have happened at the corn maze, to her surprise at her tarot reading and whatever she saw in her own crystal ball, to what happened when she first arrived and —"

"Didn't I teach you there's more than one way to see things?"

She passed her hand over the cornhusk doll, and the doll turned into a Farmer Barbie, in cute little overalls and a cute little red bandanna, holding a cute little pitchfork. Another pass, and we were back to the cornhusk doll.

"Cute trick," I said. "I guess you learned that in magic class in summer school. But what do these farm dolls have to do with starting at the end to get to the beginning?"

Mrs. Oglevee sighed and crushed the cornhusk doll, which turned to dust and fell away from her hand. "Fine. If that won't get my point across, maybe this will."

She plucked a small, boxy case out of thin air — a makeup case, just like my Aunt Clara's, just like the one Lenny had described Ginny as having in her rental trunk. I gasped. I'd forgotten about that case, which seemed to have disappeared. At least, the Rhinegolds didn't recall seeing it when the police were examining Ginny's room and it wasn't in the trunk of her rental car . . .

BAM!

The crashing sound broke through my thoughts and suddenly I was awake, looking around the motel room. No Mrs. Oglevee.

Had the sound come from inside my dream or from the real world? For a second I was disoriented — but just for a second — until I realized the motel room's window had been shattered. A breeze and a gentle wind blew in through the broken windowpanes.

And on the floor lay Ginny's old hard-side suitcase.

I didn't open the suitcase myself. I immediately called 911 from the phone on the nightstand and told them a suitcase had been thrown through my window at the Red Horse Motel.

I explained that it was a suitcase I recognized, one that had in fact been stolen from my laundromat earlier in the day — well, the previous day, since it was now nearing one in the morning on Sunday — but my explanation didn't seem to calm the dispatcher, who had a distinct and rising note of alarm in her voice as she told me to not touch the suitcase.

Which I didn't, but fifteen minutes later, I was in the passenger seat of a Mason County Sheriff cruiser, where at least I was warm while I waited for a deputy sheriff to come ask me questions. The warmth inside the cruiser made me feel guilty, though, as I stared out at all the other Red Horse Motel guests who were gathered at the far end of the motel parking lot, sleepy-eyed and grumbling and shivering in the October wind, which had gotten stiffer in the wee hours of the morning.

Thanks to the suitcase, we'd been evacuated. It could contain, an emergency worker told us, a bomb. These days, anything like a suitcase or backpack or sack was considered a possible threat. It didn't matter that there was no reason for anyone to bomb the Red Horse Motel in Paradise, Ohio. Or that I kept trying to explain to someone — anyone — that the suitcase had been Ginny's, that she'd left it for me, that it had been stolen from my laundromat, that I was more than pretty sure it was meant as some kind of warning to me.

Despite these facts, the situation warranted serious attention, Deputy Rankle had told me as he escorted me to his cruiser. You just never know, these days, he added darkly.

I wished I'd just opened the damned suitcase myself. Then I'd have known it hadn't been turned into a bomb. A HazMat team from the sheriff's department wouldn't be examining the suitcase. All the Red Horse Motel guests would still be sound asleep and the poor Rhinegolds wouldn't be worried that the motel — which represented their lives as well as their livelihood — was about to blow up.

Unless, of course, the suitcase really had been turned into some sort of bomb. Could someone have wanted me to stop asking questions about Ginny so badly that he — or she — would have made a bomb to silence me? Making such a thing wouldn't be that hard, after all, with fertilizer and other items for crude bomb-making someone could find on a farm.

Still, someone creating a home-made bomb to silence me seemed unbelievable. But then, the whole weekend had turned into one crisis after another.

The driver's side opened and Deputy Rankle got in the cruiser. He was a lanky man who looked like the almost-as-handsome brother of Mr. Azure Eyes. He said the HazMat team would know what we were dealing with in a while. Meanwhile, Deputy Rankle had questions. Had I touched or moved anything?

No, I told him, other than to tiptoe around the glass to get to my jacket, which was on the chair by the window. I'd had to shake some glass off the jacket, but then put it on as I left. (As panicked as the suitcase-through-the-window was making me, it was October in Ohio. Plus I didn't relish the idea of being interviewed while in just my Tweety Bird/kitten print PJ ensemble. I didn't tell Deputy Rankle that, though.) And of course I'd touched the door while leaving the motel room.

Had I heard anything? he also wanted to know.

Just the glass shattering, which woke me up. I didn't tell him about Mrs. Oglevee, either.

I wasn't going to tell him much more than that. After all, I'd already talked to the Paradise Police Department several times about everything — well, most everything — I'd learned about Ginny and the events surrounding her murder.

But then Deputy Rankle got a crackling call over his radio. "Situation clear. But you'll want to show your witness the contents of the suitcase."

Follow me, Deputy Rankle said, and I got out of the cruiser and did so, while emergency workers assured the Red Horse guests that the bomb scare was over and that they could go back to their rooms.

Back in my room, the suitcase now lay open on the glass-covered floor. I was still in sock feet and didn't step into the room, but peered in through the open door as Detective Rankle went in and talked to some more workers. As far as I could see, the suitcase was completely empty.

I frowned at that. Why would someone throw Ginny's old empty suitcase through my motel window?

"The suitcase was empty?" I asked Deputy Rankle as he came back out of the motel room. I hadn't told him about the stained overalls or handkerchief that had been in the suitcase — after all, I'd tried several times to be taken seriously at the Paradise Police Department about the stolen bag and its contents, and had been fluffed off.

"Not entirely," he said. And then I saw that he had donned latex gloves and was holding a note — just a plain piece of notebook paper on which had been written in large block letters:

"Stop asking about Ginny Proffitt or Guy will be hurt!"

I gasped, started shaking.

Someone — one of the emergency workers — led me to one of the benches on the walkway in front of the motel and wrapped a blanket around me. I reckon the worker was afraid I was about to go into shock.

I demanded that I be given a phone to call Stillwater, and then, seeing that the worker didn't understand, I asked for Deputy Rankle.

A few minutes later, he came back, this time without latex gloves, and sat by me on the bench while I told him everything.

I told him Guy was my cousin and a resident of Stillwater and that I was very worried. He told the emergency worker to call Stillwater to check on Guy for me.

Then I told Deputy Rankle about the first time I'd seen the suitcase, and what it contained, and how it had been stolen from my laundromat sometime after the water main break in Paradise, and how I'd figured out there was blood on the overalls and handkerchief, and how I'd finally turned in the handkerchief to the Paradise Police Department.

Then I gave him some more background: how my boyfriend and I had found Ginny's body and how I was sure she'd been murdered, and how since then I'd learned about the predictions that had made her leave the psychic fair, and how she was ill and seeking alternate treatment, and how I'd learned she'd once been married to Dru Purcell and about their business, and about seeing her with Dru at the Serpent Mound, and about Max Whitstone seeing her argue with an older woman.

All I left out was the dreams about Mrs. Oglevee.

And unlike Chief Worthy would have done, Deputy Rankle took me seriously, listening, nodding, taking notes, asking for clarification. He told me my statement would be shared with the Paradise Police Department and the suitcase and note would be examined for fingerprints, and that he'd let me know if they found out who had thrown the luggage through the window, and I should let him know if I thought of anything new.

The emergency worker came over, then, and said she'd just talked to Don Richmond at Stillwater, and Guy was fine. There'd been no disturbance at Stillwater at all.

That's when I finally broke down and started weeping.

22

"Now, you know you can spend the night with us," Greta said.

I sat in her and Luke's kitchen, sipping hot tea with lemon and honey, happy to be warm and taken care of.

I smiled at Greta. "Thank you for the tea. And the shoes." She'd loaned me a pair of navy Keds, a half size too small, but it was better than traipsing around barefoot. I'd been allowed to take my purse and van keys from the room, and that was it. The room was a crime scene — again. "And thanks for not blaming me for upsetting all your guests."

Greta waved a hand at me. "Pshaw. You did the right thing. You'd have been a foolish girl to open that suitcase up. Now, how about it. Let me make up the couch for you."

I knew turning down her hospitality would hurt her feelings, but I also saw how tired Greta looked. The weekend had been exciting for her, but it had also really worn her out. And poor Luke was snoozing in his chair, his own hot tea untouched.

"Greta, thanks, but I'm going to go over to my cousin Sally's," I said. Sure enough, she looked disappointed. I stood up, took my mug to the sink, rinsed it out.

"You sure?" Greta stood, wincing at a catch in her hip, smiling quickly to hide it.

"I'm sure," I said.

We hugged. I went out to my van, got in, and just sat for a moment, not even putting my key to the ignition, but staring around at the now quiet Red Horse parking lot. I could see my — and Ginny's — room, the yellow police tape again across its door glinting in the room's exterior light.

Okay, I told myself. Guy is okay. You told the sheriff's deputy everything you know. Just go to Sally's.

I'd called her from Greta's. She and Cherry were still awake, as it turned out, and Sally whispered into the phone she'd welcome a break from Cherry's weeping and wailing about the general misery of her love life.

I started my van, turned out onto the dark country road, and drove toward the Happy Trails Motor Home Court, which was on the northern outskirt of Paradise.

I meant to focus on my driving. I wasn't tired — the threat to Guy had taken care of that — but still, winding dark country roads can quickly slip your mind into slumber, even when you think you're wide-awake.

But still my thoughts wandered to the question: who had thrown that suitcase through my window? Someone who didn't want me to investigate Ginny's murder. Someone who thought I might be on to something. That could be any of the psychics I suspected, as well as Dru and Missy.

But the note had threatened Guy. Who knew who Guy was, how important he was to me? That would be most anyone in Paradise. Which eliminated the psychics. Who would both know of my devotion to Guy, how deeply the threat would scare me, and would also want me to back off from investigating Ginny's background and murder?

Dru and Missy Purcell.

The answers all kept coming back to them.

And yet, the answers still didn't feel right.

I turned onto Sweet Potato Ridge Road. My mind turned to another question: what had Mrs. Oglevee been telling me before my sleep was shattered by the suitcase through the window?

That I needed to look at the message from Ginny, to start at the end and work to the beginning, in more than one way. And Mrs. Oglevee had kept producing dolls dressed in a farm motif — even a cornhusk doll. And she'd been about to pick up the small makeup case that matched the suitcase, the small case I'd only heard Ginny had, that had gone missing . . .

I gasped and jolted to a stop at the next intersection. I sat there, thinking. After all, there was no traffic to hold up.

Start at the end and go to the beginning . . .

Of course. Ginny had been killed at the back corner of the maze, near the end. But what if she'd left a clue at the beginning of the maze. Maybe the small accessories case.

I could go straight, be at Sally's in five minutes.

Or turn left and be at the Crowleys' in about the same time.

I turned left.

I pulled my van alongside the road that ran by the Crowleys' farm, where woods met corn maze and field. I got out my high-powered flashlight, opened up the back of my van for something to dig around with. I settled on a tire jack, then set off down the ditch toward the maze.

The night was quiet and still, except for my steps and a few late autumn insects singing a farewell song. I could make out the Crowleys' farmhouse across the field. It was dark, of course. No lights except for the one large light that shone over the gravel driveway at the side of the house.

I was trespassing, which made me uncomfortable. And if my suspicions were true, that Ginny's note meant to look at the beginning of the maze, that she'd buried the accessories case there and that the case held evidence that would help solve her murder, then I'd have to call the sheriff's department again. The Crowleys would be rousted from their sleep. I didn't think they'd press charges for my trespassing, though.

I walked up the slope of the ditch to the field and around to the beginning of the maze, where I trained my flashlight over the rustling cornstalks. I shivered. Out there, with the fields abandoned and all the kids and Hugh and Rebecca in the barn, Ginny could have pled for mercy at her murderer's hands and never been heard over the cornstalks' husky whispers. And from the road, a passerby would not have seen what was going on in the maze. The stalks were a good two feet taller than me. From the road, the maze just looked like a stand of corn, the dried husks overlapping to create a wall.

I moved my light to the ground. Could Ginny have buried the accessories case and whatever evidence it contained before meeting her killer? I walked along, looking for signs of digging that could easily have been missed as people worked their way through the maze, focusing on maps and the kids in costume and the ribbons that marked off each section.

I realized that I'd strayed from the beginning to somewhere in the middle of the maze. And I hadn't seen any upturned earth, any signs that something had been buried along the stalks. Dammit. The ribbon near me was a blue and yellow check. If I remembered correctly, that put me in section five, right behind section two (the middle section at the front of the maze), marked with hot pink ribbon, where I'd entered. I turned around and started following the blue and yellow ribbon, turning right at each intersection, and exhaled in relief when I got back to the hot pink ribbon.

Another fifteen minutes, and I worked my way back out.

I checked my watch. It was 3:30 a.m. I'd been wandering in the front section of the corn maze for nearly forty minutes and hadn't seen a sign at all of digging.

Dammit, I thought again.

Then what else could start at the end to get to the beginning mean?

It was a riddle as frustrating as my Aunt Clara's devil riddle, but surely Ginny's riddle had an answer. She'd given it to me, expecting me to figure it out easily enough, I was sure, so that if anything happened to her, I could get to the truth.

I'd started at the end of her life and worked back to the beginning.

I'd gone to the beginning of the maze, in which she'd been murdered near the end.

What else could she mean? Where else had she been, or what else had she done, that had a specific beginning and end?

I sat down on a stump outside the corn maze and doused my flashlight and tried to think. Never mind end to beginning. Where had she been since the beginning of her visit to Paradise that might fit her riddle?

My laundromat. No specific beginning and end there.

The Red Horse Motel. That was built as four units that made up a square. No specific beginning and end there, either.

The Serpent Mound . . .

Of course. The mound was a snake effigy. It had a tail — that was the end. And a beginning — the head.

What if she'd buried the accessory case somewhere near the snake's head? She'd met Dru there. What if she'd also taken some evidence there with her that could help her blackmail him? Something to do with the coveralls and the blood on them?

I stood up and started back to my van. It was nearly four in the morning. Most assuredly, the Serpent Mound would be closed until 10:00 a.m. Trespassing on a friend's farm is one thing. Trespassing on a state memorial and national historic landmark is quite another. I would go to Sally's, get a few hours sleep, borrow some clothes from her, and go to Serpent Mound as soon as it opened.

I opened my van door and paused. I'd heard the squeak of my van door's hinges, but had I heard something else? A rustling that came from the woods and not the cornhusks?

I shook my head. I was tired and jumpy. I'd heard a raccoon or other night animal moving about. That was all.

"I still don't see why you can't just call

the sheriff with your theory. That nice Deputy Rankle you told us about," Cherry said. "Serpent Mound is in his jurisdiction, right?"

"Right," I said patiently, turning onto the road that led to Serpent Mound. "But he's probably off duty now. And after what happened at the Red Horse, with the bomb scare and evacuation, I don't want to be rousting up any more trouble. For all I know, my theory is cockamamie."

"Maybe. But tell us again about how Mrs. Oglevee gave you this idea in the first place," Sally said from behind me. She didn't even try to hide the amusement in her voice. "I like that part. Mrs. Oglevee dressed up as a cornhusk doll."

She and Cherry giggled. We were in my van at 9:45 a.m. heading toward Serpent Mound.

When I'd arrived at Sally's trailer home much earlier, she and Cherry were up and waiting for me. I told them everything. And I mean everything, even about Mrs. Oglevee. So for the first time, someone besides me did know about my Mrs. Oglevee dreams. Two someones — Cherry and Sally. Maybe that hadn't been so smart. I was sure to hear about it again. And again. And again. They'd found my nightmarish visits from our old, feared junior high teacher supremely amusing.

But I'd had to tell them about the hint I'd gotten in the dream about another way of looking at Ginny's clue — start at the end and work to the beginning — in order for our visit to Serpent Mound to make sense.

And they'd been very sympathetic and outraged about the threat to Guy.

We'd dozed for maybe two hours, and then Sally had made us a strong pot of coffee. We were fueled by caffeine, adrenaline, and lack of sleep giddiness. Plus a sense of adventure, I'll admit. In a way, we were looking for buried treasure.

We pulled into the Serpent Mound's parking lot, which held just one car and one van.

"Not too many visitors this morning," Sally said.

"Yet," I pointed out. "We want to see if we can find what we're looking for before too many people get here. After all, we're going to go off the paths into restricted areas. And maybe even dig."

I shuddered. Besides being state owned, this was, more importantly, the hallowed ground of an ancient people. If I was haunted by Mrs. Oglevee just because of, say, the mean things I'd written about her on the junior high girls' room walls, what kind of haunting would I get if I dug up part of Serpent Mound in search of an accessories case?

"Do you think it's okay I'm wearing heels?" Cherry asked. "I'd hate to twist an ankle."

I grinned. Cherry was always great for pulling me back to the here and now.

Twenty minutes later, we stood at what was the head of the serpent, according to the map we'd been given when we'd bought our tickets. We were the only people in sight.

"What now?" Cherry asked impatiently. "This dumb accessories case could be buried anywhere."

She was right. I looked around, my heart falling. We were standing on the path, looking around at fields that spread out for miles, dotted here and there with small patches of trees.

"No, not really," said Sally. "Think about it. Ginny would have wanted to put the accessories case somewhere she could re-find easily. And she wouldn't have had much time to bury it, because she was meeting Dru and because she wouldn't have wanted to get caught. So she couldn't have walked far from here. It has to be close, somewhere she could easily remember."

"One of the patches of trees," I said, excited again.

"But which one? There are at least seven," Cherry said.

We fell silent, pondering that question. I rubbed my hands up and down my arms. The wind was cold, brisk . . . and somehow urging us on, but to what? I shook my head. It wasn't like me to think that way. My weariness and the crazy events of the weekend were getting to me. And yet, the sense of being urged, nudged, somehow, by the cold wind, seemed real . . .

"I've got it!" Cherry exclaimed.

Sally and I looked at her, then at each other, reading surprise in each other's faces. Cherry never was the one who came up with answers to puzzles.

"Ginny was a psychic, right?" Cherry sounded excited. "And another word for psychic is seer, right? And we're at the head of the snake and if this earthwork snake really had eyes it would be looking straight ahead —" she pointed to a copse of trees before us, "to there."

We contemplated the patch of trees.

"Wow. That was amazing, Cherry," Sally said.

Cherry shook her head, looking befuddled. "I have no idea where that came from."

"Never mind that," I said, climbing over the railing that was supposed to keep us away from exactly where we wanted to go. "Let's go look."

It didn't take us long to find where Ginny had buried the accessories case. Just a few feet into the copse, we saw the fresh signs of digging. After all, she'd only dug this hole two days before. It had not rained since then.

We all got down on our hands and knees — even Cherry, though she was wearing a tan suede skirt and tights, despite the fact that Sally and I had told her she should wear jeans like us — and started pulling back dirt with our hands.

A few minutes later, we uncovered the top of the accessories case. I grabbed the handle and pulled.

"My grandma had a case like that," Cherry whispered.

"So did ours," Sally said.

"And my Aunt Clara," I said.

That there is a devil, there is no doubt. But is he trying to get in . . . or trying to get out?

The saying flitted through my mind, and at the same time seemed to whisper in the breeze. I shuddered. Then, slowly, I opened the accessories case.

Like the larger matching suitcase, it only held a few items: old newspaper articles. Just three.

We read them quickly, swapping, until we'd read everything, and then we stared at each other in stunned amazement at the truth we'd just learned.

Winnie, for all her good work in tracing Ginny's past, hadn't dug quite far enough into Dru's. These articles were old enough they must not have made it into the online archives.

The earliest dated article was about a man who'd gone missing from a bar in Bakersfield. There'd been a fight between a young man named Harold Thiesman and another young man named Dru Purcell, who'd just left the military, married a psychic who ran a business in Randsburg, and started life over as a fine artist specializing in landscapes. They'd been fighting over Dru's wife, Ginny, because Ginny and Harold had once dated and Dru had caught them flirting. Police had broken up the fight.

The second article was about how two days later Harold Thiesman disappeared. The police suspected foul play because a bloody knife was found by his apartment's back door. But there were no fingerprints. No evidence that could lead to an arrest warrant, although Dru Purcell had been questioned and released.

The third article was simply about how Harold Thiesman's body was still missing and the police had no leads.

"Oh Lord," Cherry said. "The bloody overalls in the suitcase . . ."

"Dru Purcell's," Sally said. "Dru must have murdered Harold and Ginny knew it, and all these years kept the overalls. How could she let Dru walk free? Especially since they divorced later? It's not like she was protecting him out of love."

"Maybe she knew enough about the circumstances of the murder to know Dru hadn't meant for it to happen — maybe it was a fight gone too far, or Dru killed in self-defense," I said, thinking of Owen's situation.

"Then why keep the overalls?" Sally asked.

"Blackmail. Maybe she thought the pants would come in handy for blackmailing Dru someday. We've already heard how nasty she was to the animal psychic," Cherry said. "And she just dropped Max, giving him no reason. She definitely had a dark side."

That there is a devil, there is no doubt
. . . I shook my head to clear it.

"She was sick. She probably dropped
Max because she knew he couldn't handle
being supportive and she just didn't want
to deal with being left," I said. "And she
needed money. So she finally decided to
cash in on the knowledge she'd had all
those years about Dru, coming here,
threatening him, hoping for money so she
could go for her radical treatments."

"But Dru — and maybe Missy — were
having none of that. They didn't want to
take money from the church to give her
and they couldn't have her tell the truth
and ruin Dru's empire, so they killed her,"
Sally said.

"And Missy could have noticed the suitcase in the laundromat before I did — I
was so busy that morning — then taken it
after I'd left to see Guy," I said. "Ginny
could have told Dru about the overalls and
the suitcase when she threatened him with
blackmail —"

"Yeah, when they met here," said Sally.
"And maybe Dru set up a meeting at the
corn maze for Friday night, knowing he
could kill her and stash the body just like he'd
done with this other fellow years ago —"

"Wait! Something doesn't make sense,

though," Cherry said. "Ginny saw something in her crystal ball just before she must have left to meet Dru. And she was really upset about it, and by the Death card in the tarot reading. Why would she come meet him if she knew he was capable of killing her, and why would she bring her crystal ball to the corn maze?"

"Dru can explain that in his confession," Sally said. "You're worrying about details instead of the big picture —"

"Ladies, are you lost?"

We all jumped, turned around, and saw the grim-faced park ranger peering down at us.

It took about an hour, but we finally got everything sorted out with the park rangers and the sheriff's department.

We wouldn't be fined for our trespassing, given our reasons and what we found, but we were sternly warned to talk to officials first, if we ever ran into a similar situation.

After we gave our statements, the sheriff's deputy — not Deputy Rankle, but a very married, middle-aged, thick-waisted Deputy Clarke, much to Cherry's disappointment — assured us that Dru would be questioned as soon as possible.

And that was it. I took Sally and Cherry back to Sally's, where they were planning to nap until Sally's boys returned from their fishing trip, and then they were all going to go to the Country Buffet up in Masonville for lunch.

I was invited to join them for the nap and the lunch, but I just asked for a cup of coffee to go. If life was back to normal, I still had my tutoring appointment with Hugh Crowley to keep. And then I'd go visit Guy.

Yep, I told myself, sipping on coffee as I headed up Sweet Potato Ridge back to the Crowley farm, that was it. Just a simple case of blackmail gone awry. A hypocritical preacher and his wife trying to protect their little heavenly empire here on earth. Very simple.

So why couldn't I shake a sense of wrongness? Why did my aunt's old devil saying keep playing in my head?

Just tired, I told myself. I just needed to get back to my laundromat and apartment, make sure Guy was okay, work things out with Owen, and then everything would be all right.

23

At first, I thought no one was home at the Crowley place. I stood on the front porch, holding the screen door open and knocking on the front door. No answer. Jeb, the Crowley's old blue tick beagle who sprawled beneath the porch swing, looked up at me lazily, and then settled back into a snorting, twitching nap. Jeb had howled at me — his tail wagging the whole time — when I came up on the porch. I petted him and he quieted down. Then he saw that I didn't have any treats, so he went back to his regular spot. If I didn't have treats or a rifle and we weren't going critter hunting, Jeb was not interested in me.

I knocked again, a little harder, and the front door came open. That surprised me. People always think folks in the country leave their doors unlocked. Not these days, unless someone is home.

I poked my head in. "Hello?"

No answer.

"Hello?" I tried again.

"I'm in here." I heard Rebecca's voice. She sounded weak and weary.

"Rebecca? It's Josie. You okay?"

"I've got me a sick headache and I'm laying down in the living room. Come on in. Hugh'll be back shortly. He doesn't want to miss his tutoring."

I stepped in, taking care not to let the screen door bang. I've never been burdened with headaches myself, but Aunt Clara used to get migraines — or sick headaches, as she also called them — and I knew any loud sound would increase the pain. I shut the door quietly behind me.

Then I turned from the small front hall to the right through the arched entry to the living room and stopped cold.

Rebecca wasn't lying on the couch. She was standing up across the room in the other archway that opened to the kitchen, where Hugh and I would do, I'd thought, our tutoring session.

But I didn't reckon I'd get to tutor Hugh. Because Rebecca had a rifle pointed right at me.

"I've already heard. Cherry called one of

her hairdressers, who called Ella, who called me. It looks like Dru did the killing," Rebecca said, "and I know folks will believe that for a while, but I also know it won't sit right with you and you'll figure it out sooner or later." She shook her head. "I'm sorry, Josie. But I can't go to jail or heap trouble on Maureen. She needs me. She and Ricky."

Although my body had turned numb and my mind cold with fear, I was able to believe that Rebecca was terrified and thought she was protecting her family. She wouldn't hesitate to use that rifle.

And I'd already started wondering about the question Cherry had asked back at Serpent Mound. Why would Ginny run out to meet Dru if she'd seen her own death predicted?

And the woman Max had seen at the Red Horse . . . his description fit Missy. But it also fit Rebecca.

"I have someone who needs me, too, Rebecca," I said. "Guy needs me. Let's talk this out. If you kill me, eventually that will be figured out, too, and that will just make things worse for you and your family."

Rebecca shook her head, licked her thin pale lips. The rifle trembled in her hands.

"No. Everyone will believe Dru killed Ginny to hide their marriage and his work in the dark arts. We were the only ones here in Paradise that knew about all of that.

"Ed and I were stationed out there, you know. Edwards Air Force Base. Dru and Ed joined up together, but then Dru didn't re-enlist. Ed came home for two weeks, married me, and off we went. I followed him from base to base — but that was okay. I had Little Ed.

"By the time Ed was back at Edwards Air Force Base again, Little Ed was eight," Rebecca went on. Her voice was sad and lost and, as I'd thought with Maureen talking about her Ricky, Rebecca wasn't, in a way, talking to me. She just needed to get the story — the justification for why she was going to kill me — clear in her own mind. After all, she had time. Hugh and Maureen obviously weren't there. The only creature who would hear the shot was probably Jeb the blue tick beagle, and he'd just wonder why he hadn't been invited to go critter hunting and then he'd go back to sleep.

"Ed wanted to look up Dru, and I agreed. We became pretty good friends with Dru and Ginny. Back then, we thought what they were doing with psychic healing and seeing was phenomenal stuff.

"Then Little Ed got sick. Kidney disease." Rebecca's voice wavered. "The doctors didn't have answers. We turned to Dru and Ginny, asked for their help. And I . . . I was so angry with the doctors — with God — that I took Little Ed out of the hospital, away from medication, up to Dru and Ginny's place. They prayed and meditated for two days while I held him . . . but he died. In my arms, he died."

Tears were coursing down Rebecca's face now. My heart clenched in reaction to what I'd just heard. I hadn't even known the Crowleys had once had a child, before Maureen.

Lots of things fell into place. Dru and Ginny's marriage breaking up. Dru turning his back completely on the psychic world, seeking redemption — after this terrible loss of Little Ed as well as his murder of Harold several years before that — in what he saw as the exact opposite of the psychic world, his own brand of fundamental Christianity.

That there is a devil, there is no doubt . . . but is he trying to get in or trying to get out . . .

Ginny had stayed with the psychic arts, embracing them as fundamentally as Dru had rejected them. That had been her way of coping with the horror of what had happened to Little Ed. Then she returned to Paradise during the psychic fair, hoping to blackmail Dru for money to pay for the alternate treatments she wanted.

Her appearance must have been a shock to Rebecca. It had to have been bad enough, seeing Dru in town all those years, knowing his secret, knowing he knew hers. But why would Rebecca suddenly kill Ginny now? Had her appearance in Paradise jolted a long-buried anger in Rebecca?

"Ed always told me Little Ed would have passed on anyway," Rebecca was saying. "A doctor who was part of the investigation after Little Ed's death told me that, too. But I still feel like by trusting Dru and Ginny . . . we killed our own son. After Ed finished his tour of duty, we came back here. We'd fallen out of touch with most everyone in Paradise. When we were young, we foolishly thought that we no longer needed any connection to people in Paradise, while we were off exploring the world outside of our hometown. So no one, except Ed's and my immediate families, knew about Little Ed. And after we came back, no one ever spoke of him. And then we were blessed with Maureen. When

Dru came back to town, Ed and Dru were never friends again, of course, but Ed told me it was only right to forgive.

"Then Ed, God rest his soul, passed on. He didn't live to see Ricky get ill, too.

"But Maureen had the good sense to follow every bit of medical advice she could. Ricky's getting the best care possible in Cincinnati. But then Ginny came here Friday night." Rebecca's voice turned bitter and hard and cold. A chill crept up my spine, warning me. She wasn't going to talk to me much longer. And when she stopped talking, she'd want to walk me out to the woods and shoot me. I glanced nervously around the room for something, anything to use to distract her. There was a display case of Hummel figurines against the wall. Maybe if I knocked it over . . .

I inched toward the case as Rebecca went on. "Ginny'd just seen in her crystal ball that Ricky would die if he didn't get psychic healing treatments from her. She'd been talking to Maureen anyway at the fair. Maureen had gone against my will, knowing how I hate psychics or tarot cards or anything like that, wanting advice, a healer, something to help Ricky no matter how wild it might seem. I'd gone to the Red Horse and warned Ginny away from us.

"But Ginny came up to the house anyway. I was here by myself, while Maureen was down in Cincinnati with Ricky, and Hugh was talking to the kids in the barn. I was in the midst of scrubbing down the bathroom."

Rebecca would have been wearing rubber gloves, I thought, probably the thin disposable kind. That's why she'd left no fingerprints on Ginny's gun.

"Ginny told me all about how she was Ricky's only hope," Rebecca was saying. "She wanted to set things right, after what had happened with Little Ed."

I shivered. To Ginny, attempting to heal Ricky after what happened to Little Ed might be setting things right before she faced her own illness.

"She wanted to do a reading again with Maureen in the crystal ball, to verify what she'd seen. And I could just see it all in a flash," Rebecca moaned. "Maureen believing her. Desperate to believe her. Taking Ricky from his treatment, him dying just like Little Ed.

"So I told her Maureen was out in the maze and we should go find her. Ginny followed me down to the corn maze and to the far corner — I know that maze like the back of my hand — and when we got to

384

the far corner, I turned suddenly, startling Ginny, so that it was easy to push her down.

"Ginny dropped her crystal ball as she fell. I was going to hit her in the head with the ball, then run back up here for my rifle, and go back and shoot her, but then a new way opened for me. A small gun came out of Ginny's pocket as she fell.

"I don't know why she had it, but I picked it up. I still had on my gloves from my cleaning, so I knew I wouldn't leave fingerprints. It seemed so . . . simple. I shot her through the head. Then I shoved her body back through the corn to the edge of the woods. I left the gun and the crystal ball near her, thinking I'd come back and just drag her and the ball and gun back into the woods later. I had to hurry because I knew Hugh would be coming to the maze with the kids, and I had to get back to the house.

"But then your boyfriend found the body. And you got to poking around. And I saw you at the corn maze last night."

I remembered the sound I'd thought was from an animal. "You were in the woods when I was out there."

"I couldn't sleep. I can't, much, these days. I walk in the woods when I can't

385

sleep. I knew you wouldn't give up until you figured out the truth, so I told Hugh that he needed to go with Maureen today, that she needed him, and I'd apologize to you for him missing his tutoring.

"I'm sorry, Josie," Rebecca said, and she truly sounded it. "But we're going to have to go to the woods now."

I glanced at the Hummel display, set myself to run into it.

"No, Rebecca, I can't let you do that."

Both Rebecca and I jumped at the sound of Hugh's voice. He'd appeared in the archway from the kitchen, right behind Rebecca.

She whirled, turned the rifle on him. "Hugh!" she cried in a strangled voice. "I thought I told you —"

"Maureen is fine." Hugh took the rifle from Rebecca's hand. She didn't fight him at all. I felt the shuddery warmth of blessed relief rush through me.

But then he looked right at me. "I heard the whole thing. Rebecca wanted you to believe she'd killed Ginny, but of course that's ridiculous. I did it for just the reasons she gave."

He looked at Rebecca. "Call Chief Worthy. We'll tell him the whole story. How I killed Ginny to protect you and

Maureen and Ricky from her wicked ways."

Rebecca wavered.

"Hugh," I said softly. "Hugh, you've sacrificed enough for this family. Hiding the truth won't help Rebecca face what she's done. And she needs to face it."

Hugh pointed the gun at me. "Josie, you have to believe me. Or so help me God." He swallowed. Tears coursed down his cheeks. "Or so help me, I'll kill you, just like I killed Ginny."

I looked at Rebecca. A war played out in the expressions on her face. She was horrified at what Hugh offered to do. Yet she was pleased at getting a way out. Yet again she was aghast at her own pleasure . . .

I fixed her with a look, ignoring Hugh at my own peril, I realized, but suddenly knowing my one chance to get out of this alive and have the truth be told.

And it didn't involve crashing over Hummel display chests.

"Mrs. Crowley, you knew my Aunt Clara. Knew her well. Prayed with her many a time," I said. "And she had a saying." I took a deep breath, and said it as somberly as Aunt Clara always had: "That there is a devil, there is no doubt. But is he trying to get in, or trying to get out."

I paused. "Either way, there's only one way to be free. Do the right thing."

Rebecca's eyes widened. Hugh moaned. Rebecca pushed the rifle ceilingward, just as he pulled the trigger.

Jeb the blue tick beagle howled at the sound of the shot.

And I crumpled to my knees.

Epilogue

Hugh's shot went into the ceiling and I fell to my knees out of relief. Hugh dropped the rifle and I grabbed it from the floor before either he or Rebecca could get it.

But Rebecca had collapsed against Hugh, and he held her up as she sobbed. He looked in my direction, and I tried to catch his eyes, but he cut them away.

I was glad to be alive, glad to know the truth, but still filled with sorrow. I kept hold of the rifle, went around Hugh and Rebecca to the kitchen and picked up the phone to call 911, yet again.

Now, a month later, life has returned to normal, more or less.

Rebecca told the whole story to Chief Worthy. She's being held in the women's penitentiary and her case should come to trial early in the new year.

Ricky Crowley's condition finally turned

for the better. His doctors say he should be home by Christmas. We're holding another chili-spaghetti supper for him at the Methodist church, though, to keep helping Maureen with medical expenses.

Dru, when confronted with what Sally and Cherry and I had found in Serpent Mound, also confessed to the long-ago murder of Harold Thiesman.

Then he gave a long interview on the Masonville CBS-affiliate channel and said he'd killed Harold in self-defense when Harold had come to his and Ginny's home and started a fight. He'd dumped Harold's body in the desert. Ginny had told him she'd burned his overalls and handkerchief, but she kept them all these years, and then, in Paradise tried to blackmail him, saying if he didn't give her the money she wanted for her treatments, she'd write out the truth in a letter she'd mail to the authorities, then kill herself, rather than facing the pain of sickness before death or hospitalization, which she feared as much as death itself.

That, I realized as I watched the interview on the TV in my laundromat while working on several shirt orders, was why Ginny had the suicide note and the pistol with her when she died.

Dru also admitted to throwing the suitcase with the threatening note through my Red Horse Motel window.

The water main was repaired, and I was able to return to my laundromat and home.

No one ever confessed to breaking into the LeFevers' bookshop, but the general belief is that it was Dru and a few of his followers.

Missy took over Dru's congregation. Despite the moment of compassion she showed during the book burning at the Red Horse — telling Dru to back down — she ruled the congregation with even more righteous fury than Dru had, trying to make up, I supposed, for his past failings and her association with him. But most folks were so soured by the extremes she and Dru had pursued, that the congregation lost about half of its members. We in the area's churches — of all kinds — took in a few of those folks. Graciously, without too much gossip over the Jell-O salads in the carry-in suppers.

I even heard of one former Dru follower who became a devout Wiccan.

The others drifted away from religion altogether, at least for the time being.

But that's the problem with going to one

extreme or another, with no room for doubts or questions. Doesn't leave you much wiggle room to grow in your faith in times of trouble.

Anyway. It turned out that Guy has type 2 adult onset diabetes. Guy does not like the diet changes this has forced, but we — the staff at Stillwater and I — are helping him cope.

Winnie and her many friends ended up gathering nearly seven hundred signatures throughout the county to get the bookmobile reinstated. The Mason County Library decided to cut back on periodical and video purchases, plus shift around some staffing hours, to let Winnie get back to running her beloved bookmobile. Those of us who depend on the bookmobile are thrilled.

Cherry got over her heartbreak about Max quickly enough, especially when she met Deputy Rankle, who turned out to be a cousin of Mr. Azure Eyes. The deputy was at the Bar-None one night, off duty, and was charmed by her story of how she helped solve the mystery of Ginny's murder. She totally reconfigured what happened with her and Max — in her version, there was no Silly Putty, and she pinned him to the floor and made him tell me about the woman who visited Ginny — but neither Sally nor I dashed her version with the truth. Deputy Rankle was a far better choice for Cherry than she'd made in a long time.

And it was kind of nice to have a law figure who actually liked me in my circle of friends, although one day Chief Worthy came into my laundromat and mumbled a weak apology about not taking my information seriously.

It took me two weeks, but I finally convinced Hugh to take up tutoring again. He didn't want to, at first, because he was so horrified at what had happened at the Crowley farm.

But I thought his brother Ed had it right. Forgiveness keeps our hearts from turning hard. And besides, I didn't really think he would have shot me. He told me his finger slipped as Rebecca pushed up the gun, and I believe him.

Just last week, he got a letter from his grandson in Seattle. He brought it to our Sunday tutoring session in my laundromat office and read it to me. Slowly, sounding out words, his hands trembling as he held the letter tightly.

And as for Owen and me . . . well, Owen came home from Kansas City on cloud nine after having visited with his son, who was, he said, going to come visit for Thanksgiving. That was fine with me. I was looking forward to meeting him.

But I couldn't say how things would eventually work out between Owen and me. We agreed we cared about each other, that we wanted our relationship to work out, but we weren't sure if we could work through our differences in communication — my need for total sharing and honesty, Owen's need for keeping the things private that seemed, to me, exactly what you should share with someone you loved.

But somehow, not knowing how our relationship is going to work out is okay, at least for now.

There are other things I don't know, either.

I'm still not sure I understand my Aunt Clara's devil saying. And I don't know how Ginny knew my aunt's saying. My guess is that Ginny knew the strange old saying independently of my Aunt Clara. A coincidence — although the LeFevers (who are expecting their first child next June) assure me there's no such thing.

I checked with the LeFevers and they said they'd never heard me calling out in my dreams and if they had, they surely wouldn't have told Ginny or anyone else about it. I told them about my Mrs. Oglevee dreams — just in general — and they told me that it's not altogether uncommon for people to repeatedly dream about a person who'd been important to them in life who'd passed on. So, in the parking lot, Ginny could have been making a guess about my having a "spiritual guide," then, based on my reaction of amazement at her divining the truth, made good guesses about just what form my guide would take.

Truth be told, I'm not sure how I feel about that explanation.

And I don't know why Ginny focused on me as the one who would implicate Dru if anything happened to her or why she played such odd games to reveal Dru's past. Maybe she didn't want to make knowing about his past too easy, in case he decided to give her the money she wanted.

Of course, she was wrong in her prediction about who her killer would be, assuming that Dru might kill her if she threatened blackmail, and she was wrong about Ricky, and about the wisdom of going to Rebecca with her predictions of his death unless he got her help.

So maybe leaving the suitcase with the

overalls and the handkerchief and its odd note with me was just a lucky guess on Ginny's part.

She couldn't have known I would be able to find her killer if something happened to her . . . could she?

I also don't know why I have dreams of Mrs. Oglevee, why she shows up to give me advice. I probably will never know.

But inasmuch as I have the gift of questioning, as Sally pointed out that day at Suzy Fu's Chinese Buffet, I have come to know that it's just as much a gift to be able to accept not always knowing the answer to everything.

PARADISE ADVERTISER-GAZETTE
Josie's Stain Busters

by Josie Toadfern
Stain Expert and Owner of
Toadfern's Laundromat
(824 Main Street, Paradise, Ohio)

Thoughts and prayers go out to the Crowley family. As we all know, they've had a tough row to hoe the past several years. But there's some good news: Ricky is expected to make a full recovery and should come home in the near future from Cincinnati's Children's Hospital!

We still need to support the Crowleys as best we can. So please mark your calendars for the dessert auction (organized by Luke and Greta Rhinegold) at St. Paul's Lutheran Church for 7 p.m., Wednesday, November 12. I know I'll be there! Mrs. Beavy is bringing three of her famous buttermilk pies, one of them a sugar-free variation.

I'll be bidding on that one for Guy, who, as many of you know has been diagnosed with diabetes 2. Thank you for all the cards and prayers. He's doing pretty well, adjusting to his new diet.

I know I speak for all the Main Street business owners when I say it's great to finally be back in business, after the water main break. In celebration of being back in business, here are this month's stain tips:

- Rust spots from water sometimes emerge on linens. Mix two quarts warm water, two cups lemon juice, and two tablespoons salt. Spread your item out on the lawn on a sunny day and treat spots with this mixture. When you see the spots start to fade, carefully wash the item as soon as possible.
- Make throw rugs look like new by adding a half-cup or so of table salt to the wash water.
- Get Silly Putty out of clothing by pouring rubbing alcohol over the putty, rubbing, and repeating until the Silly Putty disintegrates or can be pulled right off. (This works on hair, too. Just in case someone you know gets Silly Putty in his or her hair. For some reason.)
- Pre-treat collars and cuffs with cheap shampoo to prevent ring-around-the-collar stains.
- And know that one thing gets out blood better than anything else — hydrogen peroxide.

Of course, always test these tips on a hidden corner or hem of the stained item. These tips come from my expertise — but remember, it never hurts to question conventional wisdom.

Until next month, may your whites never yellow and your colors never fade. But if they do, hop on over and see me at Toadfern's Laundromat — Always a Leap Ahead of Dirt!

About the Author

SHARON SHORT's humor column, "Sanity Check," appears every Monday in the *Dayton Daily News* and covers everything from shredding pantyhose for stress relief to talking refrigerators. Her fiction credits include several short mysteries published in *Futuro Mysterious Anthology Magazine,* and *Orchard Press Online Mystery Magazine:* In addition, Ms. Short is a principal of her own marketing communications firm. She lives in Miamisburg, Ohio, with her husband and two daughters.